Mercy's Face

Mercy's Face

Donna Van Cleve

Two Story Publishing House
Hutto, Texas

Mercy's Face
Published by
Two Story Publishing House
P.O. Box 482
Hutto, Texas 78634

Copyright ©2007 by Donna Van Cleve
www.donnavancleve.com
Email: donna@donnavancleve.com

All rights reserved. To use or reproduce any part of this book in any form or by any electronic or mechanical means, including information storage and retrieval systems, written permission must be secured from the publisher, except by a reviewer who may quote brief passages in a review.

This book is a work of fiction. Names, characters, places and incidents are the products of the author's imagination or are used fictitiously.

Publisher's Cataloging-in-Publication Data

Van Cleve, Donna C.
   Mercy's Face / Donna Van Cleve
   244p. cm.
   ISBN 978-0-9787937-4-6
      1. Frontier life—Texas—Fiction. 2. Horses—Fiction.
      3. Adoption— Fiction. 4. Christian Romance—Fiction.

2007923641

On the Cover: *Dallas Fuel* photo by Cappy Jackson
Horse owned by Joe & Dee Lynn Braman of Refugio, Texas
Used with permission
Visit their websites at www.jbquarterhorses.com/
& www.cappyjacksonphotos.com
Other photo credits: Jonathan & Vanessa Roeder of Pflugerville, Texas
& Joy Watson of Cotulla, Texas

Acknowledgments

Thank you, Pete Aleshire & Sally Benford
at *Arizona Highways* for permission to use the
Stagecoach Etiquette Rules.
Ironically, the original article was published in the
Omaha Herald in 1877—the same year as the setting of this story.

Thank you, Jan Athey, Librarian for the Toy Collectors Association
Library in Strasberg, Pennsylvania, for your information about toy trains
in the 1800's.

Thank you, Joy Watson, Vanessa & Jonathan Roeder,
Joe & Dee Lynn Braman, & Cappy Jackson
for your part in making a beautiful cover.

Thank you, Clara Jo Horton,
for your sharp eyes & thoughtful input.
Thanks also to Isla Casey, Karen Thomison, & Beth Corbet
for your help & comments about the story.

Thank you, Jack, for loaning me your *Quarter Horse Journals* and
teaching me, a bona fide non-cowgirl,
about horses and cattle through the years.
I still have a lot to learn.

Proverbs 3:5-6

Author's Note
About Brownwood, Texas

The main characters in the first book, *Grace Falling Like Rain,* passed through a small town on their way home to Grace, Texas, a fictional town that would probably be located in the middle of Lake Waco today. But the lake wasn't built until the 20th century, so the town of Grace held up historically & geographically. In the second book, though, most of the story takes place in that anonymous town mentioned in the first, but I wanted it to have a name this time around.

I looked at a Texas map and found an actual town whose location and historical information dovetailed with the town in both books. That community was Brownwood, Texas. *Mercy's Face* is a work of fiction, but I used information about Brownwood from the book *Something About Brown: A History of Brown County* by T.R. Havins, which included photographs of Brownwood in the late 1800's. Some businesses and their locations around the town square in the story are entirely fictional, although I did use some actual business names, people, and stories from Brownwood's history to provide a framework for this work of fiction.

I was surprised to find the name of Jim Taylor in this historical book, which is also the name of the main character in this story. But the real Jim Taylor was known in this area to be associated with John Wesley Hardin. I used that fact to create a moment of tension, which you will read about in the story.

Brownwood, Texas has a rich history, and I enjoyed researching it for the story. I hope Brownwood's historical scholars will be forgiving with the liberties I took in using it as the main setting for *Mercy's Face.*

For my children:
Van, Vanessa & Jonathan
& the joy of having a ringside seat
to watch the wonder & adventure
all over again with my grandchildren,
Audrie & Finn

For my first family:
Dad, Mom, Joy, Joe & Bobby
& the wonderful additions of their families

For my friends,
especially Donnie, Mary Jan & Janet,
who make the effort to stay in touch
in spite of my reclusive ways

For the founding members
Of the Sisterhood of the Comfy Socks:
Christy, Susan, & Vanessa
For all your rah rah, yah yah, cha cha support,
And by the way,
it's your turn now…

&

For the late Dwight Graham
who took the time for family & friends;
My inbox won't be the same without you

Chapter 1
Fort Worth, Texas…1877

Every head turned as the beautiful woman sauntered through the hotel lobby on the way to the stairs. She smiled to herself, basking in the attention she drew—especially when men seemed to forget their female companions when she entered a room.

She walked up the stairs, swaying her hips just enough to insure she had everyone's attention. She was sick of those stairs, and the hotels, and the gambling houses. Surely Eustace would be ready to settle down soon. She stopped at Room 204. She was sick of this room, too, and hoped they could eat somewhere besides the hotel tonight. She opened the door to find Eustace stuffing something in the new leather valise she had recently purchased for him, at his suggestion.

"What are you doing?!" the woman asked.

"Ahh, my lovely Reen, back so soon?" he said calmly as he pulled the buckle tight and secured it. "I was hoping to avoid this."

"Avoid what?!" she said, feeling the panic rising in her throat.
"Why did you pack your bag? Are you… are we going somewhere? Why didn't you tell me? You know it's going to take me more than a few minutes to get my things together."

In the back of her mind she knew what he was doing, but she refused to let the thought venture forward. This couldn't be happening to her.

Eustace walked over to the chair and picked up his coat—the expensive coat she had also bought him. "You know as well as I do that this couldn't last," he said as he pulled his left arm through the sleeve, then the right.

"Couldn't last?" she said, shaking her head in disbelief. "You said you loved me!! You said we would always be together! I believed you!"

"I did love you, Reen," he said, "for a while. But all things come to an end eventually."

"We haven't been together three months, Eustace! I think the word 'always' means quite a bit more than three months!"

"You can always go back to *Daddy*," he suggested as he put on his hat—the hat she had bought him, no—that wasn't right—the hat was his. It was the new boots, the new shirt and pants she had also bought for him. "You told me you had him wrapped around your little finger."

"Don't you remember? You made me choose between my parents and you," she said, her lips trembling. "And I took their money—you insisted we had to have it to make a fresh start—that we would pay them back eventually. How am I ever going to pay them back? We've spent almost half of it!!"

"You're a smart girl—you'll figure out a way," he said as he walked towards her. "Now, if you'll pardon me, I have a stage to catch."

"You can't do this to me, Eustace!" she cried, the tears flowed freely now. "I gave you everything of me! I held nothing back from you!!" She braced her arms across the doorway. "You have to take me with you!!"

Eustace stopped in front of her, calmly put the valise down, gripped her arms and picked her up off the floor, turned and set her down behind him. He retrieved his valise and walked out the door as she started screaming and pounding his back.

Halfway down the hall he dropped the valise, turned and violently shoved her up against the wall.

"Don't push me, Reen," he said, through gritted teeth. "Why don't you try to act like the lady I hoped you would be instead of the spoiled little girl who always gets her way. If you want to humiliate yourself further and ruin your chance of bagging some other imbecile who's stupid enough to hook up with you, then keep following me downstairs. There's a good-sized audience down there to see your performance."

"You're hurting me," she whimpered.

She shut her eyes halfway through his barrage of insults—she couldn't stand to see his handsome face snarling so close to her own. But she needed to tell him something, and she was sure he would take back everything he said and take her with him. She opened her eyes and looked straight into his.

"I'm carrying your child," she said, bracing for the worst. She wasn't completely sure if that was true, but she suspected it.

He let go of her and backed away as if she were a leper.

After a moment, he shook his head and said, "You're lying."

"I wouldn't lie about—" she tried to say, but he cut her off.

"You'd lie about anything to get your way," he said, "or to get back at somebody. I heard stories about you before we met—about a lie you told a girl that sent her to her death... just because she was interested in the man you wanted."

She shut her eyes again, feeling nauseous. "But she didn't die—why do people keep saying that? She was taken by that half-breed! I had nothing to do with that!"

"But it was your lie that put her in his hands, wasn't it, dear? You're a liar and a thief, and you're just trying to trap me," he said, grabbing the valise again.

"I'm telling you the truth!" she said, this time pleading with her eyes. "You're going to be a father."

"Well, in that case, I'm living up to my name," he said.

"What!?" she asked.

"*Eustace* means fruitful," he said, turning to walk away. "You aren't the first woman who's tried to trap me that way, and you probably won't be the last."

She grabbed the first thing her hand touched and threw it as he started down the stairs. The vase shattered behind him, along with all her dreams.

She ran back to the room, slammed the door, crawled onto the bed, and pulled the covers over her head before the deep sobs came.

Four days later...

"Where is she?" the tall, dark-skinned man asked the hotel clerk.

The clerk couldn't help but stare at his piercing blue eyes, seemingly out of place with his skin.

"Is there a problem?" the blue eyes continued. "You said she was here."

"Uh, yes sir," the clerk said. "We can't seem to get rid of her. She won't come out of her room, and her bill is passed due. She gets hysterical if anyone tries to go in there. I don't know what she's doing for food. We haven't heard a peep out of her today and were considering calling the doctor or sheriff or somebody."

"Do you have a passkey?"

He nodded his head. "We're ready to see her leave, but before I hand over a key to you, I need to know who you are and what relation you are to this woman," the clerk said cautiously.

"My name is Jimmy Taylor, and her father hired me to bring her home," he said as he took out a letter of reference stating his business. "And I'll be taking care of her bill, but before that, I need you to bring some food to her room, and she'll need a woman to assist her for a little while. Can you recommend someone?"

The clerk called to a young boy walking through the hotel lobby and motioned for him to come over to the desk.

"Tommy, go to the kitchen and tell Mrs. Connor to bring a tray of soup and a pitcher of water for Room 204."

"What about hot tea or coffee?" Jimmy suggested.

"I think water would be the best choice for your friend right now."

"I didn't say she was a friend."

"Your *charge*, then," the clerk continued. "She threw an expensive vase of flowers at her gentleman friend on the day he left—by the way, that'll be three dollars added to her bill. Anyway, hot liquid of any kind might mean an additional risk to you when you face her."

"Good point," Jimmy said. "Water it is."

"Go on, Tommy," the clerk said, "do as I told you."

The young boy walked swiftly across the lobby to the dining area and through the double doors at the far side. In a few minutes, a short, stocky woman carrying a linen-covered tray shuffled over to the two men. The clerk introduced her to Jimmy.

"He's here to take our *favorite* guest home, Mrs. Connor," the clerk said, with a hint of a smile.

"Praise the Lord!" she said, acting relieved, then quickly apologized. "I'm so sorry, sir. I didn't mean to offend you."

"No offense taken," Jimmy said, smiling. "Could you help her get ready to leave?"

The woman nodded, and turned to walk toward the stairs.

"Here, let me carry that for you," Jimmy said to the older woman as he reached for the tray.

"Thank you, young man," she said. "You're definitely not cut of the same cloth as our queen up there."

Jimmy snorted. "No ma'am. She's the daughter of a friend of my father's, and her daddy had a penchant for spoiling her. I have no idea what to expect when we walk through that door, other than I know it's not going to be easy."

"You're right about it not being easy. She's had us wait on her hand and foot up until her *friend*"—and she raised her eyebrows on that word—"left. Then after that, she's just holed herself up in that room for the past four days—allowing no one inside. She even stopped ordering food. I've had Tommy leave some bread and water by the door—I didn't want her to starve," she said, and then lowered her voice to a whisper. "We're a little concerned that she's gone off her nut, if you know what I mean."

Mrs. Connor stopped in front of room 204. She looked at Jimmy, took a deep breath, and then knocked on the door.

No answer.

"Miz Reen?"

Still no answer from beyond the door.

Jimmy looked at the woman. "Did you say *mis'ry?*" *How fitting*, he thought.

"No, sir, I said *Miz Ree-nuh.*"

"Are you sure we have the right room?"

The woman nodded her head and tried again. "Miz Reen? Someone's here to take you home."

"Nobody from home knows I'm here," a hoarse voice said from the other side. "Go away."

"Here," Jimmy said as he handed the tray to her and turned and slipped the passkey in the lock.

"Mr. Taylor's come for you," Mrs. Connor said. "And we're coming in there with some food."

"Justin?" the voice asked.

Jimmy stepped into the darkened room and paused, waiting for flying objects.

Nothing.

He walked across the room to pull back the heavy drapery from the windows.

"Justin, is it really you?" she asked in a small voice, shading her eyes as she slowly sat up in bed.

Jimmy pulled back the last drapes, took off his hat and turned to face the woman.

"No, Florine, it's not Justin," he said. "It's me… Jimmy."

"No!! Not you!!" the woman said with a horrified look on her face. She let out a blood-curdling scream and promptly fainted.

Chapter 2

Mrs. Connor set the tray down on the table and walked over to the bed. "Oh, my," she said. "She doesn't seem to like you at all, Mr. Taylor."

"Yeah, I figured Florine wouldn't be too happy to see me," he said. "I'm a reminder of something she'd like to forget ever happened. And what is this *Reen* name you called her?"

"That's how Mr. Ashton introduced her—as Miz Reen. She tried to make us think they were married—but we knew better. He was a snake, that one. I knew he was trouble when I first laid eyes on him. But Miz Reen, she seemed to see only what she wanted to see, and not how things really were," Mrs. Connor said as she leaned over Florine. "Poor thing, she's thin as a rail. Her heart's been stomped on and she's afraid to face the world."

"You do realize it's the devil you are referring to," Jimmy said, "although she doesn't even look like the same snooty debutante I remember."

"She's definitely been knocked off her high horse," Mrs. Connor said, patting Florine's hand and then her face. "Miz Reen?" No response. She turned to Jimmy. "Dip that towel in the water pitcher and hand it to me."

He did as she asked, and the older woman began wiping Florine's face and arms. The younger woman came around and blinked her eyes. When she saw Jimmy, she opened her mouth to scream again, and Mrs. Connor jabbed the towel in it and grabbed Florine's right hand reaching up to grab it. Jimmy grabbed her other arm.

"You just hold on a minute, missy," she said. "We're both here to help you, so we'd appreciate you not damaging our ears again. We'll let you go if you promise to calm down."

Florine's chest heaved and nostrils flared as she glared at them. But she finally nodded her head, and Mrs. Connor pulled the towel out of her mouth and let her go.

"Get your hands off of me," she spat at Jimmy.

"Gladly," Jimmy said, raising his hands and stepping back.

"What are *you* doing here?" Florine demanded. "Why are you in my room?"

"Your father sent me to find you and bring you home," Jimmy said.

"Do you know who this is?" Florine asked Mrs. Connor as she looked at Jimmy.

Mrs. Connor nodded. "Mr. Jimmy Taylor."

"No—not his name, simpleton. Do you know what kind of person he is?" Florine asked again. "I bet you don't know that he's a savage Indian, and a kidnapper, and a lying drunk, and my daddy would never have sent someone like *him* to find me."

"I'm sorry, Florine, but that's exactly what your *daddy* did."

"I don't believe you."

Jimmy pulled out the letter of reference Mr. Locke had given him and handed it to Florine. She read it, and read it again, and then dropped her hands in her lap as a look of hopelessness swept across her face. Then the tears came.

"Why are you crying?" Mrs. Connor asked. "Your daddy wants you to come home."

"He hates me," she blubbered. "He'll never forgive me for what I did. He's hired a half-breed kidnapper to punish me."

"Oh, good grief, Florine," Jimmy said. "That's the most ridiculous thing I've ever heard."

"But you did kidnap Allie," Florine said to him as she turned to Mrs. Connor. "He really did kidnap a girl two years ago, Mrs. ... what was your name?"

"Connor," the woman said. "Now, now, you don't know what you're saying. You just need to get some food in you, and we'll get you all cleaned up and ready for travel and—"

"Tell her, Jimmy!" Florine interrupted. "You can't deny it."

"I guess I can't," Jimmy said, "but that's all worked itself out."

Mrs. Connor looked at him with raised eyebrows.

"It's a long story, but I assure you, Mrs. Connor," he explained, "the kidnappee and I are on the best of terms. She's my sister-in-law now, and I even stood up for my brother at their wedding."

"Well, then," Mrs. Connor patted Florine's knee, "that settles it. Mr. Taylor must not be too bad of a man if he participated in the *kidnappee's* wedding. Now let's get some food in you so you'll have some strength for the trip home."

"He's an Indian, too," Florine said, disgustedly. "I can't believe my daddy would want me to be in the company of this... savage. Have you heard of my family—the Lockes of Waco? Our ancestors were very close to the British throne."

Jimmy rolled his eyes and said under his breath, "Inside or out..."

Mrs. Connor snickered, and then said, "No, I haven't heard of your family, Miz Reen, but my husband's family is the potato-growing Connors from Ireland; my family's Welsh, and according to Mr. Taylor's name, I believe his ancestors are British, too, but then the other side of his family probably has more claim to this country than you do, so I wouldn't go flaunting your pedigree like it means something around here."

It was Jimmy's turn to snicker this time.

Florine sat there, shocked that the *hired help* spoke to her in such a manner.

The best response she could come up with was, "Well, I don't want him in here."

"I'd be happy to step outside," Jimmy offered, relieved to get out of that room and away from Florine. He paused at the door and told Mrs. Connor, "I'll be back in a little while."

He walked up and down the hall as he thought about the trip home, and decided he wasn't getting paid nearly enough money for the job that lay ahead of him. He tried to focus on that new stud horse the money from this *job* would buy. He had big plans to raise and train horses, and had already acquired several good brood mares from the earnings he received from breaking horses for ranchers and friends in central Texas the past two years. His father told him that he would receive an inheritance at age twenty-five, with which he planned to buy some land to call his own, but that was still five years away. He was twenty years old, or thereabouts. He didn't know the actual day or month in which he was born—his mother told him it happened in the spring of 1857.

Jimmy stopped when he saw his reflection in the mirror at the end of the hall. Florine was right—he *was* a half-breed, but it wasn't quite as noticeable since he cut his hair and dressed like a gentleman. Some folks even mistook him for a Frenchman. He never denied who or what he was, but he didn't always bring up the subject either, to avoid trouble. His piercing blue eyes always threw people off when it came to guessing his ancestry.

He was half Apache, or Indeh, as they referred to themselves. His birth father, Nantan Lupan, had taken captive his mother and older brother on a raid at their home in Grace, Texas, back in 1856. Jimmy was born during the first year of his mother's captivity, and lived among the Indeh until he was five years old. It wasn't *captivity* to him—it was all he ever knew; that is, until his mother's first husband found them. Matthew Taylor had been looking for his wife and son off and on for six years, and the confrontation meant the death of his birth father. His mother Julia would not come back to Grace without bringing Jimmy and an orphaned girl she had named Faith. His stepfather grew to accept and love Faith, but Jimmy was a constant reminder of the pain Nantan Lupan had inflicted on his family.

For a long time Jimmy never really knew where he belonged, and the difficult years at the local school and later a boarding school made him feel like he would never be accepted in the white man's world. His brother Justin had few problems stepping back into the culture from which he came, and Jimmy eventually became jealous of the older brother he had grown up adoring. That, coupled with the lack of acceptance from the only father he knew—his stepfather—resulted in a burning anger and resentment toward his family, although they had never intentionally hurt him.

Eventually, the boarding school informed the Taylors that their fourteen-year-old son had become more than they could handle, so Jimmy returned to Grace. Most young men his age had less schooling than he and were already out doing a man's work. At home Jimmy came and went as he pleased, answering to no one, and his angry disposition had everyone walking on eggshells around him. By the time he was eighteen, his regular bouts with the bottle usually culminated in disastrous results. The breaking point happened on the weekend his parents celebrated their thirtieth wedding anniversary.

Jimmy's brother Justin and their uncle, John Stockton, were escorting a young lady by the name of Alexandra Blake back to their hometown of Dalton in South Texas. They planned to stop over in Grace to attend the anniversary celebration. Jimmy had no reason to celebrate his parents' anniversary—his festering wounds reminded him that his stepfather's posse killed his birth father, although he remembered little about Nantan Lupan. He did witness the killing when he was five years old, and although he didn't understand what had happened, the experience left him with a terrifying sense of loss. As his growing up years became more difficult, Jimmy grabbed hold of that offense and brandished it as an emotional weapon, especially to provoke his stepfather.

Jimmy chose to dishonor his parents by going on a three-day drinking binge. He barged in on a family dinner the night before the ceremony and managed to offend everyone there. He knew from the moment he saw Allie and Justin sitting together that he could hurt his brother by hurting Allie. Several shameful incidents later resulted in Jimmy's banishment from his home. He was ready to cut and run, but a last chance encounter with Allie down by the river scared her enough to run away from him. He tried to stop her from running over a dangerous patch of rocks alongside the river, but just as he reached her, she jerked her arm away from him and fell and struck her head. He figured he had done enough harm previously that he would be blamed for that, too, and his brother would probably kill him, so he decided it was time to leave for good. But he needed to buy some time to get away before he was blamed for Allie's accident, so he made it look like she had fallen in the river and then took her with him, at least to get a head start on his brother. When he had put enough distance between them, he planned to send Allie home.

Brilliant plans under the haze of alcohol dim into stupidity when sobriety hits. Jimmy realized that he had gone too far this time, but he had already set the course and had to see it through. His concern for himself shifted to a concern for Allie and getting her back home safely. A violent clash with a band of Apaches waylaid that plan, and Jimmy almost paid for it with his life. But throughout the ordeal, he watched Allie continue to exhibit grace and forgiveness—even after all that had happened. And she told him she was determined to help him come back home and reconcile with his past and his family. It eventually happened with the help of Allie and his brother Justin, but not without tremendous pain—physically and emotionally. It was through God's grace that he was able to turn things around.

After he returned home, Jimmy had some penance to pay for the bad choices he had made, but for the first time in his life, he was at peace with himself. And for the first time he could remember, Jimmy had a good relationship with his family—especially his stepfather. His mother had always loved and defended him, but he had even pulled away from her through the years. He felt like he was seeing his family with new eyes, and enjoyed working with them and getting to know them. He saw a future for himself and had a direction to work towards in his life, and it felt good.

Jimmy's thoughts drifted back to the image in the mirror and of the trip that lay ahead of him.

I don't know if I want to do this. Taking Florine home will be like strapping myself to an angry she-wolf, he thought to himself.

But immediately, the thought of Allie and what he had put her through came to mind. The realization of it hit Jimmy like cold water on his face.

All right, all right—I get it—she was strapped to an angry wolf herself, and she survived. I don't deserve any easier a time than she had.

He decided to go downstairs and take care of Florine's debts.

The hotel ought to be paying me to take her, he thought ruefully, and immediately he felt a twinge of guilt. It stopped him in his tracks.

"What was that?" He questioned himself aloud. "Can I not have even one foul thought to myself anymore?"

But he knew what it was and shook his head.

"Dang it, I've gone and picked up a conscience somewhere."

He stomped down the stairs muttering to himself. "Lord, you'd better not be turning me into a dandified sissy."

Chapter 3

Jimmy walked up to the counter and rang the bell since no one seemed to be around. After all of an extraordinarily short amount of time, he slammed his palm down on it again.

The clerk came through a door behind the counter with a handful of papers.

"Yes sir!" he said, "What can I do for you?"

"I need to settle Florine's account," Jimmy said gruffly.

"I'm glad to see you're still in one piece," the clerk said, smiling, "but it doesn't look like it was pleasant for you."

Jimmy realized it wasn't the clerk's fault for his cantankerous mood. His frown loosened up a bit as he shook his head. "I would've rather tangled with a rattlesnake," he said, "but at least I could've shot the snake."

The clerk laughed out loud as he shuffled through the papers and then slid the bill over to Jimmy. "Mr. Ashton paid the bill up to the day he left, and Miss Reen's been here four more nights. They spent quite a bit of money while he was here, but Miss Reen hasn't spent anything on food since he left. How's her health?"

"Her voice and temper are just fine, but she did look like she needed to eat something," Jimmy said. "I think Mrs. Connor's getting some food down her."

Jimmy pulled out some bills, and a crumpled piece of paper fell out from among them. He opened it up and looked at the familiar writing. His sister Faith had written down a verse and given it to him not long after he reconciled with his family. He had carried it with him ever since, but wasn't sure he understood it. He read it silently again.

Trust in the Lord with all thine heart and lean not unto thine own understanding; In all thy ways acknowledge Him and He will direct thy paths. Proverbs 3:5-6

Trust. Now that was a word he was trying to get more familiar with. He had depended on himself for so long, it was hard to open himself up and let others in—other than Faith. She always had his back. Then Allie came along and forced her way into his mind and heart, and eventually broke down his defenses. He smiled at the thought as he folded up the note and put it in his pocket. Then he settled up with the clerk, which included a bit more for his trouble.

"Where's the nearest stage office?" Jimmy asked. "And do you know when the next stage goes south?"

"Four blocks down on this side of the street," the clerk said as he nodded his head toward the direction of the station. "The next one should be leaving around noon."

"I appreciate your help, sir," Jimmy said, shaking the clerk's hand.

Jimmy walked outside and looked around. The sky was the same color of blue. It was the same dusty street he had ridden down just a half hour before. The street was filled with people going about their everyday business. But everything was different somehow. Maybe it was the recently acquired burr under his saddle that gave everything a dismal look.

He had been searching a month for Florine—first in the Houston and Galveston area where he tracked her and Ashton after leaving Waco. Then he came up to this part of Texas and had already spent a week in the territory, first in the Dallas area and now in Fort Worth, when he finally got a tip last night at a gambling house in a seedy area the locals called *Hell's Half Acre*. A fancy dressed couple that fit the description of Florine and her escort had been regularly visiting the place up until a few nights ago. Jimmy figured that meant he had missed them again—that they had already left town, but he also learned at which hotel they had been staying, so he decided to check there. Maybe someone had heard where they were headed next.

He was surprised to hear that the woman was still there—by herself. Abandoned was the term used. Although Jimmy didn't personally know Florine's recently departed beau, it spoke volumes about his lack of character when he heard that Eustace Ashton had deserted her far away from her home and family. No woman—even someone as difficult as Florine—deserved to be left alone to fend for herself.

He thought he would feel relieved once he found her, but the feeling of dread had waylaid the feeling of relief.

"Lord, help me," he said under his breath as he stepped down onto the street and walked up to his horse.

Forty-five minutes later Jimmy walked back into the hotel lobby with one ticket in hand. He had left his horse at the stage office so he could drag Florine and her trunk back there. No, that wasn't quite right, although he grinned at the thought. He would drag Florine's trunk and escort her back to the stage office. He took the stairs two at a time and stopped at Florine's door, which was ajar. Mrs. Connor was stripping the bed.

"Where is she?" Jimmy asked.

"Taking a good long soak downstairs," Mrs. Connor said. "That poor girl—she was skin and bones."

"Did she eat something?"

"Yes, sir, after complaining about you for at least ten minutes," the older woman said. "She sure doesn't like you."

"The feeling's mutual, but that's irrelevant," Jimmy said. "Do you think she's up to traveling soon?"

Mrs. Connor nodded her head. "She was pretty weak, though, and she said she felt sick to her stomach, but getting some food in her seemed to help. I'll pack up some bread and hardtack for her—it might help settle her stomach on that bumpy ride ahead of her."

"The stage leaves at noon—do you think she'll be ready?"

"I'd better get down there and push her along—our queen will probably want to soak for hours," Mrs. Connor said, and then looked around the room. "But I think I have just about everything packed up in here."

"I really appreciate your help," Jimmy said as he offered her several dollars.

"Oh, pshaw!" she said, shaking her head and refusing it. "You're probably going to need it for the trip home."

"I insist—" Jimmy said. "You earned it."

"All in a day's work," said the proud woman, leaning over to pick up the linens.

"Well, it's been a pleasure meeting you, Mrs. Connor," Jimmy said as he slipped the bills under the soup bowl on the tray.

"Likewise, I'm sure, Mr. Taylor," she said as she looked up, "and you leave that tray right there—I'll carry it downstairs later."

Jimmy smiled and said, "Yes, ma'am."

"Why don't you take her trunk down and wait for us in the lobby. I'll bring Miz Reen and her traveling bag down shortly."

"Sounds like a good plan."

At eleven o'clock, Jimmy decided to drag the trunk over to the station office to save time. He was ready to climb the walls by the time Mrs. Connor escorted Florine to the lobby at 11:45. She was dressed in her Sunday finest and turned every head in the lobby. The lavender satin dress fit close to her form until it flared just below her hips. Jimmy would have taken a second look if that face, body, and dress had been on someone else.

"The stage leaves in fifteen minutes, Florine," Jimmy said impatiently.

"I do not want to talk to you," she said, looking a little peaked.

"Fine, but I need to get you on that stage, and it won't wait for us."

"I will not sit next to you, either," she said.

Jimmy chuckled resignedly and looked away. "Fine. Let's go."

Florine turned and thanked Mrs. Connor for her help, and for the sustenance she had been leaving by the door the past several days. Mrs. Connor's mouth dropped open before she regained her composure.

"I'm sorry if I came across as rude and ungrateful," Florine said. "It's been a difficult few days lately."

Mrs. Connor patted her arm and told her that it was all right. Then she dropped Florine's overstuffed bag in front of Jimmy and threw her arms up in the air, startling Florine.

"Oh, my stars, I forgot the package for the road! Wait here, and I'll be back faster than a bird can swallow a worm," she said over her shoulder.

"We need to go—" Jimmy said, but the woman had already run towards the kitchen.

Almost before the door swung shut, she came out again, tying a napkin into a bundle. She handed it to Florine and told her it would help settle her stomach on the bumpy ride ahead.

Florine seemed uncomfortable as she accepted the package. Mrs. Connor smiled sympathetically and patted her arm again.

"I had an upset stomach earlier," Florine felt obligated to tell Jimmy. "But why am I telling you?"

She turned and walked out the door.

"It was nice to make your acquaintance, Mrs. Connor," Jimmy said, touching the brim of his hat.

"Likewise, I'm sure," the older woman said.

"And you are a gem among jewels for what you've done this past week."

"Go on now," Mrs. Connor said, blushing from the praise.

Jimmy smiled as he picked up Florine's bag and stepped out the door. The smile disappeared when he turned to see the back of Florine's dress flouncing down the street. And with her head held particularly high, who would ever have known that this woman had just been jilted?

But everyone knew.

Chapter 4

Bad news traveled fast. Jimmy saw women staring at her and whispering as she walked along about ten paces in front of him. Some of the men were blatantly ogling her.

Florine came to the end of the boardwalk to step into the street when a man walked up to offer his arm. Florine stepped back at first, but the man smiled politely as he spoke.

"Allow me to assist you across the street, madam," he said.

Florine looked warily at him at first, and then said, "No thank you."

"But, I insist," the man said and took her hand.

Here we go, Jimmy thought as he walked up to them and said, "The lady doesn't need your help."

The man took one look at Jimmy and dropped her hand as he said, "Are you with *him?*"

Florine stiffened at the remark. "No, I'm not, and I would be happy for you to assist me across the street," she said as she offered her hand to the stranger and turned her back to Jimmy.

Jimmy exhaled slowly. *You don't know what you're getting yourself into, Florine,* he thought to himself.

He watched them until they were about halfway across, and then followed.

On the other side another man walked up to Florine and insisted on *helping* her, too. She declined and turned and thanked her escort, but he continued to hold her hand on his arm.

"I have to catch a stage," she said, beginning to feel a bit alarmed when he wouldn't let go of her arm.

"So soon?" the man said. "I was hoping to get to know you better."

Jimmy walked on past them towards the stage office, without a passing glance.

"And I would really enjoy getting to know you, too," said the second man as he took off his hat. "It's been some time since we've seen as pretty a lady as you in town."

"Thank you, but I'm going to be late for my stage," Florine said a little loudly, watching Jimmy.

He kept walking.

She began to panic.

"I thank you kindly for your help, but I don't need it anymore."

"How about coming over to the Half Acre and having a drink with me," the first man said. "That's where I first saw you last week—in the Longhorn."

"I don't go there anymore," she said. "Let go of my arm, sir," she demanded, and then called out, "Jimmy!?"

Jimmy stopped, but didn't turn around.

"I'm... uh, with him," Florine pointed her bundle toward Jimmy; her velvet purse dangled on her arm.

"He doesn't seem too concerned," the second man said.

"What's a fine lady like you doing with a..." he said as he looked at Jimmy and fumbled around for the right word, "what in the hell is he, anyway?"

Jimmy turned around and walked back to the three. His face was dark and angry; his blue eyes burned pale against his skin. He set down the bag without taking his eyes off the men before he straightened up to his full six-foot two-inch height. The fingers on his right hand instinctively curled into a fist.

"Tell them what I am, Florine," he said firmly, never looking at her, but glaring at one man and then to the other.

Florine swallowed, feeling danger dancing all around them.

"Well, he's uh... a... friend of my family."

That opened a door for the other two men to step away with their pride intact.

"Well, why didn't you say so, Miss," the first man said. "We wouldn't want to come between friends now, would we?" He looked to the second man who was nodding his head furiously.

You have a pleasant trip to wherever you're going, ma'am," the first man said to Florine, backing away, and then nodded to Jimmy.

The men turned and walked quickly back across the street.

Florine stood there trembling.

"I'm glad to know I've been promoted from half-breed kidnapper to friend of the family now," Jimmy said as he picked up Florine's bag and started to walk towards the stage office.

"Jimmy?" she said, wanting to understand what just transpired.

"We have a stage to catch, Florine," he said over his shoulder.

She hurried to catch up with him. She was on the verge of tears now.

"Why were those men being so forward with me?" she asked.

"I think you know why," Jimmy said, keeping his eyes straight ahead.

He heard a sharp intake of breath. When she spoke, it was barely a whisper.

"Because I'm a fallen woman now? How would they know that?" She looked around at the people on the street for the first time, noticing that most of them were staring at her.

"News travels fast," he said, "—especially scandalous news."

She stopped. "I think I'm going to be sick."

"Don't be so dramatic, Florine. You had to have known how people would react to you—especially men."

"Was that why those men offered to help me across the street? Was that why they wouldn't let me go?" Her eyes widened as she answered herself. "Because they think I'm a... "

She cried out as she turned and stumbled into a side alley. Jimmy could hear her retching.

He felt a pinch from his conscience, but brushed it aside. He followed her down the alley.

"Get out of here!!" Florine yelled. "I don't want you to see me."

She doubled over again.

"If you miss this stage, woman, you're going to have to ride on the back of my horse with me," Jimmy said as he walked back towards the entrance to the alley.

She straightened up.

"Wait!! You're not riding in the stagecoach with me? But what if some other man approaches me?" Her face was as white as a sheet.

"So you might have some use for me after all, *Miz Reen?*" Jimmy taunted as he walked back to hand her his kerchief.

Florine grabbed it, and then stopped and looked at it, front and back.

"It's clean," Jimmy said. "I took all the Indian off of it, too."

That caught her by surprise. "That's not why I did that."

"But you didn't want me near you earlier."

Florine thought for a moment. "I... I'm sorry about that." She looked down, refusing to look him in the eyes. She then wiped her face and asked, "Are you just going to put me on the stage and leave me?"

"I think you can handle yourself just fine."

"I don't even know how to get home."

"I'll be going the same way that you go. I'm just not leaving my horse up here," Jimmy said.

"Oh," Florine said, relieved. "I understand about your horse. It broke my heart to leave my horses."

"Heart?" Jimmy couldn't help but say. *You have a heart?*

"What?"

"Are you able to walk to the stage office now?" Jimmy asked.

"I think so," Florine said, but on the third step, her legs crumpled beneath her.

They missed the stage.

Chapter 5

Florine sat weeping in the stage office. She had been crying for a good ten minutes. "I'm sorry, Jimmy. I didn't mean to get sick on you."

Jimmy looked down at his stained boot. "That's all right, Florine. These boots have had worse stuff on them."

"I tried to tell you to put me down," she said.

"But you fainted again, Florine," he said. "I couldn't let you just fall on the ground. You're weaker than you thought."

"And I made us miss the stage," she sniveled.

"We'll just take the next one," he said.

He felt uncomfortable around a crying woman, but a sick, crying woman was vastly worse.

"Stop your crying now—look here, I'm going to walk over to the window there and exchange the ticket for the next stage."

"I can't stay in this town another minute," Florine sobbed, "not with everyone talking about me and men approaching me for the wrong reasons."

Jimmy asked the clerk if he could exchange the ticket for the next stage.

"Tomorrow's Sunday," the clerk said. "The next stage won't come through until Monday morning."

Florine wailed even louder. Passersby paused in front of the stage office to see what all the commotion was.

Jimmy leaned toward the clerk and said in a low voice, "You have to help me, sir—I'm begging you—tell me there is some other means of transportation out of this town... **today**."

"Well, the train is an option, but it won't make a run south until Monday, too," he said, then furrowed his eyebrows as he thought. "The only other means I can think of other than horseback is by buggy or wagon."

"Where can I get a buggy?" Jimmy asked.

"They're not cheap, but there's a smithy the next street over and north about five blocks. He sells and repairs carriages, and he probably has a used one he'd be willing to let go of."

"That sounds good," Jimmy said and nodded toward Florine. "Can Miss Locke stay here while I go over there?"

The clerk nodded and said, "Tell Jabus that Adam sent you." He looked over at the distraught Florine and lowered his voice. "You just be sure to come back for her, you hear?"

"I will," Jimmy assured him. He walked over to Florine and asked if she would mind going home in a buggy. She shook her head, no.

"The trip will take longer, and there may not always be good accommodations along the way. Are you up for it?"

"I can do anything as long as we leave this town today," Florine sniffed.

"Even sit next to me?"

Florine nodded her head. "Just get me out of town."

"Then I'll be right back. Don't you go anywhere."

Florine nodded and blew her nose in his kerchief.

Jimmy found the blacksmith shop easily enough, but learned that the only carriage available at that time was a newly built funeral coach. Jabus said he would let it go for a very reasonable price since the undertaker left town and reneged on the agreement.

"Is there another place around here where I could buy a buggy?" Jimmy asked.

"There are several blacksmith shops, but the few of us who build carriages or have them shipped in have a waiting list for new ones. Sometimes I get a used one to re-sell, but the demand right now is far greater than the supply."

Jimmy paced back and forth trying to decide. *Lord, this is getting harder by the minute.* He wasn't sure what to do. He didn't know what would be worse—going back to face Florine empty-handed, or to show up with a funeral hearse to take her home in.

Jabus could tell he was considering it. He told Jimmy he hadn't bothered installing the glass since he had no offers to buy it, but it did have the curtains, and he demonstrated by pulling back the dusty black cloth to show the inside.

"I don't know," Jimmy said. "Florine would have a fit."

"It's taller than the normal hearse—a person could even sit up inside of it," he said. "And it's big enough for two people to sleep in it."

Jimmy almost choked when he said that.

"It would only need to sleep one; that is, if I could get her in it while she's still breathing."

Jabus chuckled at Jimmy's comment. He had no idea Jimmy was actually telling the truth.

Jimmy walked around the long black carriage. The workmanship was impressive—he had never seen such a fine carriage. And it *was* big enough for Florine to sleep in at night, if need be—and up off the ground. It had plenty of space to store supplies, including Florine's trunk.

"And it's never been used?" Jimmy asked, convinced Florine for sure wouldn't step foot on it if it had carried even one dead body.

"I swear," Jabus said. "And it even has lanterns along each side if you need light at night. It's one of my finest creations, and I'm willing to sell it for what the materials cost me."

"Can those two bay mares in the far pen pull a carriage?" Jimmy asked.

Jabus said they were trained to pull, and he would let them go if Jimmy would buy the hearse.

Jimmy thought for a moment longer, then made a decision.

"Well, I'll take it if you'll clean it up and make sure it's fit for travel, and hitch up the horses while I go get some supplies," Jimmy said.

"It'll be ready for you," the man assured him.

Jimmy rode back down the street to a dry goods store he had passed on the way to the smithy's place. He planned to tie his own horse to the back of the wagon since Demon had never pulled anything before, and now wasn't the time to attempt to train him. He was too tetchy anyway. He thought of Allie and smiled. She had told him he needed to change his horse's name, but he just hadn't gotten around to it. His life was different now, though, and Demon deserved a more fitting name. Maybe he would come up with a good one on the trip home.

Jimmy ignored the stares in the store and began to stack up a substantial pile of supplies, including blankets, a roll of canvas, oil for the lamps, food, cooking utensils, and containers for water—separate, of course. He figured Florine would refuse to drink after him. And he grabbed a few more handkerchiefs, assuming she would need those, too, as emotional as she was. He also added some basic tools and supplies for carriage and horse maintenance. Jimmy had been shoeing and training horses for years, and he knew how to take care of them. Horses were what he knew best, and he thought again of the stud horse he would buy after he collected his bounty for bringing Florine back to her parents in Waco. He would have to keep that foremost in his mind to survive this trip. He was glad Mr. Locke's pockets were deep, and he had been generous with his expense money. Jimmy was using most of it in an hour's time.

The thought of the trip taking longer didn't set well with him, but he realized it might be best for them to travel alone, avoiding the stares, questions and potential trouble of a very pale, flaxen-haired woman traveling with a man of questionable heritage, according to most folks. He frowned at the thought, and then almost chuckled when he thought of Florine having to sit next to him the whole trip now.

Jimmy walked back to the counter and looked over the stack of merchandise to make sure he had everything they would need. The clerk looked uncomfortable.

"It's cash only," he told Jimmy.

Jimmy nodded. "Tell me what I owe you."

The clerk added up everything and hesitantly told Jimmy the amount.

Jimmy paid him in bills, and told him to keep the coins. The clerk's demeanor went from suspicious to surprised to quite pleasant after the sales transaction.

"I'll be back in a little while to load it up," Jimmy said.

"Yes sir," the clerk said cheerfully, "I'll be happy to help you."

Jimmy was back at the stage office in a little over an hour. The clerk gave him a relieved look—like he thought Jimmy had abandoned the overwrought woman to his care. Florine almost smiled at him, like she had been thinking the same thing.

"So we're really going to leave this town today?" she asked.

Jimmy nodded. "The carriage seat doesn't have a cover, though. Your fancy hat won't provide enough shade from the sun. Do you have a parasol?"

Florine nodded, yes. "In my trunk—right on top."

Jimmy opened the trunk and retrieved the parasol.

"I'm going to load your things, Florine, and then I'll come back for you," Jimmy said.

The clerk came out of his office to help Jimmy with Florine's baggage. Outside the door he stopped when he saw the funeral hearse sitting in front of the building next door.

"Is that what I think it is?" he asked.

"Yes—it's the only thing I could find on short notice," Jimmy said. "But it's never been used, and Jabus said he hadn't even finished it, so Florine probably won't even recognize what it is."

"Then you might ought to wait until dark to leave," the man suggested, "because she *is* going to recognize it."

"But look how much we can store back here—and it'll be protected, too," Jimmy said, trying to convince himself he didn't do so badly after all. The clerk helped him load the trunk into the back of the funeral wagon, and they started walking back to the stage office.

"This is going to be harder than I thought," Jimmy said. "But she wanted to get out of town as quickly as possible."

"I don't envy you," the clerk said, chuckling.

"Are you a praying man?" Jimmy asked.

The man nodded.

"Then I would really appreciate a prayer lifted up on my behalf in the next few moments," Jimmy said.

He stepped just inside the door to face Florine. She stood up, holding her purse and her bundle from Mrs. Connor in one hand, and the parasol in the other.

"Florine, I need to tell you something about the carriage we'll be riding on," he began.

"Are there many people out there?" Florine asked.

"There's quite a few."

Florine met him at the door and unfurled the parasol before she stepped outside. She held it close to her face, hoping no one would recognize her.

"Let's just get this over with—take me to the carriage," she said.

Jimmy walked in front of her and stopped beside the coach. Florine waited for him to help her up, and once seated, she continued to hide behind her parasol.

"Hurry!" she snapped at Jimmy.

Jimmy untied the reins and walked quickly around the horses to step up into the seat beside her. He started the horses down the street, and with a slight smile, nodded to the clerk shaking his head and grinning as he stood in the doorway.

For a while down the street Florine saw people staring and pointing at them—some were even laughing.

"What horrid people!" she said. "They all know about me!"

"It's not always about you, Florine," Jimmy said, "good *or* bad."

"What are you talking about?" she asked. "Just look at them looking at us!"

"We do make quite a pair," he said.

"We're *not* a pair," she corrected.

"Thank God," he said under his breath. "What I meant is that people are probably just reacting to the two of us traveling together."

Florine thought a moment. "Of course! They're probably wondering why I'm in the company of an Indian."

"So I'm back to Indian instead of family friend?"

"You know what I mean," Florine said. "You can't help what you are, and you know people think that way. Maybe they don't know about my recent misfortune after all."

"I wouldn't call it *misfortune*."

"And what would *you* call it?" she snapped back at him.

"A poor choice," he said quietly, "and I'm an expert at that."

Florine opened her mouth, and then shut it. She wasn't expecting that answer. She had been working on a retort for what she assumed he would say—that her behavior was scandalous and she was responsible for losing her reputation.

But then her conscience came forward again and whispered that it was the truth. Her proud posture slumped forward. That was the thought that had haunted her the past four days. Her future was ruined. She had not only humiliated herself, but she had disgraced her parents who had done nothing but love her and provide her with the best of everything.

She had finally admitted to herself that it was fear that had caused her to run away with Eustace Ashton. All of the girls she had grown up with were married now. Florine was so afraid she was missing out on life... on love. At twenty-three, she thought she was past marrying age and could see nothing but a future as a spinster—beautiful, of course, but lonely. The one man she had loved for years and had held out for was lost to her. She used to imagine her future would be with Justin—Jimmy's brother. But he had chosen someone else.

What is so horrible about me? she asked herself. Many had told her that there wasn't a more beautiful woman in Waco than she. She knew how to dress. She knew how to carry on polite conversation. She knew how to make a man look good by simply being on his arm. She had plenty of interested men in her past, but the young ones never stayed around for long. Several years before, she had overheard a conversation in a powder room when someone said, "Most men don't have deep enough pockets or the patience of Job to put up with Florine Locke." At the time, she had simply told herself those were the words of some old jealous biddy, but now she wondered if that was the truth. She had refused several proposals from old, wealthy men who wanted to relive their youth by buying a beautiful wife half their age. She couldn't marry someone she didn't love.

She had everything right on the outside, but what was wrong on the inside? Was Eustace right? Was she just a spoiled little rich girl?

They rode the rest of the way out of town in silence. Jimmy chanced a glance at Florine, who seemed to be lost in thought—no, it was more than that. She looked grief-stricken.

He handed her one of the canteens of water. "This one's yours; I have my own."

"Thank you," she said quietly.

"Are you all right?" he asked.

She shook her head, yes. "I'm just glad to be out of that wretched place," she said as she turned around to look back. "Good riddance."

She noticed the covered top of the long carriage for the first time.

"What kind of carriage is this?" she asked. "Is it used for hauling freight?"

"You might say that," Jimmy said. "I figured we needed something big enough to carry all your stuff."

Florine frowned at him.

"That was a joke, Florine," he said.

"Oh," she said uncomfortably.

Florine looked back again and even stood up in her seat.

Jimmy held his breath, waiting for the explosion. But it never came.

"Your horse is beautiful," she said. "I wouldn't have left him either."

Jimmy exhaled and nodded. Florine almost sounded human.

"You like horses?" he asked.

Florine nodded her head.

"I need to change his name," Jimmy said.

"What's his name?"

"Demon."

Florine nodded. "I think he deserves a better name than that."

"You're right," Jimmy said.

"I'll come up with a better name for him, but I'll have to watch him a while—you shouldn't name him just anything," she said. "It needs to fit him."

"Well, his name did fit him in the beginning, but he behaves better now. He's powerful, but I can keep him under control."

Florine actually smiled, although not at him. She was thinking about something, and the transformation in her face was amazing.

"What are you thinking about?" he asked, looking forward again.

"Demon reminds me of a horse we used to have," Florine said. "My dad bought two horses when I was sixteen years old—a gentle old mare for me and a stallion for him. His name was Rogue, and his behavior fit his name. Daddy told me to stay away from him—that he was unpredictable and dangerous, but telling me that I couldn't do something made me want to ride him that much more. I didn't want the old, gentle nag. I wanted to ride the stallion."

"You!? Wanted to ride a stallion?"

Florine nodded. "Doesn't sound too lady-like, does it," she said matter-of-factly.

"Did you ride him?"

Florine grinned and nodded. "When Daddy wasn't around."

"Did he ever throw you?"

Florine shook her head, no.

Jimmy hated to admit it, but he was impressed.

"I sweetened him up with carrots and apples or molasses bread for a while until he got used to me coming around," she said. "Then I began to brush him and rub him until he got used to me touching him. Then I eventually got a halter on him and was able to lead him around—"

"Was he broke?"

"Yes, but my dad said that only a man could ride him—that he was too tough to handle. But he became so used to me being around him that I was able to ride him bareback in a very short amount of time."

"You weren't scared of him?"

"No."

"Have you ever been thrown from a horse?"

Florine nodded. "Yes, when I was younger. But my grandfather made me get right back on." She stopped and smiled again. "If my father had been there, he probably would've given in to my crying and not made me get back on the horse. He has such a tender heart. And I probably would've quit riding from then on. But my grandfather was tough and wouldn't baby me."

She thought for a moment. "That doesn't sound like a grandparent, does it? They're usually the ones who do the spoiling, but Papaw was different. He was the only one in my family who stood up to me." She paused, remembering. "I miss him terribly," she said wistfully. "He was the one who told me how important names were—that a name should say something about a person. So years later when Rogue came, I renamed him King. From then on he seemed to behave differently, too—like he finally knew he was something special rather than a rascal."

"I hope you can come up with a good name for Demon," Jimmy said, "before we get back home."

"A good name," Florine started. "Home…"

And then she was silent. Jimmy ventured looking at her again. A tear was rolling down her cheek.

"What's the matter?" he asked as he pulled a new kerchief out of his pocket.

She took it without a second glance this time.

"I can't go home."

Chapter 6

"Of course you can go home—that's why I'm here," Jimmy said, "to take you home."

Florine just shook her head and continued to weep.

"Why can't you go home?"

"I can't tell you," she sobbed, "and I can't face my parents."

"Your parents will forgive you. I did so much worse than you ever did, and my parents forgave me," Jimmy said.

"It's different for a girl."

"I don't understand."

Florine shook her head again and looked away.

After a little while they met a wagon coming towards them, but it stopped ahead of them. The two men took off their hats as Jimmy and Florine rode by.

Florine was still dabbing her eyes, and Jimmy nodded a solemn greeting.

"Now that's more like it," Florine sniffed. "It's encouraging to see that there are still a few gentlemen in this territory."

Jimmy had to look away to wipe the grin off his face.

They rode along in silence for the next couple of hours.

"I need to stop," she finally said.

"Why?" Jimmy asked. "Are you sick again?"

"No, and a lady shouldn't have to explain herself."

The look on her face told him.

"Oh, sure—let me find a good spot with some privacy so you can... so I can..." Jimmy stopped right there, not sure how to finish that sentence gracefully.

"Shut your mouth," Florine said, frowning.

That worked.

Jimmy pulled the horses to a stop, climbed down, and walked around the front to help Florine down. He noticed his fingers almost met around her tiny waist. And she sure smelled good. He didn't want to notice things like that, so he dropped her a bit too quickly and had to steady her.

Florine frowned at him again and marched off to the nearest cluster of bushes.

Jimmy headed the other direction and was back at the coach before Florine. He started pacing from one end of the hearse to the other. He knew his time of reckoning was at hand.

"What… is… that?!" Florine said behind him, in a voice that would scare the dead.

Jimmy froze in his tracks and turned to face her. She was furious.

"Now Florine, it was the only thing I could find to get us out of town," he began, "and you know how bad you wanted to get out of town."

She couldn't catch her breath. But then it didn't stop her from yelling.

"It's badly—how *badly* I wanted to get out of town," she corrected him, missing the point altogether. "We rode out of town in a FUNERAL HEARSE!!??"

A covey of quail were startled out of some nearby grass.

"Yes, ma'am."

"So when we were leaving town, the people were pointing and laughing at this contraption and not necessarily that they knew about my soiled reputation?"

"I'd say it was a little of both."

She stomped around, muttering unintelligible words and then whirled to face Jimmy again.

"And those men back there weren't being polite because a lady was present. They were simply showing respect for the dead?"

Jimmy nodded. "I reckon so."

"And you didn't have the guts to tell me, Jimmy Taylor?" she said.

"I was afraid you would react like this."

"And you expect me to ride into Waco on a funeral hearse for the whole town to laugh at me, too?"

"I hadn't thought that far ahead, Florine—I just knew you were desperate to get out of town."

She walked up to him and shouted up at his face.

"I have never been so humiliated in my life! How could you do this to me? You probably think I'm the stupidest woman you've ever met."

Jimmy had had enough. He hollered right back in her face.

"Stupid? No! Spoiled, self-seeking, self-serving, vain, hateful, greedy, and too pretty for your own good—I've thought all those things, but I've never, ever thought of you as stupid! And contrary to your self-centered logic, I didn't buy this *contraption* just to embarrass you, Florine, but there wasn't anything else available. I figured it was more important to you to get out of town as soon as possible by whatever means than to have to stay another night!

"You don't make it easy for people to be around you for any length of time, Florine! Nothing's good enough for you. I imagine you would've found fault with that stagecoach, too, and made life hell for everyone on it. I'm sorry you were humiliated, but my part in it wasn't intentional. I can't say the same for your part in humiliating yourself. That was your own doing!"

Florine stood there wide-eyed and trembling. Earlier she had asked herself what was wrong with her, and she got her answer. She turned and ran back towards the brush to get away from the words that still lingered in the air. But the words followed her, taunting her. She didn't want to hear those words—she didn't want to face them. She ran blindly as tears filled her eyes and spilled over. She stumbled over an exposed root and fell. She rolled to her side, pulled her knees up and put her hands over her face as she wept.

The shame was all over her again, and she was back in the hotel room trying to hide. And at that moment, she didn't want to live. She couldn't face her future, but even more so, she couldn't face the truth about herself. She hated herself. She hated that her parents never said no to her—that they never gave her boundaries for her behavior. She took it as far as she needed to go to get her way, and she knew that meant misery for those around her if they tried to say no. She hated her weaknesses—that her insecurities led her to disregard all reason and sense of propriety. She had thrown her life away on an illusion of love and security.

She *was* stupid, she thought. And everybody hated her. Justin. Eustace. Her parents. And now a half-breed Indian. She couldn't even impress Jimmy. He saw right through her.

After a few minutes, something touched her arm. She flinched away. She heard him sigh resignedly.

"Florine, I'm sorry," Jimmy said quietly. He really wasn't sorry he said what he said, but he thought it might silence the condemning voice hollering inside his head at the moment.

"Why are you sorry?" she said in a crushed voice. "It was the truth."

"I'm sorry I hurt your feelings," he said. "Come back to the wagon. We'll eat something, and you'll feel better."

"Just... leave me here."

"I can't leave you here, Florine. It'll be getting dark in a few hours, and we need to be getting on down the road."

"I can't go home," she whimpered again.

"We'll talk about that later."

"I'm tired," she said, weary of the turmoil she had been carrying around in her head for days.

"I'm not," Jimmy said, grabbing her hand. "Here, put your arm over my shoulder."

He picked her up and carried her back to the hearse and set her down. She stood there looking at the hearse.

"Has this wagon carried dead people?" she asked

"Nope. It's brand new—not even finished," Jimmy assured her as he pushed aside the curtain and dug around for some food. "The person who ordered it left town, so it's never been used. I promise, Florine, it was the only thing the smithy had that I could buy so we could leave town today."

She peeked inside. "You bought a lot of stuff, I see. It does look like it could hold a lot of... freight."

He looked at Florine with a quizzical frown.

"That was a joke, Jimmy," she said wearily.

Jimmy almost grinned as he handed her some soda crackers and jerked meat. "It's a well-built wagon, and I figured we could make it work. And why do we care what those people thought about how we chose to leave town? What are they to us?"

Florine nodded slowly as she took a bite of a cracker. "It seems like I've had that backwards—I've been worrying more about the opinions of strangers rather than the feelings of those who care most about me."

"I know what you mean," he said. "I hurt my family bad before I turned things around in my life."

Florine looked at him. "Badly," she corrected him, but this time she heard what he said. She had treated her family badly, too. "I know you don't like me, and even though you're being paid to bring me home, I believe you have my best interests at heart, and... I'm... sorry for demeaning you earlier today."

Did Florine Locke just apologize to him? That made him uncomfortable. He turned and began securing the supplies.

"Don't worry about it," he said gruffly.

"It won't happen again."

He smiled warily and closed the curtains. He figured it was only a matter of time before Florine got her dander up about something else.

"We'd better get going," he said. "You can finish that on the way."

He helped her back up on the seat, noticing that Florine's fancy dress was torn and dirty.

"Your dress is torn," Jimmy said.

"That's all right—it's just a dress," she said.

That didn't sound at all like Florine.

He walked around the horses and climbed up beside her.

"I probably should be wearing black anyway," Florine said with a half smile.

Jimmy chuckled. "Now that was a good one." He handed her another kerchief. "Now wipe the tears and dirt off your face, and we'll be on our way."

"I can't go home, Jimmy," she said again.

"Why?" he said as he started the horses forward.

Florine was silent.

"What other option do you have?" he asked. "Where can you go?"

She shrugged her shoulders.

"Can you support yourself? Do you have money?"

She shook her head "Not much. I'm ashamed to admit it, but we took almost a thousand dollars from my father—I knew where he kept some money at the house. Eustace convinced me that we needed it to make a new start, but he also assured me that we'd pay back my parents the money we borrowed as soon as we established ourselves somewhere."

"Borrowed?" Jimmy asked. "I think that's called stealing."

"I know—I really thought we would eventually pay them back, but then we spent over half of it on traveling expenses and new things for Eustace, and his gambling. He was sure he could triple the remaining money at the card table."

"Gamblers always believe that."

"Now I know, but it wasn't until after he'd left that I realized he had taken the rest of my father's money. He left just enough for the stage fare back to Waco."

"How thoughtful of him."

"I don't know how I couldn't see what he really was. My mother tried to tell me, but I thought she just didn't think he was good enough for me."

"He wasn't, Florine."

"I don't know... we probably deserved each other."

"You got the worst end of the deal."

"More than you know..." she said as she began to weep again.

Jimmy tried to be patient, but this crying every time he turned around was getting old. He exhaled loudly.

"I'm sorry," she said. "I'm not usually such a crybaby."

He just nodded his head and let her cry again. It unnerved him still, and he didn't like it, but he was getting used to it. The worst thing about her crying was that it distracted him, and he didn't see the four riders coming until they were right on top of them.

He started to wave a greeting until he noticed their guns were drawn.

"Stay calm," he said quietly to Florine.

"Why?" she said as she blew her nose. Then she saw them. "Oh!" she wailed even louder. "What more can happen to me?"

"Calm down, Florine," Jimmy said, not taking his eyes off the men. "What do you want?"

"What do you have?" a big, red-faced man spoke up.

Two of the men rode their horses around to the back of the hearse.

"Hey, Cullen—this is a casket wagon," one of the men said.

Florine continued to weep. The men looked at each other and then to the one called Cullen. They seemed uncomfortable all of a sudden.

Cullen cleared his throat and spoke up. "Who'd you lose?" he asked Jimmy.

"Her man," Jimmy answered, nodding toward Florine.

Florine looked at Jimmy, "You don't have to go and tell everybody." And she cried even louder.

Cullen holstered his gun, took off his hat, and turned and swiped it at the man next to him to do the same. The other two rode their horses along the sides of the hearse back up to the front.

"I'm sorry for your loss, ma'am," Cullen said.

Florine nodded from behind her kerchief.

"She's got a purse, Cullen," one of the other men said.

Cullen glared at him. "What did I tell you earlier, pea-brain!?"

"Sorry, boss. It won't happen again. But she's got a purse!"

"You can have it," Florine said and held it out for them to take. "He left me with nothing!"

Cullen looked her up and down, noting her torn and soiled dress. One of the men started his horse forward to grab it, and Cullen swiped at him with his hat.

"We don't disrespect the dead or the grieving."

"That didn't stop you from shooting—"

"Shut up, Hank!!" Cullen interrupted.

"Hey—you said we're not supposed to be using our real—"

"Just shut up! All of you!" Cullen said. "Y'all talk worse than a bunch of women."

He turned back to Florine, who still held out the purse.

"No ma'am," Cullen said. "You keep your purse, and we'll be on our way."

The men walked solemnly by the funeral wagon. Cullen donned his hat as soon as he passed, and then they took off in a trot towards Fort Worth.

"Thank you, Lord," Jimmy said under his breath as he looked behind them. He looked at Florine sitting there wide-eyed. "We dodged a bullet there. We'd better put some distance between us before they decide they don't need any loose witnesses running around."

"Witnesses to what? But they didn't rob us."

He started the horses forward at a good pace.

"I don't think we were their first victims, and now we know two of their names."

"Is that what Mr. Cullen was getting so upset about?" Florine asked. Jimmy nodded.

Florine turned even paler. "Jimmy?"

"What?"

"What do you think they would've done if they had found out we weren't carrying a body?"

"I don't think they'd have been too happy with us," he said, "but I'm not going to dwell on that. I'm just going to get us on down the road."

Florine thought for a moment. "Jimmy?"

"What, Florine?"

"Did I remember to thank you for getting a funeral hearse to take me home in?" she asked.

Jimmy turned and grinned at her, and then they both started laughing.

"Why are we laughing?" she said. "I'm shaking so bad I can't even think straight."

"Badly," Jimmy corrected her.

Florine snickered.

"And come to think of it, you didn't even have to lie," Florine said.

"He asked the right question, so I didn't have to," said Jimmy. "He just made the wrong assumption. And you sure put on a good show with your bawling."

"What show?"

"Oh, never mind," he said. "But I think he actually felt sorry for you."

"That's because he doesn't know me," she said dejectedly.

"People can change, Florine," Jimmy said. "Just look at me."

Florine turned and looked at him. Those eyes—those piercing blue eyes. He had Justin's eyes. Why hadn't she noticed that before? She looked away.

The sun was getting low on the horizon by the time Jimmy found a good place to stop for the night. They had crossed a creek and left the road to follow alongside it for a while until they were well out of view from the road. Jimmy went back and covered their tracks for good measure. He didn't want any unwelcome guests to come upon them during the night. He came back and unhitched the horses, watered them, and hobbled them so they wouldn't wander off too far.

Florine sat atop the wagon and watched Jimmy handle the horses. She wasn't sure what she was supposed to do. She didn't realize they would be sleeping outside. She had never slept outside before, much less near a man she barely knew, and now that the moment was here, she couldn't do anything but sit there.

Jimmy came back to the wagon and began rummaging around through the curtained window in the side. He pulled out the blankets and the tarpaulin.

"Would you like to get down and stretch your legs?" he asked.

Florine shook her head, no.

"Where would you prefer to sleep?" he asked.

"Where are you going to sleep?" she asked back.

"On the ground here by the wagon."

"What about snakes and ants and... other things?"

"What about them?" he asked.

"Aren't you worried about them crawling on you?"

Jimmy shook his head, no. "I've probably slept outside more times than I have inside. If something crawls on you, just squash it or brush it off."

"Oh."

"I can clear out some of this stuff and you can sleep in the wagon if you want," he said.

"I'm just fine right here," she said.

"That bench seat is going to get a little hard and cramped before the night's over with," he said.

"Just hand me a blanket, and I'll be fine," Florine said.

Jimmy handed her a blanket. Then he laid out the tarpaulin beside the wagon, wadded up the other blanket for a pillow and laid down on his makeshift bed.

"Good night, then," he said.

"Good night," she said.

The wagon creaked as she tried several different positions—all uncomfortable. She sat up and looked around in the quickly fading light. The darkness scared her, or was it the isolation that bothered her more? She leaned over and looked at Jimmy, who seemed very much at ease stretched out on the ground.

"Jimmy?"

"What?"

"Do you think we could light one of these lanterns?" she asked.

"It'll just draw insects."

"Oh."

She jumped when something began yipping and howling uncomfortably close.

"What is that?!" she asked.

"Coyotes."

"Will they attack us?"

"Nope."

"Well, why are they making that noise?"

"They're probably bothered that we're here, or they might be greeting each other—I don't know. Go to sleep."

"I've never slept outside before."

"Really?"

"I never knew it was so noisy."

"Seems quiet to me. I guess I'm used to it."

"And dark."

"It's dark when you shut your eyes anywhere," Jimmy said. "Just shut your eyes and pretend you're in your own bed at home."

"All right," she said. But she was convinced she would never be able to go to sleep.

Jimmy woke before sun-up the next morning to find the wagon seat empty. He quickly looked around in the gray light, concerned that Florine might have wandered off—until he noticed a slender hand holding onto the bar on the back of the wagon seat. Sometime during the night she had crawled onto the top of the hearse and gone to sleep.

The corner of his mouth turned up when he thought about what the folks in Waco would say if they saw the stylish Miss Locke right now. He felt something else—pity, maybe? But then he told himself that she had put herself in this situation. She was due for some comeuppance in her life.

But the feeling was still there. He knew that her life had changed drastically for the worse. She had committed the unforgivable sin in some folks' eyes. He didn't know if she would survive the scandal in her hometown, and if she did, things would never be the same for her.

But that wasn't his problem. He was hired to bring her home, and that's as far as he planned to get involved. Put her in Mr. Locke's care, collect his pay, and get out of there.

He folded up the tarpaulin and blanket and stuffed them in the hearse. He built a fire and put some water on to boil for coffee. He mixed up some dough for camp bread, not bothering to be quiet about it—hoping Florine would get herself up.

She didn't stir.

After his second cup of coffee and third piece of camp bread, Jimmy realized she wasn't going to wake up on her own. He climbed up the side of the wagon and leaned over the seat.

"Florine? It's time to get up—we need to be on our way."

She just groaned and tried to roll over away from his voice, letting go of the back of the seat.

Jimmy was tempted to let her roll off the hearse to wake her up, but decided the fall might be a little far. He grabbed her arm.

"Florine, be careful—that's a long ways down."

She opened her eyes sleepily and frowned at him, trying to pull her arm away from him.

"What are you doing?" she said. "Let go of me!"

Jimmy let go about the time she jerked away from him. Her eyes widened when she started falling backwards with nothing to stop her. She screamed as her face disappeared over the side of the hearse.

Chapter 7

Jimmy lunged over the seat and grabbed for her legs rising quickly up in the air to follow her head and torso—already over the side of the hearse.

He caught her legs in time, but wasn't quite sure what to do next, other than to try to get the screaming woman to shut up.

"I swear, Florine!" he shouted. "I'm going to drop you if you don't shut up!!"

She shut up.

"I've got you, so just reach up and grab my arm and pull yourself up," he said.

"I can't," she said, reaching up. "I don't have the strength to pull myself up."

Jimmy growled and leaned back, pulling Florine back onto himself on the top of the hearse, and none too gently. He attempted to untangle himself from her legs and the mass of satin and petticoats.

"Ouch!" she said, bumping her head. "And don't you dare look until I get myself presentable!"

"Presentable for what?!" Jimmy said. "We're out in the middle of nowhere, Florine."

"For you," she said.

Jimmy looked at her. "Am I supposed to be flattered?"

"No—," she said impatiently, pulling her dress down around her. "I didn't want you to be tempted."

"Tempted for what?" he asked, frowning.

"You're a man, and men have carnal thoughts."

Jimmy leaned his head back and snickered disgustedly as he helped Florine up to a sitting position. "I don't care to take advantage of you, Florine, so get that out of your vain little head."

Jimmy turned and climbed over the seat and down onto the ground, leaving Florine on top of the hearse.

"You don't?" she said under her breath. "Well, then would you help me down?"

"I wouldn't want to be tempted," Jimmy said over his shoulder as he walked toward the horses. Then he stopped and turned around. "It's about time you learned to help yourself. Breakfast is on the campfire, and after you eat, I'd appreciate you cleaning everything and packing it back in the wagon while I hitch up the horses."

"But I need to..."

"You have fifteen minutes, then we'll be back on the road," Jimmy said, "whether you're ready to go or not."

Florine just sat there on the hearse with her mouth agape.

After a moment, Jimmy hollered, "Now you have fourteen minutes!"

Florine started moving.

Few words were spoken the first couple of hours on the road. Florine felt justifiably put out for a while, but when she cooled off and tried to start several conversations, Jimmy had little to say. He seemed offended, but she thought *she* had more reason to be offended than he did after he refused to extend common courtesy to her earlier—he didn't help her off the hearse, he didn't help her with breakfast, he didn't clean up the campfire and breakfast dishes he had dirtied, and he didn't allow her ample time to get ready to travel. And her daddy was paying him to bring her home. Surely he could be a little more helpful.

But then to tell her in so many words that he didn't desire her like a man would desire a woman was even more humiliating. Who did he think he was? He should have jumped at the chance to desire her. If Jimmy, whom she thought no proper woman would be interested in, didn't want her, then that meant she had become an undesirable—no man would ever want her again. But those men on the street still wanted her, she recalled, and something inside her went dark when she remembered why.

Florine's shoulders slumped again and her head bowed forward.

Jimmy noticed the change in her posture... again. Florine's demeanor had gone from pompous to poor, pitiful me in a matter of minutes. She was as clear to read as trail sign.

"What's wrong, Florine?" he asked.

"Nothing."

Jimmy left it at that. He knew Florine probably wanted him to dig it out of her, but he chose to remain silent. He could tell something was bothering her, though.

She couldn't stand his continued disregard.

"Why would *you* of all people not want *me*?" she asked.

Jimmy laughed. "Is that what you're stewing about?"

Florine glared at him.

"Oh—it should be an honor for someone such as myself with a much lower social status to have lustful thoughts towards someone as beautiful and highly regarded as you—a descendant of the Lockes of England," he said in a mock British accent.

"How dare you speak to me like that!" Florine said.

"Have you ever had one single thought apart from yourself?" he couldn't help ask.

"What?"

"You know, putting someone else's feelings or needs before your own—like maybe your parents, or a friend, or even a stranger that needs some help."

"Of course I have," Florine said indignantly as she sat there trying to remember an instance when she thought of someone else before herself.

Nothing came to mind except for… Eustace, but she wasn't about to mention that humiliation. She kept silent.

"I don't know if you are even capable of thinking beyond yourself. And heaven help anyone who gets between you and what you want."

"Why are you talking so mean to me?" Florine asked, on the verge of crying again.

"There you go again—it's all about you and your feelings," Jimmy said. "Why can't you hear what I'm saying? Did you think I didn't notice this morning that you assumed I was up on that hearse trying to ravish you when I was just trying to keep you from falling off?"

Florine didn't know what to say, so she fell back on a phrase she used all of her life when things didn't go her way.

"I hate you!" she said vehemently.

"Well, Miss Locke, I have to admit I've never met anyone quite as undesirable as you, no matter what stock you have descended from," Jimmy said. "But I have to congratulate you—it took almost half a day before you reneged on your apology. I'll try my best not to touch you anymore."

Florine wouldn't look at him. Why did she ever agree to ride home with him on a wagon, and a funeral hearse at that? And why did she ever apologize to him in the first place?

Those were the last words spoken until they stopped for a break around midday.

Jimmy's conscience had not let up on him since the heated conversation with Florine, but he kept arguing with himself that he was justified in telling her the truth. As he rummaged around in the back of the hearse for something to eat, he finally acquiesced to the still, small voice shouting inside his head. It took him a while, though, to think of something nice to say.

"Thanks for cleaning up the breakfast dishes this morning," he said without looking at her.

She thought for a moment and responded in a matter of fact tone, "Thank you for fixing breakfast." And after an uncomfortable pause, she asked quietly, "Can I help you do something else?"

Jimmy turned and looked at her, and he realized she was trying. She *had* heard what he said earlier, even through the angry words.

"Florine, I'm sorry—"

She shook her head and stopped him from continuing. "You were right again, Jimmy, although painfully so. I couldn't recall one memory of me putting anyone else first, and that's horrible. I don't want to be that way."

Jimmy nodded. "I'm sorry to have been so blunt with you."

"Maybe I can't hear otherwise," she said with a half-smile. "Please be patient with me, and I'll try to be of more help to you."

"Let's eat something quick, and tonight we'll take the time to cook an actual meal for supper. I'll watch for game along the way."

Florine pasted a smile on her face as she reached for the biscuit and jerky Jimmy offered her. "I hate to tell you this, but..."

"What?"

"I don't know how to cook," she admitted, biting into the biscuit.

"It's about time you learned then," Jimmy said. "You do realize you're going to need this skill when you get married and have children, right?"

"We always paid someone to do that for us at home," Florine said, and then suddenly looked away, panic-stricken.

"Don't worry, Florine, it's not that hard. I can teach you a few things before we get back to Waco," he offered.

"I can't face my parents," she said as her bottom lip began to quiver.

"Why?" Jimmy asked. "What is so bad about going home?"

The tears began to spill from her eyes. She tried to speak, but couldn't get the words out for the sobs that overtook her.

Jimmy grabbed her by the shoulders. "What is it, Florine? I'm sure we can work it out."

She shook her head, no.

"Tell me," he insisted. "It can't be that bad."

She leaned her head down into his chest—she couldn't look at him when she sobbed, "I'm … going … to … have … a …ba… by," finally admitting the secret she had dreaded telling anyone.

Jimmy didn't know what to do except hold her while she wept again.

A baby.

That changed everything.

And he was wrong. He had no idea under heaven how to work that out.

After a few minutes, Jimmy leaned back and said, "We'll think of something."

"Do I disgust you?"

"Why would you say that?"

"Because it will soon be evident to the world that I am a woman of loose morals."

"The world can be pretty unforgiving, but believe me, I've done worse."

"It's different for a woman, Jimmy," she said. "It's not fair! Eustace could just walk away from this problem, but I can't."

"The baby isn't the problem, Florine," he said. "The problem happened before that. The baby's a responsibility."

Florine looked at him. "I haven't really thought about the baby as being a *someone*—I've just been thinking that my father will never forgive me for ruining my reputation… and his. I didn't mean to hurt my parents this way."

"You have another life to consider now. Start thinking that way and what's best for you and your baby. We all do things we regret," Jimmy said. "But don't keep making more mistakes—you need to think things through before acting on something. Let's eat the rest of our meal on the road. We'll figure something out."

She nodded, and let him lead her over to the step to help her climb up on the seat. She felt immensely lighter for some reason, even though she felt her life, as she knew it before, was over.

Jimmy wished he hadn't been so hard on her earlier. She was in what his mother referred to as a *delicate state*, and he didn't know how in the heck he was supposed to take care of her now.

"Are you going to be all right?" Jimmy asked.

Florine nodded.

Lord, help me, Jimmy said under his breath as he walked around the horses to his side of the hearse. *I don't know how to help her.*

They passed the first stage stop at mid-afternoon and Jimmy asked Florine if she would like to stop there for the night. She seriously considered it—the thought of sleeping on a bed was tempting, but she was afraid of facing anyone and their questions, so she declined. Jimmy talked to the rancher and learned that the stage had been robbed yesterday, and a man was shot. Jimmy kept that information to himself—Florine was overly emotional as it was, and he felt like they were passed any danger from the outlaws. He watered the horses, and they headed down the road.

Along the way, Jimmy shot some quail for their dinner. When they came to a shallow running creek well before dark, he decided that was a good place to stop for the night. After he unhitched the horses and led them downstream to water, Florine gathered an armful of branches and a good-sized log for the campfire. Jimmy came up and tried to take the firewood from her, insisting that she sit down and rest. She finally let him take the log from her arms.

"I can carry this just fine—I'm not completely helpless," she said. "And besides, I've been sitting all day, and I told you I was going to start helping more."

"Don't overdo it," he said.

"I'm fine, Jimmy."

"And I can cook our supper while you rest."

"You're not trying to get out of giving me a cooking lesson, are you?"

"No—I just thought it might be too taxing on you."

"I'm going to have a baby, Jimmy—it's not going to kill me if I do a little work."

Florine stopped and thought about what she said. "Did I actually say that?"

They both laughed.

"Cooking lesson number one, it is," Jimmy said.

He began by retrieving the quail from the wagon to show her how to dress them and prepare them for cooking. When he saw her face go pale, and she put her hand to her mouth, he decided he had better take care of the birds himself.

"Why don't you go down by the creek and wash up, and when you come back, I'll show you how to make gravy," he suggested.

Florine couldn't get away from there fast enough. She grabbed a few items out of her trunk, including a sturdier cotton skirt and a simple, but elegant, long-sleeved white blouse to change into. Her satin dress had been miserable to wear in the heat of the day. She had learned the hard way that certain fashions and fabrics were not for everyday travel—especially by hearse. She smiled as she turned and looked back at the funeral wagon as she walked toward the creek. It really wasn't as bad for traveling as she once thought… if she could just forget what it was. And come nightfall, she planned to sleep in it this time around. She cringed remembering her hysterical reaction to Jimmy touching her that morning when he tried to keep her from falling off the top of it.

She walked upstream where she had some privacy, and sat down and took off her boots and stockings. She watched the water for a moment as she thought about Jimmy's words. She looked down and put her hand gently on her stomach. There was a life inside there—someone she was responsible for. She realized for the first time that this little someone could love her, and she could love it back. She wouldn't have to worry about putting on airs for a baby. Her heart began to beat faster. Her baby! She was going to be a mother! Her mind filled with images of holding her baby and dressing it. She determined in her heart that she would be a good mother. She wouldn't spoil this baby.

She sighed. How could she teach her baby something she knew little of? She had been pampered and spoiled herself. How could she unlearn a lifetime of indulgence? Jimmy seemed to see things clearly—maybe she could learn from him. And the thought haunted her again—why didn't he think she was desirable and worthy of love?

She shook that out of her head when the thought occurred to her that maybe she shouldn't focus on being desirable now as much as becoming a better person for her baby. Deep down she was beginning to realize that it had more to do with fixing herself on the inside rather than how she looked on the outside. The outside was perfect, and yet that didn't seem to be enough for the baby's father, or Justin years ago, or even Jimmy now.

She peeled off her soiled satin dress and held it out in front of her. Then she reared back and threw it in the stream. In a poignant moment, Florine felt like she had let go of a lot more than that dress. She watched it for a moment and...

"What in the Sam Hill did I just do?" she said as she splashed through the shallow water after it. "That's an expensive dress!"

She stepped back onto the bank and wrung out the dress as best as she could and draped it over a branch. Then she pulled the combs out of her hair and shook loose her long, blonde tresses. She picked up her lavender soap and stepped into the cool water and waded out until it was almost knee high. She sat down in the shallow creek and let the water wash over her. It felt so good after two hot, dusty days on the road. She hoped Jimmy wouldn't mind her sitting there relaxing just a little while longer.

A good half hour had passed and there was no sign of Florine. Jimmy was getting a bit worried. How long did it take a girl to *wash up*? It usually took him all of five minutes to take a whole, plunge-in-the-water bath. Just *washing up* took half that time.

He had fried the quail in some beef tallow, and it was time to make gravy, but he was waiting to show Florine how to do it. He decided to go check on her to see if she was all right. She might have slipped and fallen in the creek. He pulled the skillet off the fire and set it aside.

As he walked toward the creek bank, memories haunted him of the grief he had caused his brother two years before by making him think that Allie had drowned. He regretted that to this day, not realizing at the time the agony he had put his family through with that self-serving stunt. And as vain and selfish as Florine was, her behavior still didn't hold a candle to the reprehensible things he had done. He had told himself that he never would've done those things if he hadn't been drinking, but that didn't ease his conscience. He knew that no one had forced him to put the bottle to his lips.

Jimmy stepped up his pace. The little voice inside his head pricked him again about how critical and judgmental he had been towards Florine.

He was almost running by the time he came upon her. He pulled up quick when he saw that she was standing beside the creek buttoning her blouse. He tried to look away, but he couldn't. Surely that wasn't the same woman he had brought this far. He watched her lean over to step into her skirt. Her long, damp hair fell forward over her shoulders and hid her face for a moment. She pulled it to one side as she sat down to put on her stockings and shoes. Her face looked content—almost smiling.

She hadn't heard him walk up. He stepped back out of sight.

"Florine?!" he called out. "Are you all right?"

"I'm fine!" she answered. "I just need to get my shoes on, and I'll meet you back at the campfire."

"It's getting dark—don't tarry!"

"I won't," she said. "Thanks for checking on me."

Chapter 8

After a few minutes, Florine came back to the camp. Her hair was still damp and left down. A simpler, but expensive-looking brown skirt and white blouse had replaced the fancy lavender dress. Jimmy thought she had never looked more beautiful. He watched her drape the fancy dress on the hearse.

"I'm sorry I took so long," she said. "I don't remember a bath ever feeling that good, and I'm an expert at taking baths."

Jimmy just smiled and nodded, looking away so she couldn't read his thoughts. He watched the fat drippings start to sizzle.

"Oh! I forgot about the gravy," she said, squatting down beside him. "Now tell me what you're doing. Something sure smells good."

Jimmy agreed, but it wasn't the food he was referring to. He could hardly think straight with the smell of her perfume wafting under his nose. He shook his head clear and tried to focus on making the gravy.

"You need to heat up your grease—usually a few spoonfuls of the drippings from the meat you've fried. Sprinkle in some flour and stir it for a little while to let it cook. Then add your liquid—milk if you want milk gravy, or water, which is what we're going to use," Jimmy said as he poured some water in the skillet. He handed her the spoon. "Keep stirring so it doesn't get lumps. Vestal used to say if the gravy has lumps, then just call them dumplings."

Florine giggled as she stirred. "Vestal's been with your family a long time, hasn't she?"

"She came with my parents when they moved here from Illinois. I guess we're her only family."

"Did she teach you how to cook?"

"Some," Jimmy said, "but mostly I just watched her cook while I was waiting to get something to eat. I didn't sit down to dinners much with my family after I came back from boarding school—I'd get something from Vestal and take off," he said as he paused and smiled. "She never fussed at me for not waiting to eat with the family." The smile disappeared as he continued. "I also learned a few things at the boarding school when I was assigned kitchen duty for misbehaving, but mostly I learned it just cooking for myself—trial and error, although I don't know all that much," Jimmy said. "The gravy looks like it's done—add a little salt and pepper if you have it."

"That didn't take long, and it didn't seem so hard to do," she said, tucking that thought away in her mind. "What was boarding school like?"

"Hell," Jimmy said matter-of-factly.

"I'm sorry," Florine said.

"I've learned to let it go." He said as he fixed her a plate.

Florine tasted the quail and gravy and camp bread. "This is wonderful," she said. "We had a good cook at home—Matilda, but I'm sure I didn't thank her nearly often enough."

"It's never too late."

Florine nodded and ate in silence for a while. "If my father can find it in his heart to forgive me, he'll still send me away."

"How do you know that?"

"That's how my family handles mistakes—we sweep them under the rug as if they never happened. Perfection doesn't acknowledge or tolerate mistakes."

"He won't be able to ignore a baby."

Florine shook her head no, and a sadness swept over her face. "I just realized something, too."

"What's that?"

"He won't let me keep my baby."

"How do you know that?"

"Because the baby will be a reminder to him and the rest of our town of the mistake I made, and we're the Lockes of Waco, remember?"

"Whose ancestors were close to the British throne," Jimmy couldn't help but finish.

Florine smirked and rolled her eyes. Then she looked around the camp and beyond. "That sounds so ridiculous out here—but I've heard that for as long as I can remember. It's like we have no identity standing on our own merits—it was always our family name and the connection to our ancestors that was valued."

"Are you considering giving up your baby?"

"I don't know," she answered truthfully. "I'm just trying to get used to the idea that a baby exists. But for a moment back at the creek, I liked the feeling of being a mother, which is not like me at all. I can't stand being around crying, fussy children. And they're everywhere!"

Jimmy laughed. "I hear it's different with your own, though."

"I even found myself making plans for this baby," Florine said, and tears filled her eyes. "But I don't think I'll be able to follow through with them."

"Why not?"

"If I kept this baby, Daddy would disown me, and I can't support myself—I don't know how to do anything except…" she paused, looking for a better choice of words than 'to make a man look good,' "…dress well. And even if I could work somewhere, who would take care of the baby?"

"Well, we have a couple of days to think about it before we get back to Waco," Jimmy said. "How'd you like your dinner?"

Florine looked down and was surprised to find her plate empty. "Where did all that food go? You're a good cook, Jimmy Taylor."

"Thank you, ma'am. Tomorrow morning we'll have cooking lesson number two," he said. "We're having pancakes for breakfast. They're pretty easy."

"I love pancakes," Florine said as she watched Jimmy start to straighten up.

"Give me your plate, and I'll go wash these."

She started to hand it to him and stopped. It was about high time she learned how to do that, too. "Why don't I go wash the plates?"

"It's getting too dark to see, and I don't want you to step on a snake going to the creek."

"But I need to learn this stuff, remember?"

"All right," he agreed. "I'll light a lantern and come with you."

Jimmy grabbed one of the lanterns from the hearse, lit it, and walked Florine down to the creek so she could rinse off the plates while Jimmy washed out the skillet.

"This isn't so hard," she said.

"It would be if you let the food dry on the dishes," Jimmy said. "It's best to do them right after you eat. And let me tell you something about taking care of a skillet. Some people never let water touch a cast-iron skillet, but Vestal always washed hers with soap and water. She told me that the important thing is to not let the water dry on it or it'll rust. And then you have to cure it after you clean it, and you do that by keeping it greased."

They walked back up to the campfire, and Jimmy set the skillet on the fire to dry it, and then he wiped the inside of the skillet with a little lard and set it aside.

"There's so much I need to learn," Florine said.

"Well, that'll help us pass the rest of the time before we get to Waco," Jimmy said. "Now, where do you want to sleep tonight?"

Florine told him she wouldn't mind sleeping inside the hearse, so he unloaded some of the supplies to make room for her. She opened her trunk and pulled out a few petticoats and dresses to make a padding before spreading out her blanket. Then she found her most chaste-looking nightgown and a shawl and went behind the wagon to change into her sleeping clothes. She draped her clothes on the side of the carriage seat before crawling into the back of the hearse.

"Well, Jimmy," she said as she tried to find a comfortable position, "this is definitely a first for Florine Locke." She pulled the curtains across the opening, shutting out the lamplight.

Jimmy smiled as he unrolled his blanket on the tarpaulin between the hearse and the dying campfire. He reached up and turned down the oil lamp on the side of the carriage. He stretched out and turned over on his back, watching the stars and thinking about the woman a few feet from him. She didn't seem to be the same person that went to the creek earlier. They were
actually civil to each other that entire evening, and Jimmy found himself looking forward to the next conversation.

The wagon stopped creaking as Florine finally settled herself in.

"Just bang that cured skillet by the window to wake me up."

"All right."

"Goodnight, Jimmy."

"'Night."

Chapter 9

Jimmy opened his eyes just before dawn. Something had been lingering near the edge of his mind all night and finally came forward.

"Florine!" He jumped up and banged on the side of the hearse with his hand. "Wake up!"

She moaned loudly. "Go away," she said sleepily. "I'm tired."

"Florine! I know where you can go."

"What?"

"I know where you can go to have your baby, and you can even earn your keep there."

Florine sat up and opened the drapes. "What are you talking about?"

"Get up, and I'll tell you about it while I get the fire going."

Florine crawled slowly out the back of the hearse. She grabbed her blanket and wrapped it around her before limping stiffly over to the campfire. Jimmy pulled her trunk close and patted it.

"Have a seat." He began stacking some branches on the ashes of the previous night's fire.

"Now, what are you talking about?" she asked.

"I know where you can go," he said as he lit a fire. "I don't know why I didn't think of it as soon as you told me—I guess I've never had to deal with a situation like this. But several years ago I met this storeowner in a town west of here. They didn't have children of their own, but were fixing to take in three kids whose parents had died. Since then I've visited them a number of times passing through, and each time they had taken in more children, and I think they're up to ten or eleven now. I'm sure Mrs. Samuel could use the help."

"Help with what?" Florine asked.

"With all the children."

"I told you how I feel about being around children."

"What else are you going to do?"

Florine just sat there. She had no idea what she could do except go home and hope her father would forgive her and let her stay.

Jimmy poured some water into the coffee pot and set it close to the flames.

"If you decide to keep your baby, you're going to have to learn something about kids," Jimmy said.

"I haven't completely thought that through, yet. I don't even know if I would make a good mother."

"Well, you have an option now—I could send a letter of introduction to the Samuels if you want me to. I'm sure their door would be open to you. They're good people, Florine. You could learn a lot from France."

"You mean *Frances*."

"Her name's France, like the country, and she's pretty remarkable."

Florine felt a pinch of jealousy as she listened to him compliment this other woman. "What does she look like?"

Jimmy thought a moment. "She's short and has dark red hair and a bundle of energy, and seems to accept people as they are—"

"Petite and auburn-haired," Florine interrupted. "So you're saying she's pretty."

"I guess so—for an older woman."

"Oh—so she's old?" Florine looked relieved.

"Yeah, she's probably in her thirties," Jimmy said as he noticed her reaction. "Are you jealous of her?"

"Of course not!" Florine said. "Why in the world would I be jealous of some old married woman?"

But all of her life, Florine *had* felt that every woman was her rival. She had no close women friends, and now that she thought about it, there were very few she could even call friends. But there were plenty of interested males who called on her when they needed a beautiful woman on their arm to impress people in social situations. But few had stayed around for any length of time—except for Eustace. She thought her future was set with him, but that dream went sour. Her thoughts drifted back to Jimmy talking.

"…I tell you this, older woman or not, if France Samuel was unattached, I'd be knocking at her door," Jimmy said.

"What?! Why would you be interested in an older woman?" Florine asked.

"It's not her age or even so much her looks, Florine," Jimmy said, "although she's attractive. But from the moment I met Mrs. Samuel, she accepted me for who I was and treated me with respect. She even made my grandmother feel welcome and comfortable in her home. And I don't know of anyone else other than my mother who could've done that."

"Your grandmother?" Florine asked. "When would she have met your grandmother?" Her eyes widened. "This happened when you and Justin were bringing Allie home, didn't it?"

Jimmy nodded as he used his handkerchief to lift the lid off the pot and poured in a handful of coffee. He replaced the lid and let it boil for a moment longer before using his kerchief to move the pot to the side of the fire. He lifted the lid again and poured in a little cold water.

"Why did you boil the water just to put cold water in it?" Florine asked.

"To settle the grounds. You want to try it this morning?"

Florine shook her head. "I can't drink it."

Jimmy smiled, remembering that Allie couldn't drink coffee either. He poured himself a cup.

"Why'd you smile?"

"You just reminded me of someone who couldn't drink coffee either."

"Allie."

Jimmy looked at her and nodded. "You'd like her if you got to know her."

"She hates me," Florine said, "and I guess I don't blame her." *What was it about Allie that the Taylor brothers loved?* Florine thought. *I'm much prettier than she, and yet I never stood a chance with Justin after he met Allie.*

Florine looked down, remembering again the fool she had made of herself over Justin for years. And to drive in the final nail of Justin's contempt for her, she told Allie a lie that put her in harm's way—into Jimmy's hands. She told Allie that Justin was down at the river that Sunday morning, but he actually wasn't. Florine just wanted her to know that she knew Allie and Justin had sneaked off to the river the night before. But Allie believed her and went down there to find him.

When Allie didn't show up on the front porch with everyone else to load up for church, Florine had to tell Justin where she thought Allie might have gone. Justin followed her tracks down to the river and found blood and signs that looked like she had fallen in the river and drowned.

But she hadn't drowned. Jimmy had taken her. Florine looked up at him.

"Why did you take Allie that day?" she asked. "Why did you make everyone think she had drowned?"

Jimmy took a swig of coffee and thought for a moment. "Mainly because I was half-drunk and not thinking straight," he began. "The day before, Matthew and Marcus had told me to leave town and to not come back until I'd straightened up my life, but I hadn't left yet. I'd had some encounters with Allie before she showed up at the river that morning—encounters I'm ashamed to admit. And I frightened her again—"

"Why did you treat her that way?" Florine asked. "Was she rude to you?"

Jimmy shook his head. "I didn't even know her, but I knew she was special to Justin, and I guess I was trying to get to Justin through her. But it went from bad to worse. She turned and ran away from me along the riverbank. I tried to stop her, but she pulled away and fell and hit her head pretty hard—knocked her out and put a big gash on her forehead. I couldn't take her back to the house—I wasn't even supposed to be there. If Justin saw me carrying her up to the house bleeding like she was, he probably would've killed me before I could have explained what happened.

"I needed to get out of there quick, but I couldn't leave Allie unconscious on the riverbank—she could've fallen in and drowned. So I decided to take her with me—just until I could buy some time. I knew they'd be looking for her soon, and Justin would've followed our trail and found us in no time." Jimmy paused and shook his head. "I'll always regret doing this, but I made it look like she'd slipped into the river to get them looking the other direction until I could get far enough away. Then I planned to send her home."

Jimmy stared at the fire for a moment.

"It didn't occur to me at the time how horrible that was—what I put my family and Allie's family through. But I was leaving for good—I never planned to come home, so I didn't care what it did to them. By the time I'd sobered up good, I realized the mess I'd gotten myself into, but by then, I didn't know what to do except keep going. A couple of days out, I decided to leave Allie with a family I trusted, but their place was abandoned when we got there. When we tried to leave the next morning, a band of Apaches raided the place and saw us leaving. We tried to run, but they shot me out of the saddle. Allie came back and put herself between me and the braves trying to kill me. She told them I was Indeh—that I was the son of Nantan Lupan—my birth father, and they recognized his name and spared our lives."

"She came back to defend you?" Florine said. "After everything you put her through?"

Jimmy nodded. "I didn't deserve it, but she saved my life."

"What happened then?"

"They pulled the arrows out—"

"Arrows? You were shot more than once?"

"Twice—one in the shoulder and one in the leg, and a bullet went through my side here," he said as he touched his waist.

Florine sat there wide-eyed. "How did you survive?"

"An old man doctored me, and they tied me to my horse that first day," he continued. "I've never hurt so bad in my life."

"Badly," Florine corrected.

"Badly or whatever—all I knew was that it hurt like hell," Jimmy continued. "Allie even rode behind me to hold me up that first day—I don't remember much about the first couple of days, except for the pain."

"Where did they take you?"

"The band split up and left us with a handful of braves. We moved every day, but stayed in the same general area until the others had finished raiding. Then the whole group headed north to their home camp. It was there that I met my grandmother, Nah-kay."

"Did you recognize her?"

"No, but she knew me. I didn't learn who she was until after she took us to her tipi. When she was checking my wounds, she tried to get me to take off my pants, and in the process of telling her 'no,' I called her 'grandma.' She recognized that word and kept pointing to herself and trying to say it. Allie asked her if she was Nantan Lupan's mother, and Nah-kay understood his name and nodded yes."

"And then Justin found you."

"Yeah."

"What kept him from killing you?"

"He almost did," Jimmy looked at her, "except Allie got in between us."

"Of course—Joan of Arc to the rescue again," Florine said sarcastically as she looked away and sighed. "I don't understand that—she should've hated you."

"But she didn't," Jimmy said. "She forgave me, and she seemed to see what I could be and not necessarily what I was. I probably would've left Grace and never come back if it wasn't for her."

"A real saint." *How could I have competed with that?* Florine thought to herself.

"You'd like her if you got to know her," Jimmy said again.

"I don't think her kindness would go so far as liking me," Florine said. "We were both after the same man, remember? I'm sure she hates me."

"You don't know that."

"Yes, I do," she said. "And Allie's not going to help me with my problem. Tell me about the Samuels—where do they live?"

"A town called Brownwood," Jimmy said. "The community has grown and Mr. Samuel has expanded his store and can't help at home as much as he used to, so Mrs. Samuel has her hands full with all those kids. In fact, my sister was considering an offer to go work for her. I haven't been home in over a month, so I'm not sure if she accepted it."

"Faith hates me, too," Florine said.

"Oh, Florine," Jimmy said, exasperated. "Not everyone hates you. Have you ever tried to get to know my sister?"

Florine looked at him and shook her head.

"Because she's Indeh?"

Florine didn't answer.

"Do you really believe you are of more value than my sister?"

"No, of course not," she said a little too quickly. "I really haven't given it much thought, and besides, I'm older than she." Florine quickly changed the subject. "Weren't you going to show me how to make pancakes?"

Jimmy nodded his head as he looked at her. Florine looked away—she couldn't bear to see the disappointment in those blue eyes. *Why should I care?* she thought. *It's only Jimmy.*

But for some reason, she did.

Chapter 10

The rest of the trip to Waco was tolerable for Jimmy. Florine had drawn a line in the sand from day one about the differences between them, but after their conversation about Faith, he knew she thought the Indeh were beneath her. He didn't hate her for it. He felt more of a disappointment—that she had walled herself off because of a prejudice that had been passed on to her. He treated her with respect, though, and resigned himself to get her delivered safely to her father. Then he could put all of this behind him.

Jimmy could even be charming when for a moment he forgot who he was accompanying. And Florine actually showed some semblance of a witty personality—especially when she talked about horses.

Before they knew it, the suspension bridge leading into Waco loomed ahead of them.

"Stop, Jimmy!" Florine said.

"We're almost there."

"Matilda's husband sometimes does maintenance work on the bridge," she said. "I can't be seen by anybody that knows me."

"But I thought you didn't care about that any more."

"For my parents' sake—I'm sure they've been devastated by all the gossip floating around about me. I don't need to stir up any more humiliation for them by me making a grand entrance riding into town on a hearse," Florine said. "I'll just crawl in the back until we get to my house."

"All right," Jimmy said as he climbed down and walked around to help her down. He opened the curtains to scoot things around to make a spot for Florine to hide.

"I forgot my parasol," she said, hearing a carriage coming over the bridge. "But someone's coming."

"I'll get it," he said as he quickly lifted her up to climb through the window and shut the drapes behind her. He walked over to the carriage seat and grabbed the parasol and came back beside the window as a buggy began to pass by.

"Here you go," he said, and her slender, white hand reached out from behind the black drapery to grab the parasol.

A woman in the passing buggy screamed, and Jimmy jumped a good foot before whirling around to see what the commotion was. The driver of the buggy urged his horse forward as the couple both made the sign of the cross and stared back at him as they passed by.

He realized they must have seen Florine's hand from behind the curtain and felt obligated to holler, "It's not what you think!"

But the buggy was rushing down the road away from them.

Jimmy couldn't help but laugh out loud.

"What's going on?" Florine asked as she parted the curtain.

"I think we frightened the dickens out of those folks," he said. "They must've thought I had raised the dead or something when I passed you the parasol."

Florine giggled.

"They'll sure have something to talk about for a while. I'm glad they're heading away from town," Jimmy said. "Otherwise, I might have some powerful explaining to do. I guess we'd better be more cautious going into Waco."

"I'll be careful—I don't want to cause a scene in town," Florine said as she shut the drapes again. "There'll be a big enough one at my house."

"You'll get through this," Jimmy said as he climbed up to the wagon seat.

Ten minutes later, Jimmy turned the horses up the drive that led to the Locke's house, a stately two-story mansion with massive columns on a large porch in the front. He pulled the horses to a stop as Matilda stepped through the grand front door. Jimmy waved at her, but she quickly disappeared back inside.

"We're here, Florine," he turned his head and spoke to the back of the wagon.

Florine peeked through the drapery. "Go to the back of the house—there are too many eyes in this neighborhood."

Jimmy walked the horses to the back of the house as Matilda and Mrs. Locke came outside on a smaller back porch.

"I've brought your daughter home, Mrs. Locke," he said as he started to climb down from the wagon seat.

Mrs. Locke took one look at the hearse, let out an anguished cry, and fainted in Matilda's arms.

"What is it with these Locke women?" Jimmy said under his breath, and then realized Mrs. Locke had assumed the worst. "It's not what you think, ladies!" Jimmy said as he started towards the porch. "Florine's fine!" Then he decided he had better help Florine out of the hearse first, so he turned back to help her out of the window opening.

"Mother?" Florine called out as she hurried to the porch. "Mother! I'm all right." She knelt down beside Matilda, who was sitting on the porch cradling Mrs. Locke. "Is she going to be all right?" Florine asked tentatively. "She looks so much older than the last time I saw her."

"Worry tends to do that to a person, Miss Florine," Matilda said. She patted Mrs. Locke's face, and the older woman's eyes fluttered open.

She looked earnestly at her daughter. Tears filled her eyes, but a small smile and a look of relief swept over her face.

Florine began to cry. "Oh, Mother, I'm sorry! I'm so sorry for the trouble I caused you and Daddy. I never meant to hurt you. I was so stupid to believe that man. You were right about him, Mother."

Matilda helped Mrs. Locke to a sitting position, and she opened her arms to her daughter. Florine fell into them, still weeping.

"My beautiful daughter's home, Matilda," she said. "Everything's going to be fine now."

Florine caught Jimmy's eye, and they both knew everything wasn't going to be fine. She buried her face in her mother's shoulder. The other news could wait.

Her mother held on a while longer, then pulled back and said, "Now let's get you inside. Are you hungry? Why do you smell like smoke? And look at your hair and clothes—has anyone seen you like this? Where have you been? And why have you come home in a funeral hearse of all things?"

"I'll explain everything, but can it wait until later? We're tired and would like to get a bite to eat."

"Of course, dear. Help me up."

Florine and Matilda helped Mrs. Locke on her feet, and they walked towards the door. Florine looked back at Jimmy.

"Come on, Jimmy."

Mrs. Locke looked sharply at Florine. "Mr. Taylor may have other plans, Florine."

"I'm sure he does eventually, Mother, but he needs to be paid, and I'd like for him to be here when I face Daddy."

"But Florine…"

But Florine interrupted her. "Come on in, Jimmy—Matilda can fix you something to eat." Florine leaned forward and turned to face Matilda. "And you are a wonderful cook, Matilda, and I appreciate you taking such good care of us all these years."

If Matilda had been wearing false teeth, they would have fallen right out of her gaping mouth. And Mrs. Locke was staring at her daughter like she didn't recognize her.

The corner of Jimmy's mouth turned up as he followed the ladies inside. Maybe there was some hope for Florine yet, he thought to himself.

Matilda and Florine led Mrs. Locke to one of the beautifully upholstered settees in the parlor. Florine sat down beside her.

"Can I bring you some water, Mrs. Locke?" Matilda asked. "And do you think you'll need your smelling salts?"

"It's '*may* I bring you some water,' Matilda," Mrs. Locke corrected her, "and yes, you *may* bring me some water, and no, I do not need my smelling salts. Will dinner be ready by the time Mr. Locke arrives at five-thirty?"

"Yes, ma'am, everything will be ready," she answered and then looked at Florine and Jimmy. "*May* I bring you some water, too?"

"Yes, Matilda," Florine said. "That would be wonderful. Thank you."

Again, Matilda stared wide-eyed at Florine before turning to go to the kitchen.

Jimmy caught Florine's eye and nodded toward Mrs. Locke before offering to help Matilda with the water. Florine pleaded with her eyes for him to stay, but he shook his head and followed Matilda out of the room.

"What was that about?" Mrs. Locke asked, noticing the signals between her daughter and Jimmy.

"I have something I need to tell you, and I probably should do it before Daddy gets home."

"If this is about that wretched man that kidnapped you, I don't want to hear about it. You're home now, safe and sound, and that's all that matters," Mrs. Locke said, "although I have questioned the sanity of your father a number of times since he hired another kidnapper to find you and bring you home. I don't know what he was thinking."

"Jimmy's no kidnapper, Mother," said Florine in his defense. "Well, actually he was, but he's a changed man now. And Eustace didn't kidnap me either. I made that dim-witted choice all by myself. I wish now that I had listened to you."

"Well, I'm sure you've learned from your mistake, and we can just go on from here. We've recently begun planning the Cotillion—you can help with that since you are a former queen, and—"

"Mother—I can't," Florine interrupted.

"Of course you can, dear," she continued. "I have some wonderful ideas for the theme—"

"No, Mother—I've been trying to think of the best way to tell you this," Florine began, and then started crying again, "but there's just no best way. I've hurt you and Daddy so badly, and now that I've come home—"

"Oh, darling," her mother interrupted, "if you're worried about what people will say, we'll come up with something that will smooth everything over—like… you're a widow now. Yes! That's believable, and you know, the hearse parked outside may work to our advantage. I'm sure people in town have already noticed it. We can get a headstone and have a small service…"

"That is preposterous, Mother!" Florine said. "And that means I would have to take the Ashton name, and I never want to be associated with that man ever again, much less have my baby carry that horrible name…"

Florine stopped when she realized what she had said.

Her mother's face paled.

"Oh, no, Florine—not that," her mother said in a breathless whisper. "Your father will never stand for that."

Matilda and Jimmy walked through the door carrying the glasses of water.

"We'll never survive the scandal," she said as her eyes fluttered shut, and she leaned into Florine.

Florine looked at Matilda. "I think Mother's going to need her smelling salts now."

Chapter 11

Mrs. Locke was helped to her bed where she chose to stay the rest of the evening. Two distressful shocks in one day were more than she could handle.

Jimmy unloaded Florine's belongings from the hearse, and she asked him to take the funeral coach away from the house before her father arrived. She directed him to the livery stable shared by the residents of the neighborhood.

When Jimmy came back, Florine had Matilda serve him a plate of food in the kitchen. He looked at the single plate and then looked at her.

"Please don't misinterpret this, Jimmy," she said. "I know you're hungry, and I want to make sure you get something to eat before my father gets home. I'm not sure how he's going to react or what's going to happen or if I'll even be allowed to stay here."

Jimmy nodded his head. "I understand. But you need to eat, too."

"I don't know if I could keep anything down right now," she said anxiously. "I'm really worried about facing my father. I had hoped Mother would stand up for me, but I guess it's going to take some time for her to adjust to all this."

Matilda stopped stirring the soup and set the spoon down. She walked over to Florine and said, "I'll stand with you if you want me to."

Florine smiled and reached out to hug Matilda. "You dear, dear soul. How have I missed seeing you all these years? I know I've taken you for granted and have been so dreadful at times, and yet you're willing to stand up for me even when my mother won't. But there's more to this than you realize."

"Everyone makes mistakes," Matilda said as she hugged her back and turned back to her cook stove. "Let me know if you want me in there when you talk to your father."

"I will, Matilda."

Jimmy sat down to eat. "Sure you won't join me?"

Florine shook her head, no. "I'd better go freshen up and change before Daddy gets here. Appearances are everything around here."

At five-thirty sharp, Mr. Locke walked through the back door into the small vestibule.

"What's for dinner, Matilda?" he called out as he hung his hat on the halltree and walked into the kitchen.

He stopped dead in his tracks when he came face to face with Jimmy Taylor.

"You find her?" he asked when he finally got his breath.

Jimmy nodded.

"Is she all right?"

Jimmy nodded again.

"Thank heavens," he said, visibly relieved. "Where is she?"

"In the parlor, waiting for you."

He looked towards the door to the dining room, took a deep breath, and took a couple of steps before stopping again.

"I'll be back to settle up with you in a little bit," he said.

"I'll be right here."

Mr. Locke nodded and walked out of the room.

Florine heard her father call out to Matilda, as he did every evening after work. She smiled at the memory and then started trembling. She was used to getting her way with him, but this was different. She knew her father and his pride. Their name and reputation meant everything to him. She stood there watching the French doors he would be walking through.

Mr. Locke stepped into the parlor and looked at Florine.

Nothing was said for a moment.

Florine broke the silence. "I'm so sorry, Daddy. I'm so sorry I hurt you and Momma."

He held out his arms to her and she ran to them.

"I was afraid I'd never see my little girl again," he said.

"I was so stupid, Daddy," she said through her tears. "I was so afraid nobody would ever want me, and I'd end up alone."

"Why would you think that, princess? You're the most beautiful girl in Texas."

"Every daddy says that about their daughter."

"But in my case, it's true."

"I've learned it takes more than beauty for a man to love a woman. And I really thought he loved me. I believed everything he said."

"Well, you're home now, and everything's going to be fine."

"But I need to pay you back what we took—what Eustace took when he left me alone in Fort Worth."

"He abandoned you?"

Florine nodded.

"What kind of low-life vermin would leave my beautiful, helpless daughter alone so far from her home?" Mr. Locke said angrily.

"I don't even want to think about him now, Daddy," Florine said. "And I'm determined to work on the *helpless* part of me, too. I plan to make myself useful in some way from now on. And I'm going to pay you back somehow."

"You were born for somebody to take care of you, princess. And don't you worry about the money, although if I ever come across that poor excuse for a man, I'll take it out of his hide."

"Let's not talk about him anymore, Daddy," Florine said.

Mr. Locke remembered his wife and looked around. "Where's your mother? Have you seen her yet?"

Florine nodded. "She's not feeling too well and went to bed. I think the shock of seeing me was more than she could handle." *And she couldn't face what I'm about to tell you.*

"Well, I'm hungry," he said. "Let me go settle up with Jimmy so he can get on his way, and we'll sit down and eat dinner." He started to walk toward the receiving foyer to the other drawing room where Florine knew he kept a hidden safe.

"Daddy?" Florine said. "I need to tell you something."

He stopped and turned around and looked at her. "You really are the prettiest girl in the territory, princess." He waited for her to speak and when she didn't, he asked, "What did you want to tell me?"

Florine took a deep breath. "I'm... I'm just really glad to be home."

"I'm glad, too, Florine."

Mr. Locke walked briskly back through the house with a fat envelope in hand. Jimmy stood when he came into the kitchen.

"Is everything all right?" he felt compelled to ask Mr. Locke. "Is Florine all right?"

"Of course she is," he said. "Why wouldn't she be? She's home."

Jimmy just looked at him, thinking this was easier than he thought it would be.

"Here's what we agreed on," he said as he handed him the envelope, "and just keep any extra expense money you have left."

"I bought a wagon and a couple of horses, Mr. Locke, as well as some supplies for the trip. I left it at the livery."

"You brought my daughter all the way home from Fort Worth in a common wagon?" he said in an irritated tone.

"It wasn't a common wagon, sir."

Matilda snickered, and then cleared her throat to cover it up.

Jimmy continued. "Florine can explain what happened. I just wanted to let you know that it's there, and it belongs to you now if you want to sell it and get your money back."

"Where did she sleep at night?" Mr. Locke asked. "And where did *you* sleep at night? I'd better not hear of any impropriety on your part. You were just supposed to escort the stage to make sure she got home safely."

"Florine can tell you what happened," he said and then paused. "And why did you hire me in the first place if you were worried about any *impropriety* on my part?"

Mr. Locke just glared at him. "You've been paid. I think you just ought to leave."

"Tell me—I'd really like to know," Jimmy said. "Why did you hire me?"

"I heard you were a good tracker."

Jimmy nodded. "And you weren't concerned for your daughter's safety because of my history?"

"Your father explained what happened," Mr. Locke said.

Florine walked into the room "Explained what?"

"Nothing, Florine. Jimmy was just leaving."

"Jimmy took good care of me, Daddy," Florine said and turned to Jimmy. "Thank you for everything, Jimmy. I don't know what would've happened to me if you hadn't shown up back there."

"Is everything all right?" he asked her.

Florine nodded and walked over to him and started to shake his hand, but then suddenly hugged him.

"It will be," she whispered in his ear.

Mr. Locke bristled.

Jimmy pulled back and looked at her. "You know where to get word to me if you need anything."

She nodded and looked into those blue eyes.

Jimmy turned and looked across the kitchen at Matilda.

"Goodbye, Matilda," he said. "Thanks for the meal."

He grabbed his hat and walked out of the house.

Florine stared pensively after him. "Oh! Jimmy!! I forgot to tell you!" she called out as she followed him out the door.

"Florine!" Mr. Locke said sternly.

Florine kept going.

Jimmy stopped and turned around. "Tell me what?"

"Brave!"

"Brave?"

"Yes—what about *Brave* as a new name for Demon?"

Jimmy thought about it for a moment and then nodded his head. "I like it."

Florine smiled.

Jimmy grinned back. "I knew you'd come up with a good one."

Mr. Locke called out from the porch, "Florine, get back in here!"

Florine stood there looking at Jimmy, trying to think of something else to postpone his leaving.

"We're friends now, right?" she asked tentatively.

Jimmy smiled at her and nodded his head, yes. "Take care of yourself, friend," he said as he turned to walk away.

Mr. Locke's voice carried across the yard when he said to Florine, "Don't tell me you're interested in him, too!"

"What are you talking about, Daddy?" she said, still watching Jimmy walk away.

"I thought I'd picked the one person to find you that I would never have to worry about you throwing yourself at him."

Florine was horrified as she watched Jimmy pause in his steps, then walk on. He had heard what her father said. She whirled around to face her father "How could you say that in front of him, Daddy?!"

"He's not one of us, Florine."

"Jimmy!" Florine called out as she turned around.

But he was already gone.

Chapter 12

The sun sat low on the horizon when Jimmy rode Brave into his hometown of Grace. He was bone-tired and ready to be home. He passed by Kimball's Mercantile Store, which belonged to his sister Jenny and her husband Marcus. He recalled the night of his parents' thirtieth wedding anniversary party. The whole town was at his family's home that evening. Earlier that day, Marcus and Matt had told him to leave town for good after they had learned of his shameful behavior toward Allie. So Jimmy thought he would leave a goodbye calling card by breaking into the store to take some supplies before leaving. He ended up doing some ransacking while he was there, too.

After Allie and Justin brought him home weeks later, he confessed to the vandalism and agreed to work at the store for a solid month. He even drove the supply wagon to Waco several times for Marcus to make up for the mess he had caused that night. He shook away the memories—another stupid stunt from his angry past.

The anger—the deep, burning anger that was destroying his life was gone. He still had moments of exasperation—thoughts of Florine came to mind, but he was able to control his temper now. He knew his bouts with the bottle usually culminated in a lack of self-control, and he didn't like that feeling now. He hadn't touched a drop of liquor since his time with Allie.

Allie… thinking of her always brought a smile to his face.

Allie had shown him that religion wasn't just a social event where everyone went to church just to feel superior and self-righteous over everyone else. Well, some folks may have felt that way—the entire Locke family came to mind this time. Or that religion wasn't there just for people to feel good about themselves for being charitable, although he knew that was the case for some people, too. Allie showed him that true religion was about a relationship with God through his son Jesus. She called it *grace*, which was still something he was trying to grasp the meaning of. It was so hard to think of it as a free gift when nothing came free in this life. But it meant so much to Allie and his brother Justin that they had named their first child, a baby girl…Grace.

Allie told Jimmy that knowing Jesus helped her to not be so self-centered—Florine's face appeared again in his thoughts—but rather to try to put others before herself. Jimmy remembered how Allie had risked her life to save his own on more than one occasion.

That wasn't normal.

Jimmy looked at the three-storied red brick home as he walked Brave up the drive. A huge porch led up to the second floor. The porch roof created a balcony on the third floor. Part of the first floor—Vestal's domain was underground. Up until two years ago, he had never felt like it was his home, but now it was a place of comfort and refuge for him.

As Jimmy came around the corner of the house, Vestal stepped out of the bath house with a load of folded linens. She jumped and dropped the pile of sheets when she saw him.

"Jimmy Taylor!" she said as she grabbed her chest. "You 'bout scared me to death!"

Jimmy laughed as he climbed off his horse.

"You had better get over here right now," she said sternly.

Jimmy tied Brave to a hitching post and walked over to Vestal. "I'll pick them up, Vestal—I didn't mean to startle you."

"No, I don't want you to pick them up, although I'll let you since my back's been giving me fits," she said. "I mainly need you to give me a hug."

Jimmy laughed again as he wrapped his arms around Vestal. "Hello, Vestal. How's my sweet champion?"

Vestal grinned as she hugged him back. "It's about time you got yourself home, boy. It's been downright dull around here without you."

"Where is everybody?"

"Well, your mom and dad are over at Matt's right now. I expect them back any minute," Vestal said. "And you'd better check in with your grandmother before you go to bed. And Faith went to Brownwood several weeks ago."

"She took the Samuel's offer?"

Vestal nodded. "She was so excited about teaching those kids."

"I think that was a good decision for her. She's kept herself cooped up in this house for too long," Jimmy said. "And you would love the Samuels, Vestal. They're about as good as they come."

"That's what your father said. He took Faith over there himself to make sure she was going to be all right. He thinks this is just what she needs to get her out of her shell."

"Working with all those children is bound to do that," Jimmy said.

"Are you hungry, sweetness?" Vestal asked.

"I ate supper in Waco, but I wouldn't turn down a piece of pie or cake if you have any," Jimmy said.

"I always have some kind of confectionery on hand. Your father has a sweet tooth, you know."

"Good. Well, let me take care of my horse, and I'll meet you in the kitchen," Jimmy said as he picked up the dropped sheets and handed them to Vestal.

"I guess this means you found the girl, then," Vestal asked.

Jimmy nodded.

"And I guess this means you're going to get your stud horse soon, huh."

Jimmy grinned and nodded.

"I'll have a big slice of cake waiting for you, and we'll celebrate."

"You're the best, Vestal."

Chapter 13

Jimmy walked into the pen and whistled as he held out his hand. The horse walked over to him and took the apple slices. Sometimes he just rewarded him with words of praise and a rub, but he always made it worthwhile for the horse to approach him.

Jimmy worked with him for most of the morning and then climbed up on the corner of the fence to watch the stallion pacing around the pen. It had been a week since he had bought the horse and brought it back to Grace. He was halter broke, but had never been ridden. Jimmy planned to take his time training this one.

Matthew Taylor walked up to the pen.

"You did good, son," he said, watching the horse. "That's a fine horse."

"Thanks," Jimmy said. "I still can't believe he's mine."

"Demon's not too happy about it, is he," Matthew said, noticing Jimmy's other horse snorting and prancing around two pens over.

"Florine gave Demon a new name," Jimmy said. "She thought I ought to call him *Brave*."

Matthew smiled and nodded. "Florine came up with that? That's not bad for her."

"Yeah, I thought having to take that woman home would be the end of me, but the last half of the trip turned out fairly pleasant. But it didn't take her long to revert back to her old self after she got around her daddy again."

"Langston's a sharp businessman, but he's lacking when it comes to dealing with people."

"Appearances are everything, I was told, and I didn't fit into their picture too well."

Matthew looked at Jimmy. "Did Langston mistreat you?"

"Nah, it doesn't matter," Jimmy said, shrugging his shoulders. "He paid good money, though, and I'm looking at the fruit of my labor."

"I'm going to have a talk with him next time I'm in Waco," Matthew said.

"No, Dad, don't worry about it," Jimmy said. "I'll probably never see him again."

Two days later, Langston Locke drove his lathered horse up the drive to the Taylor home just before dark. He climbed down out of the buggy and marched up the steps to the front door and pounded on it.

Julia Taylor opened the door to an angry man.

"Langston! What is the matter?" she asked. "Is Hazel all right?"

He calmed down a bit when he saw Julia. She had that kind of effect on people. She was a beautiful woman, tall and slender, silver-haired and with those striking blue eyes that seemed to peer into one's soul.

"My wife's fine," he said. "I'm sorry for calling on you unannounced like this, but I need to talk to Jimmy."

"He's out working in the barn," Julia said. "If you'll take a seat in the parlor, I'll go get him."

"Don't bother—I'll find him," he said as he walked through the door and past her, heading toward the stairs.

"Is something wrong?" she asked as she followed him.

"Florine's gone again, and I think Jimmy knows where she is."

He paused for a brief moment where the stairs split and chose the one going downstairs to the right. Julia followed him.

"What are you talking about?" she asked. "Jimmy had nothing to do with her leaving again—we know nothing about that. He's been here the whole time, other than when he went to pick up a horse last week."

"I didn't say he had anything to do with her leaving—but I believe he knows where she is, and he's going to tell me." He said as he walked out the back door and down the steps.

Julia didn't know whether she should find Matthew or follow Langston to the barn. She decided she'd better find her husband, but not before she issued a warning.

"LANGSTON!" she said in her sternest voice.

He stopped and turned around to face her, shocked to hear the gracious Julia Taylor yell at him. He had never seen this side of her. Those blue eyes were blazing, and she looked something akin to an angry mother bear.

"I don't know what you plan to tell my son, but you had better not disrespect him or threaten him or touch him in any way, or you'll have me to answer to. Do you understand me?" Julia said.

"And that goes for me, too," Matthew added as he stepped up beside her. He had heard all the commotion from upstairs.

Julia breathed a sigh of relief.

"What's this about, Langston?" he demanded to know.

Langston was still reeling from Julia's barrage in defense of her son. He decided he had better calm down and use a little more tact in addressing Jimmy.

"I'm sorry, Julia," he said. "I'm just worried about Florine. She's run off again, and I think Hazel was in on it this time, but she swears she doesn't know where our daughter went, other than she thought Jimmy knew something about it."

Jimmy heard all the hollering, and walked quickly up to the house to see what the matter was. He stiffened when he saw Mr. Locke talking to his parents.

"I knew something about what?" Jimmy asked as he stepped up to face him.

"Florine's disappeared again, and run off in that hideous funeral hearse you brought her home in."

"What? When did she leave?" Jimmy asked.

"Some time early this morning," he continued. "She usually sleeps late, so I don't see her before I go to work. I didn't know she'd left until I came home for dinner. On top of that, I didn't even have dinner because Matilda's mother is sick or something so she didn't even come in today."

"Why did Florine leave?" Jimmy asked.

"I think you know why, and I'd rather not discuss this in front of your parents."

"Mom, Dad, would you excuse us for a moment?" Jimmy asked his parents.

"I'll have Vestal fix you something to eat, Langston," Julia said decorously before she and Matthew started to step back inside. "And you're welcome to stay the night."

Mercy's Face

"Thank you," he said, relieved to see the old Julia back. He watched them until they closed the door.

"Someone had to have gone with her," Jimmy said. "Florine can't handle those horses by herself."

"I know, but nobody knew she was even in town except..." he stopped, "Matilda and Rune..." He slapped his forehead. "That's why Matilda didn't come in today." He began pacing back and forth. "How dare she usurp my authority in my own home... and after all I've done for her. Well, she can just stay gone."

"Matilda doesn't strike me as the kind of person who would do anything without being told," Jimmy said. "Do you think Mrs. Locke had anything to do with that?"

"She would never go against me," he said, and paused a moment, thinking. "And Bill Williams also knew Florine was in town, but he wouldn't have anything to do with her leaving."

"The Ranger?"

Mr. Locke nodded. "Hazel was telling Florine about a young man who was shot when he tried to stop some men from taking his wife's wedding ring during that stage robbery south of Fort Worth. They thought it was chivalrous, but the man can't even walk now—what's so chivalrous about that?"

"Do you realize your daughter would've been on that stage if we hadn't missed it back in Fort Worth?"

"But you would've been there to protect her."

"I probably would've gotten myself killed," Jimmy said. "There were four of them, and I'm not that fast with a gun. But what did that have to do with Ranger Williams?"

"Oh—Florine said she needed to talk to Bill about that robbery—that she might have some information for him. She gave him a pretty good description of most of them, and even remembered two of their names," Mr. Locke said. "They sent that information all up and down the stage route and to all the sheriff's offices in the territory. Those men won't be running around Texas much longer without getting caught."

"That was a brave thing she did," Jimmy said.

"I advised her against it—she shouldn't have gotten involved."

"But surely everyone on the stage was able to give a description, too, right?"

Mr. Locke shook his head. "The men's faces were covered—I don't know why they let you and Florine see them."

"They must have come up on us too fast," Jimmy said. "You shouldn't worry about them finding out what she did. They probably don't even remember they ran into us. Now tell me why Florine ran off again."

Mr. Locke looked away. "Too many people know us here in Texas so I was going to send her away—to my cousin's back east—until after... you know, and then she'd return and everything would be back to normal."

Jimmy noticed he couldn't even say the word *baby*.

"Florine told me she wanted to keep it," Mr. Locke said as he shook his head. "But that's just unacceptable."

"So you gave her no other alternative?" Jimmy asked.

"There *is* no other alternative," he said doggedly. "But to help her make the right decision for all of us, I told her I would forget about the money she and Eustace stole from me, if she would do the right thing."

"And if she didn't choose your decision, what would happen then?" Jimmy asked.

"I simply told her that she would be responsible for paying back the thousand dollars," he said.

"So you threatened her," Jimmy said.

"Of course not!"

"But you know Florine can't make that kind of money on her own."

"She's just not thinking clearly about the consequences of her actions. She can't keep this constant reminder of her indiscretion."

"It's called a baby, Mr. Locke—your grandchild."

"That's no grandchild of mine—something out of wedlock doesn't count."

"I guess that means I don't count either," Jimmy said.

"I'm not here to argue with you, Jimmy. Hazel said Florine mentioned somebody that you knew might help her, but she wouldn't even tell her mother. So I just want to know who these people are so I can find my daughter."

"How would I know?" Jimmy said. "I'm not one of you, remember?"

"So you're not going to help me?" Mr. Locke said, ignoring the comment.

"I think you need to give Florine some time to decide what she wants to do with her life, and whether that baby is going to be a part of it."

"What if something happens to her?" he said. "I'll pay you if you'll go get her. You don't even have to tell me where she is."

Jimmy shook his head. "She'll just keep running away if you force her to do something she's not ready to do. I think you need to give her time to decide what she believes is best for her and the baby."

"Can you promise me she's in good hands?"

"If she's heading where I think she's heading, then, yes, she couldn't be in better hands."

"If she makes the wrong choice," Mr. Locke said, "then I've lost my daughter forever."

"It doesn't have to be that way," Jimmy said.

"Yes, it does," Mr. Locke said determinedly. "And if anything happens to Florine in the meantime, I'm holding you personally responsible, Jimmy."

Chapter 14

Rune pulled up in front of the general store and handed his wife the reins.

"Well, this is the third store, surely it's the right one," he said. "But I'll make sure."

Matilda turned around and said, "Florine, I think this is it."

Florine peeked out of the back of the hearse at the store. She saw the name *Samuel* on the sign.

"This is the one, Matilda," she said. "Samuel was the name Jimmy gave me. I knew I'd recognize it when I saw it."

She crawled to the back of the hearse and climbed out and stretched. She looked around and saw that the store sat on the town square. It dawned on her for the first time why it was called the town square—it literally was square. Businesses surrounded what looked like this small town's court house. She realized this must be the center of the town—the streets seemed to radiate off of it like spokes on a square wheel.

The square was full of activity—men visited under the trees near the court house, wagons and horses passed to and fro. She remembered the reaction of the people seeing something move in the back of the hearse in Waco, so she decided to step around to the side of the hearse facing the store.

A few minutes later, Rune walked out of the store with the proprietor. The storeowner's eyes widened when he saw the hearse, but he gave Matilda a friendly smile.

Rune introduced them. "This here's Matilda, my wife," he said, pointing to Matilda. "And this is Florine." He pointed to her. "Ladies, this is George Samuel."

George nodded towards a beautiful young woman looking rather hot and tousled standing beside the funeral hearse.

She smiled hesitantly and said, "Hello."

"Nice to meet you folks," George said as he looked from one end of the hearse to the other. "I must say, I've never consider traveling in one of these before, but it looks like it's working fine for you."

Florine said, "Jimmy Taylor bought it to bring me home from Fort Worth."

"Jimmy Taylor? My goodness—how's that young man doing?"

"He's doing fine," she said, "and he told me that you and your wife might be able to help me."

"Sure—if Jimmy said so," he said. "How can we help you?"

Florine felt embarrassed all of a sudden and wasn't sure how to bring up her dilemma with a stranger, and a man at that.

"Is your wife around, Mr. Samuel?" she asked. "I'd like to talk to *her*."

"France is at the house," he said, noting her uneasiness.

He gave them directions to his home, and said he would see them this evening.

A few minutes later, Florine and the Bishops walked up to the Samuel home, a large rock house with a porch spanning almost the entire length of the front. As she knocked on the door, she could hear the sounds of children from somewhere behind the house. After a moment, a young woman answered the door.

"Hello," Florine said. "I'm looking for Mrs. France Samuel."

"Florine?!" the woman said.

Florine stared at the young woman for a moment before recognition set in.

"Faith! It's been a while!" Florine said. "I forgot that Jimmy told me you might be working here now."

"What are you doing here?" Faith asked, flabbergasted to see her.

"Uh… I've come to… talk to Mrs. Samuel," she stammered and looked at Matilda. "And this is Matilda and Rune Bishop, also of Waco."

"Come on in," Faith said as she stepped aside. "I just never expected to see *you* of all people here.

"I never expected to ever be here," Florine said.

"Mrs. Samuel is out back with the little ones."

Faith asked them to have a seat in the parlor and said she would go and fetch Mrs. Samuel. Rune and Matilda sat down, but Florine walked around the room looking at everything. The furniture was nice, but simple. A large braided rug covered the middle of the floor. Something cooking smelled good, too, and she realized how hungry she was.

Florine had forgotten about the possibility of Faith being here. She had hoped that Matilda and Rune would be the only ones outside of the family… and Jimmy, who knew about the baby. Florine had told her mother she would run away again if her father forced her to leave Texas to give up her baby. She mentioned that Jimmy knew of a good place where she could stay and have her baby, and that's where she decided to go. Her mother gave in, but only at the insistence of sending the Bishops to escort Florine. She told her daughter that she wouldn't be able to keep anything from her husband, so she forbade Florine to tell her where she was going.

Florine felt that Faith had no reason to show her any consideration in keeping her secret since she had never gone out of her way to befriend her. Florine still hadn't decided if she should keep the baby or not, and if not, she wanted as few people to know about it as possible. She knew the Bishops were loyal and discreet, but she felt she would have to work on her relationship with Faith to insure her confidentiality.

Florine realized this situation was getting more complicated by the minute. Why did one indiscretion seem to lead to another quandary, then another? She looked at Matilda, who looked exhausted.

"Have I remembered to thank you for coming with me?" she asked her.

"At least five times, Florine," Matilda answered. "I'm glad we got you here safely, but I just hope I have a job when I get back to Waco."

"I know Daddy's going to be mad when he finds out you helped me, but he won't stay mad for long—he loves your cooking too much, Matilda. And he can't stay mad at you and Rune when he finds out that you came only at Mother's insistence, and for my protection. And—"

A piercing scream from the back of the house interrupted her. They looked toward the windows as the screams continued and then glanced at each other before they all headed the direction of the shrieks. Someone had to be dying by the way it sounded. They walked quickly through the dining room and kitchen and out the door onto the back porch. Florine pulled up short when she saw Faith and Mrs. Samuel wrestling with a pint-sized banshee. Mrs. Samuel struggled to take a basket away from the writhing girl.

82

Mercy's Face

"You *will* give Emma the basket, Caitlin," Mrs. Samuel said, trying to pry it from the little girl's fingers. "You have your own basket; we don't take things that belong to someone else."

It took both Faith and Mrs. Samuel to wrest it away from her. Mrs. Samuel turned around and handed the basket to another girl while Faith continued to hold Caitlin. When Faith let go of her, the little girl threw herself on the ground and continued to scream and kick her legs. Faith started to reach for her again, but Mrs. Samuel stopped her.

"Just let her be, Faith," she said, wearily shaking her head. "Maybe she'll wear herself out this time. We have to have the resolve to outlast her—for her sake, and for ours."

Florine stood there wide-eyed, watching the scene. She looked beyond Mrs. Samuel to see four other young children of various ages standing in the rows of a garden. They all stared at the little girl crying and wallowing around on the ground. Florine was tempted to turn and walk away right then, if what she just witnessed was an indication of life in this house. She was convinced *she* didn't have that kind of resolve.

About that time Mrs. Samuel noticed the three strangers standing on her porch watching them. She looked at Faith for an explanation.

"That's what I was trying to tell you when Caitlin took Emma's basket," said Faith.

"Well, stay here with the kids—they know what to do, and just keep an eye on Caitlin—make sure she doesn't run off and hide again," Mrs. Samuel said. She walked up to the newcomers and introduced herself. "Let's step back into the house so we can hear each other over the din," she continued. "I'm sorry you had to witness that. Caitlin hasn't been here long, and she's really struggling living in a new home and family."

Florine thought that was an odd way to put it. All she saw was a spoiled little brat throwing a fit. They followed Mrs. Samuel back into the kitchen.

Florine introduced herself and the Bishops and told Mrs. Samuel they were from Waco. She stopped to gather her thoughts, but it was hard to think with the unnerving sound of the screams from the little girl outside.

"How long will she keep crying?" she couldn't help but ask.

"Until she figures out it's not going to help her get her way," Mrs. Samuel said. "Here, sit down—can I fix you something to drink?"

"Yes, and it's *may* I—" Florine started to correct her before she caught herself.

Matilda glared at her.

Florine covered her discourtesy by asking, "May I… help you with that, Mrs. Samuel?"

"No, but thank you for offering, and please call me France."

She poured each of them a glass of water, and as she handed a glass to Rune, he asked if he could water their horses. France told him he was welcome to take them around to the barn. As he walked out, Matilda also excused herself.

"You can stay, Matilda," Florine said.

"You need to talk to Mrs. Samuel, uh, France alone," Matilda said. "We'll be waiting outside for you."

"And tell Rune there's hay for the horses, too, if he wants to feed them." She turned to face Florine. "Now, what can I do for you?"

"You have such an unusual name… France," Florine said. "Jimmy Taylor told me about you, and I tried to tell him it was *Frances*."

"You and half the world keep trying to fix my name," she said. "So you know Jimmy? My goodness! What is that handsome young man up to these days? I am so grateful he referred his sister to us. Faith has been a huge help to me."

"You do look like you certainly have your hands full," Florine said.

"Honey, this isn't half of them," said France, smiling.

A shiver ran down Florine's spine. She really didn't like the thought of working with children, but she didn't have a choice. She hoped France had something else she could do for her.

"Jimmy told me you might be able to help me. I'd like to come work for you, if that's possible."

"I can always use more help—we're up to twelve children now that Caitlin has joined us—and she's a handful, but we just don't have the money to pay for a second helper here at the house."

"What about the store?" Florine asked. "Could Mr. Samuel use the help?"

"If you don't mind me being honest with you, Florine, you sure don't look like you've had much experience working."

"But I can learn," she said. "I really need to be able to work."

France reached across the table and took Florine's hands and gently turned them over and touched them. They were as soft and smooth as a baby's skin.

"Sweetie," she said softly, "what's the real reason you're here?"

Florine could feel the rough calluses on the older woman's hands as she touched hers. She suddenly felt ashamed again, not wanting to admit her failings to this woman—this lady Jimmy thought so highly of. Florine looked down as her lip began to quiver.

"I'll work for nothing, France," she said in a whisper. "I just need a place to stay until…"

"Until the baby comes?"

Florine looked up at France and nodded.

"Are you going to keep your baby?"

"I'm not sure," she said, "although a big part of me wants to. But my father said if I choose to keep it, I'll have to pay him back the money Eustace and I took from him before we left Waco."

"Eustace is the baby's father?"

Florine nodded.

"And where is he now?"

"He took the rest of the money and left me in Fort Worth."

"Some people will lie and cheat to get what they want," France said. "And Jimmy came to your rescue?"

Florine smiled. "Yes, well, no—if you count the fact that my father hired him to find me and bring me home."

"Well, let me talk to George about putting you on at the store. You ought to be able to earn a fair amount before the baby is due. You're not very far along, are you?"

Florine looked hopeful as she shook her head.

"Now, how much money are we talking about?"

"Almost a thousand dollars."

"Oh, my stars, honey," France said, wide-eyed. "That's a huge amount of money!"

"But if I work really hard—" Florine began, but France interrupted her.

"It would take you years to earn that kind of money working at the store—and that's if you saved every penny of it. You'll never be able to do it in the amount of time you have."

"I won't?"

France shook her head. "A thousand dollars…" she said as she thought for a moment. "Then your daddy doesn't intend for you to keep this baby, right?"

"No, I guess not," she said. "But I want to be the one to make that decision."

"Well, we're a little crowded right now, but George is almost finished with the new addition on the back of the house—our second building effort in the past two years. We've already allowed the older boys to sleep in the bottom room although it's not quite finished. We'll squeeze you in somewhere. What do you know how to do?"

Florine thought for a moment, but nothing came to mind.

"Can you cook?"

Florine's face lit up. "Jimmy showed me how to make pancakes and gravy and camp bread."

"All together at the same time?" France laughed.

"No, in separate meals, but I think I might be able to remember how."

"Anything else?"

"I used to do needlework—filled up my hope chest preparing for marriage, but I wasn't very patient about it."

"Preparing for marriage or the needlework?"

"Both, I guess," Florine said, "but I was referring to my needlework."

"Great! So you can handle a needle. We do lots of sewing around here."

"But I'm not very patient with it…"

"Patience is a learned skill, and you said you could learn, right?"

Florine nodded. "And I used to be good with horses, although I haven't ridden in over a year."

"Horses? You?" France smiled. "I never would've guessed it."

"Jimmy couldn't believe it, either."

"How do you know Jimmy?" France asked.

"Our families have known each other for years, although I never really paid much attention to him," Florine said. "It was his older brother that I was interested in."

"Ah, Justin," France said. "I don't blame you there, but I hear he's taken."

"So you know Allie, too," Florine said and then paused for a moment. "I think both brothers were in love with her."

"Allie is an exceptional young lady," France said, "but Jimmy's a good catch, too."

"I don't know where I'd be if he hadn't found me in Fort Worth," Florine said. "I'd kind of given up on everything. But Daddy made it very clear that Jimmy's not one of us."

"Do you agree?"

"I did, at first, and not in a nice way, but now that I've gotten to know him, I'd still have to agree with my daddy."

"Florine!"

"I mean, he's better than us, France," Florine explained. "I treated him so badly at first, but Jimmy was nothing but a gentleman to me on that trip. I have to admit he hurt my feelings when he quite bluntly told me how spoiled and selfish I've been all of my life. But when I thought about it, I realized he was right. Somehow being around him made me want to change, though—to be better at something. But for a while I couldn't see past his parentage and his earlier mistakes."

"I'm glad you've gotten to know him," said France.

A movement in the window caught Florine's eye. A tangle of white-blonde hair and half of a dirty, tear-streaked face peeked around the frame of the open window. The face watched for a moment before disappearing from sight. Florine continued to talk to France, but was startled when the little girl suddenly appeared at her side. Caitlin climbed up in her lap and gently laid her head on Florine's chest.

If a snake had crawled up on her lap, Florine's face would have looked no different.

Chapter 15

*F*lorine sat there stiffly as she looked up at France and whispered, "What do I do?"

France smiled and said, "Just hold her."

"I don't even know this child," she said as she awkwardly put her arms around the now calm tempest.

"She seems to think she knows you," France said. "You must look like someone she misses very much."

Florine swallowed and mouthed, *"Her mother?"* to France.

France nodded.

"Did you know her?"

France shook her head. "But look at the color of her hair—not very common around here, and it's very similar to yours."

Florine looked at the mass of white-blonde hair. Her own hair was the same color when she was a little girl. It had turned a golden blonde as she aged, but traveling in the sun recently had begun to lighten it again.

Caitlin suddenly felt limp in her arms. Florine gently lifted a lock of hair covering the little girl's face and discovered her eyes shut.

"She can't be asleep!" Florine whispered. "How could she fall asleep so fast?"

"I think she's exhausted from fighting us every step of the way these past two weeks," said France, "or maybe she finally feels safe. Would you mind holding her for a little while? I have so much to do, and it's hard to keep an eye on her while I'm working. This way I know she'll be safe and not tearing up something."

Florine nodded.

"And we have some rearranging to do to fit you in here," France continued. "What about Matilda and Rune?"

"They can stay in the wagon until they head back," Florine said.

"Are you sure?"

Florine nodded again and smiled. "I know Rune will be glad to get to sleep in it with his wife rather than on the ground like he's had to do the past several days."

"Well, it's a beautiful carriage—if you can just forget what it's used for. How in the world did you end up with a funeral hearse?"

"I'd caused us to miss the stage in Fort Worth," Florine explained, "but insisted to Jimmy that we had to leave town that day. It was the only thing he could find, and I threw a hissy fit when I realized what it was, but he assured me it's never been used for a funeral. The wagon maker said the person who had ordered it left town without paying for it, so Jimmy got it for a good price. I've actually become quite attached to that wagon myself—it's really not bad to travel in, and it's covered, and there's room to sleep two in it."

"Well, it definitely holds more than a buggy, doesn't it," France said, smiling. "We have to borrow the neighbor's wagon to haul all the kids to church, but sometimes it's not available. It's not a bad walk for most of us, but it's a little far for the little ones." She glanced at a clock on the wall and walked over and put some more wood in the stove. "Mercy, I have to get busy. You'll have to excuse me, but if you need anything, just holler."

Florine grinned at France.

"What'd I say?" France asked.

"For a second there, I thought you were referring to me. That's my middle name."

"*Holler* is your middle name?"

Florine chuckled. "No... *Mercy*. My grandfather always called me that because I was named after my grandmother."

"Are your grandparents still living?"

Florine shook her head, no. "My grandmother died when I was little—I don't remember her. But I knew my grandfather well. He lived with us up until I was fifteen, well, until he died."

"Grandparents are special people, aren't they," said France. "I wish I'd had the chance to know mine better. And I really do have to get busy, Mercy."

Florine smiled and nodded as she watched France walk out of the room. She took a deep breath. *So, it's begun,* she thought to herself. She looked around the kitchen—part of her home for the next five or six months. The walls were painted white. A large enamel stove stood to the right of a fireplace on the far wall. Something stewed noisily in a large pot on top. Various other pots and pans hung on the wall around the stove along with several shelves containing filled jars and tins. To the left of the fireplace was a waist-high cabinet with a cistern pump mounted on it. She could see the top of a large round bowl that sat beneath it in a dry sink. Open shelves above the pump held an assortment of dishes. On the adjacent wall next to the cabinet was a tall open cupboard that held more dishes—lots of dishes. Another wall of shelves held food—lots of food in mason jars and cans and more tins.

In a little while, Matilda came through the back door and stopped suddenly when she saw Florine holding the sleeping wild child.

"Good heavens!" she whispered. "I could've sworn it was your mother holding you as a little girl."

Florine smiled at Matilda.

"How did you do it?"

"Do what?"

"Calm her down?"

"I didn't," Florine said. "She just climbed onto my lap and went to sleep. I'm not sure why."

"Well, I have to say that little girl reminds me of you at that age."

"Because she looks like me?" Florine asked as she gazed down at Caitlin's peaceful little face.

"No, mainly because she acts like you did at her age."

Florine frowned at her. "I wasn't that bad, was I?"

Matilda smiled and nodded her head, yes. "But your parents never let you cry as long as Caitlin cried earlier—they always gave in to your demands. You need to pay attention to Mrs. Samuel so you won't make the same mistake with your own child."

Florine looked away, still frowning. She didn't like hearing about her faults, especially from the hired help—*Stop it! That's the old Florine talking.* She looked back at Matilda, who had put up with her all these years. Change comes hard, she realized.

She took a deep breath and said, "I know you're giving me advice,

Matilda, but it does kind of hurt my feelings when you tell me those things."

Matilda pulled out a chair and sat down as she said, "I didn't say it to hurt your feelings, Florine. I was just being honest with you because you're more willing to listen now. You never did that before. For most of your life, it was just your way and nothing else. But I think you want to change now, and that means being willing to let others show you sides of yourself you don't see. It's like watching each other's backs, looking out for each other so we don't embarrass ourselves or keep making the same mistakes over and over again. You need to learn to take things with a grain of salt."

"What exactly does that mean?" Florine asked. "I've always heard that, but I've never understood it."

"Well, in this case," Matilda explained, "it means don't get angry and shut out what's being said. If it's something that will help you, then accept it and use it. If it's not, brush it away and don't be offended. It always helps to know the motive of the person that's offering the advice, and if it's someone who cares about you, then they're just trying to help."

Florine listened and tried to take it in. "Like when you tell me if there's food in my teeth?"

"Something like that," Matilda said, chuckling. "And you know I love you, Florine—that I want what's best for you."

Florine looked at her and smiled. "That does make it easier to hear."

"I just wanted to tell you that Rune and I will be starting back home in the morning," she said.

"So soon?" Florine said, feeling a little panicky at the idea of being left alone here.

"You're going to be all right—this place is going to help you in more ways than you know," said Matilda.

Florine nodded. "But I've been thinking, too, which means I need you to ask Rune to do something for me. It'll involve some work and a little change of plans for you, though."

Florine told Matilda her idea, and the older woman thought about it for a moment and decided it was a good plan. It also meant an easier trip home for her, and she especially liked that. She left to tell Rune, but said she would be back to help Mrs. Samuel fix supper.

After a while, France came back to the kitchen and picked up Caitlin and whispered for Florine to follow her. France carried Caitlin through the dining room where Florine saw Faith working with a young boy at the table. France walked through the parlor to an alcove with two facing doors. She entered the open door to the right, which contained three beds and a dressing table that took up most of the floor space. France softly kissed the little girl's forehead before she laid her gently on one of the beds.

The gesture surprised Florine. She had seen little about that child that was worth loving.

Three other young children were already down for naps. Two still had their eyes open. France put her finger to her lips to warn them to stay quiet.

"Emma," she whispered. "If Caitlin wakes up and gets out of bed, come get me or Faith."

Emma nodded solemnly.

"I hope she'll sleep a while longer," said France as she led Florine out of the room. "That's one of the two original bedrooms in the house. Faith stays in that room with the four youngest children." She nodded toward the other door facing them and said that it was her and George's bedroom, and then walked across the parlor and out through a newer-looking door into a windowed hallway. Florine saw some unfinished stairs at the end of it, blocked by a chest of drawers and some wood crates stacked beside the steps, along with a small mountain of board lumber taking up the remaining space beside the stairs.

France opened the door to the first room and told Florine that this was the first part of the house that George had added on. She said the four older girls stayed in here. It looked larger than the other bedroom, but Florine figured that was probably because it had only two beds in it. She closed the door and walked down the hall.

"And the four older boys have already moved in here," she said as she stepped through an empty doorway. "George has to put in the door and finish the walls and ceiling, and then it will be complete."

Florine looked up to see bare rafters exposed, but she could see light coming in from a window up above. She asked France where the stairs led to.

"The middle of the attic is tall enough for another room, which we plan to do next when George can find the time to finish it. We thought that might be a good room for Faith—to give her a place to call her own," France said as she started to walk back down the hall to the middle room, "and now, you, too. But until then, we'll just move one of the girls from this room to sleep with Faith, and you can sleep in here with the others."

"With the children?" Florine said a little too high-pitched. "I have to sleep in the same room with children?"

"It's that or the barn," said France, smiling, "and the children don't bite, Florine. I told you we were a bit crowded."

They returned to the dining room and interrupted Faith as she listened to the young boy reading slowly.

"Faith, when you're finished with R. James' lesson, why don't you start peeling the potatoes and carrots for the stew," she said. "Katherine and Lorelle can help you when they get home from school."

Matilda came in through the back door. "I make a mean pan of cornbread," she said.

Florine told France that Matilda was a wonderful cook.

"It's what I do best," she said, "and it's a little crowded in this kitchen with all of us in here. Why don't you let me fix supper for you tonight."

"Oh no, Matilda—you're my guest!" France said. "I couldn't."

"That's all I've done for the past twenty years, and I wouldn't know what else to do with myself around here," she said. "Please let me do this one thing for you."

France looked at her, and then looked at Florine.

"She's the best—you don't want to turn down this offer," Florine said.

"Well, I do have a lot of mending to do," said France, sighing. "But I feel terrible…"

"Don't you dare!" said Matilda. "It'd be my pleasure to do this for you and Mr. Samuel tonight."

France smiled wearily. "You are an angel."

"All right, then out my kitchen. We'll call you when dinner's served."

"Come on, Florine," said France. "I might as well put you to work, too."

She took her to the front bedroom and had Florine sit down at a table beside a window. France brought out a basket full of clothes and set it in front of the table. She told Florine she was able to make all the children's clothes when they had adopted their original three, but as the family grew, the chore became too much for her. She started accepting hand-me-downs from neighbors, but most of the pieces needed mending, or buttons sewn on, or socks darned. She placed a pin cushion on the table and a box of spools of thread and buttons of every color and size. She looked around the room for something, but eventually gave up and asked Florine if she would mind threading a needle for her.

"I've misplaced my glasses," she explained.

"You don't look old enough to wear glasses," Florine said.

"I'll be thirty-six next month," France said unabashedly. "But it's always been hard for me to see up close. When I was younger, I used to hide when I read because I didn't want anyone to see me in those hideous spectacles. Me and my vanity. Now it's not necessarily my vanity that I have problems with—it's my memory. I can't seem to remember where I put them last."

Florine giggled. "Well, I did notice a pair of glasses on a table in the parlor... the one by the rocker."

"Thank you, Florine!" she said as she left the room and returned a moment later with her glasses. "I usually leave them in the kitchen where I read my Bible before everyone gets up, but they weren't there."

France pulled her chair close to Florine and showed her how to do a straight or running stitch to sew material together. She said it wasn't the strongest stitch and tended to break and separate with wear, and that a back stitch was sturdier and wouldn't pull out as easily.

"And that's probably what we need to use on the parts of the clothes that get the most wear," she said, "like the sleeves or pants crotch and back seam."

France also showed her how to sew a blind or whip stitch, which was used to hem edges of materials. She said her favorite stitch was the slipstitch, which hid most of the stitch inside a fold.

After an hour of sewing, they had emptied the basket, other than a pile of socks that needed darning. France said she would show her how to darn socks later.

"Now that didn't take long," said Florine.

"No, but look behind you," France said.

Florine's eyes widened when she turned to find three more baskets of clothes as full as the first.

"But we accomplished so much in such a short time," said France, "and my sewing chore already feels much lighter. You handle a needle quite well, Florine."

Florine smiled. It felt good to be complimented on something useful for once.

"Some of the children are down to only two outfits that fit them well, and the boys, especially, are growing out of their clothes almost as soon as I can put them on 'em! It would be a huge help to me if you can come in a little each day and work on this mountain, and maybe that would give me time to start cutting out and sewing some new clothes now and then."

Florine assured her that she would. She stood and stretched, feeling a pinch in her shoulders from sitting and bending over too long.

"I'd better go see if I can do anything in the kitchen," France said. "Come on in the parlor and relax a bit before we figure out where we can put you and your things."

France came back through the parlor a moment later, saying that Matilda had run her out of the kitchen again, so she asked Florine if she wanted to walk down to the store with her. Florine agreed, and France let the others know where she would be for a little while. They stepped outside to walk the couple of blocks back to the store.

France told Florine that she and George had moved to Brownwood about ten years before, and had intended to buy some land and raise cattle. George ran a freight supply wagon to earn enough money to buy the land, but the freight business was so successful that he ended up using the profits to build a dry goods and grocery store. She said that rampant cattle rustling in the area had convinced George that they would see little money gained from ranching, which was much harder work any way.

"Is Mr. Samuel a cowboy?" asked Florine.

"Well, he likes to think of himself as someone who could've been a good cowboy if he'd had the chance," France said, "but to tell you the truth, that was probably the greatest deterrent in his dream of being a rancher. He just hadn't spent much time around livestock, other than a few farm animals. But I think every young boy imagines himself as a rough and tough cowboy at some time in his growing-up years."

Florine smiled when she tried to imagine the mild-mannered George Samuel on a bucking bronc.

Before they reached the town square, they walked alongside a two-story building. From the overhang at the corner, a rooster crowed loudly above them. Florine jumped a good foot from fright.

France grabbed her arm to steady her and said, "I'm sorry, sweetie, I should've warned you about Sentry."

She turned around and shooed the bird away, threatening to put him in her next stew pot.

"Sentry?"

"That silly ol' rooster sits up there all day and crows at everyone walking by. He thinks that's his job. But I don't even notice him anymore."

"I thought roosters only crowed at sun-up."

"Yes, they do, but if you pay attention around our house, you'll hear ours crowing every hour on the hour when they're not sleeping—I don't know if they're trying to impress the hens or what," France said as they continued to walk across the next street. "But like ol' Sentry, we've had them so long, I don't even hear them anymore. Familiarity tends to make things disappear. I mean, if a hippopotamus stood in our yard long enough, I wouldn't see him after a while."

Florine giggled at her sense of humor.

France started talking about the businesses in Brownwood.

"Would you believe we have two newspapers in our town? And we have our own grain mill, and two cotton gins were built this year due to more people growing cotton in our area. And we're more fortunate than most towns in that we have a cane mill twenty miles from here. That means we always have molasses stocked on our shelves. There's talk of getting the railroad to come through here, but George said it's still some years away. But that will make such a difference in the supply lines and connecting us to the bigger cities. George couldn't leave the store for days at a time, so he eventually sold his freight business to a friend here in town."

They stepped up on the boardwalk and passed the post office. France said that the post office had originally started in someone's home, but had moved to the town square in recent years, which helped bring customers their way since their store sat right next to it. She stopped in front of their store and told Florine that Brownwood also had two hotels, two saloons, a blacksmith shop, and three other general stores—Mr. Samuel's competition. She said Mr. Smith had a sturdy safe in his store that he had allowed local people to keep their money in, and that eventually turned into the bank for the community. France pointed to a new building on the west side of the square. The sign said *The Pecan Valley Bank*— and she said it was less than a year old.

France said the two-story courthouse had also been completed within the past year. The jail was on the bottom and the courthouse was the top floor.

The building looked small to Florine—not huge like Waco's

courthouse, but she noticed it was made out of the same material as the Samuel's house. France also mentioned that Brownwood had a boot and shoe shop on the square if she ever needed use of one.

"And we also have the Lone Star Furniture Store, and they even make coffins. I'm sure they'll be eyeing your hearse—it's much nicer than their wagon," she said with a wink. She looked around the square again. "Let me see… we also have a barber right next to the furniture store, a dentist, a photographer, a bakery, and plenty of lawyers around town. And the public school only opened three years ago. I'm so thankful it's here—I don't know if I could ever teach all of those children what they need to know about reading and writing and arithmetic. Faith has been such a help with the little ones. And I would be remiss not to mention our churches—although they're scattered from here. I credit them for turning this place from a lawless frontier town to the refined, civilized community it has become."

Florine thought she was joking again and almost laughed out loud before she caught herself when she realized that France was serious about that last statement.

"…and that's all about our town in a nutshell, but you'll have time to learn more about it in the days to come," she was saying as she turned around, "—so let's go on inside."

When they stepped through the door of the store, France told Florine to look around while she talked to her husband.

George smiled and raised his eyebrows in question to France as she strolled over and kissed him on the cheek in greeting.

"Can I talk to you in your office, sweetheart?"

They walked back to a room in the back, and George shut the glass-topped door before speaking.

"I know that look, France," he said, "and the kiss usually precedes you asking if you can take in another child."

"But this is different, George," she began, but he interrupted her.

"We've talked about this, honey, and you know we can't squeeze in another child—we can barely take care of the ones we have now."

"But it's not a child, it's another helper," she said, leaning against the desk. "Florine's here to help us."

"You know we can't afford to pay another helper," he said. "And we're not even paying Faith what she's worth to us."

"It's not going to cost anything for her to help us at the house,"

France said, "but I was hoping you could also use some help part of the day down here."

George leaned over and looked out the glass panel of the door. He could see Florine looking at the fabrics. "For what? To dress pretty clothes on?"

"George!"

"What in the world can she do? I don't need another burden to carry, France—I have a big enough load right now. And I can't be spending my time training someone and then have to turn around and watch them every minute or fix the mess they've made. I really need good help down here."

"She doesn't have much experience, but she can sew, and she wants to learn. I think she's the kind of person that can do anything well if she just sets her mind to it."

George looked through the door again. "Are you sure, France? Or are you just hoping?"

France smiled a crooked smile. "I guess a little of both—but she's really in a bind, and I think she'll be a help to us, too. Caitlin's even taken to her."

"What?! What do you mean?"

"I think Florine reminds her of her mother," France explained. "Caitlin was throwing a walleyed fit when Florine came, but something odd happened when we were sitting in the kitchen talking. Caitlin came in and crawled up in her lap and went to sleep."

"You're foolin' me!"

France shook her head, no. "So I think she's going to be a huge help with our biggest little *challenge* right now—she just doesn't know it yet."

"Now if she could bring some peace to our household taming that little imp—"

"George!!"

"...I'd definitely figure out some way to use her here."

"You would?"

George nodded.

France grabbed him around the neck and gave him another kiss.

George laughed and hugged his wife. "You know I can't say no to you. You seem to make it all work out."

"I knew I married a smart man," she said.

George pulled back and quietly asked, "But why is she really here, France? She doesn't look like she belongs in a small town, and I don't think she's lived the kind of life we're used to. She looks rather pampered, if you ask me. Are you sure she's not going to be a greater burden than help to us?"

France looked back at Florine, now rearranging the cans on a shelf.

"I wondered that myself," she said thoughtfully, "but I just have a feeling about her, and she really needs our help. She's going to have a baby, and the father abandoned her."

"She's not married?"

France shook her head, no.

"You know how people are going to talk, France."

"Well, they'll just have to talk. Everybody makes mistakes, honey, but that baby isn't a mistake."

"You're right, although many would argue with you about that," he said. "She's going to keep it, though, isn't she? We can't afford to take in any more children, France."

"She wants to, but how is she going to support herself and the baby? It's so hard for a woman by herself."

"It's not easy for a man to work and raise a child by himself, either. Remember Caitlin's father?"

France nodded. "I wonder if he really will be able to take care of her eventually. She sure misses him. But everybody needs help at one time or other, don't they?"

"And bless the folks that happen to run into France Samuel when they need help," George said as he reached over and took her in his arms. "Did I tell you how much I love you today?"

She shook her head.

"Or how proud I am to have you for a wife?"

She shook her head again.

"Well, I do, and I am," said George, pulling her close. "And I'm sure the Lord will help us figure out something. He's never failed us."

France kissed him again on the cheek. "And I'm so grateful Cassie Franklin broke her toe before you took her to the barn dance, and you ended up taking me instead," she said.

George laughed. "You're never going to let me forget that, are you. By the way, Florine's friend Rune was here earlier buying some paint. Do you know what that's for?"

France looked surprised. "No… that's odd. What would he need paint for? Well, I guess we'll find out later. Let's go tell Florine the good news."

Chapter 16

The Samuels walked back through the store and found Florine talking to a couple of ladies over a collection of hair combs.

"The snoods and flat hairstyles are definitely passé," Florine was telling them. "The popular style today is to arrange as much of your hair up on top of your head—you see how mine is styled?" Florine turned her head this way and that to demonstrate. "And these combs are just perfect to help hold it in place."

"I'll take two," one of the women said, picking up several.

"Well, I'll take four—my Gertrude will need a couple of them, too," she said to her companion. "You know how thick and beautiful her hair is."

"Ah, Mr. Samuel," Florine said as France and George walked up to them. "These ladies would like to purchase some of your lovely hair combs. And I think you should order some polished cotton for your fabric collection—it's the rage in Dallas."

George's mouth dropped open before France elbowed him to put it back in place.

"Of course, ladies, follow me to the front," he said.

The ladies thanked Florine for her help and followed George to the front of the store.

"Did I upset Mr. Samuel?" Florine asked quietly.

"You definitely shocked him, girl, but in a good way," France said, chuckling. "He was wondering how he could use you here, and I think you answered that question. You're a born salesman, Florine."

"You think so?" she asked, quite pleased with herself.

"You had those ladies eating out of your hand."

"Well, I do know fashion… oh, and I re-sorted the canned goods alphabetically."

France laughed. "Now, I'm sure that will impress George, too, because I know he appreciates any show of initiative. He hasn't found anyone available that he's been willing to hire for more than a few odd jobs. Some people tend to sit around and wait for him to tell them exactly what to do. He doesn't have the time to stay onto somebody every moment of the day. There's work to be done all over this store—even if it's just dusting the shelves, but you wouldn't believe how many folks seem to be blind to simple work all around them that needs to be done."

"I have a good eye for decorating, too," Florine said.

"Good for you!" said France. "I knew you had talent. But I need to give you a word of advice. Please don't do anything major without clearing it with George first. He's the boss, and he'll probably agree with you most every time, but it shows that you respect him enough to get his advice or approval. Do you understand?"

Florine nodded.

"Well, the children should be home from school by now, and I need to get back to check on the boys," said France. "I asked them to clean out the barn after school, but their idea of clean is quite a bit different than my idea of clean. Why don't you stay here and familiarize yourself with the store, if you'd like. George closes at five o'clock, and you can walk home with him. We'll have supper ready soon afterwards, too."

"I'm starting today?" Florine said, excited about the possibility of having a real job.

"Honey, you started when you sold those ladies some hair combs," said France. "But there's much more to it than that."

"I know, but I want to work and learn," she said and then laughed. "And I can't believe I just said that!"

"Why?"

"My daddy always told me that I was born for someone to take care of me. Up until recently, I felt like I was pretty useless—but fashionably so, and that there'd always be someone to wait on me," she said. "I hate to admit it, but I've treated some people rather badly."

"God has a way of putting us in situations that will sand off the rough edges in our lives—if we let Him," said France. "But it's not necessarily an easy or comfortable process."

Florine nodded. "Do you think it would be all right if I re-arranged some things in the store window? I have some ideas…"

"Go ask George—I'm sure he'll say yes. Mercy! Look at the time," said France.

"It's a little after four," Florine said, and then caught herself. "Oh! I did it again. Sorry!"

"I may just start calling you Mercy—I love that name."

"I used to hate it," Florine said. "I thought it was too old-fashioned, but I never minded that my grandfather called me that. He used to tell me that names were important—that a good name should mean something to us. But I'm not sure what mercy means, other than to make somebody let go when they were twisting your arm."

"I'll tell you later," said France, "because I have to run now. I'll see you at supper."

France reached over and squeezed her hand. "I'm glad you're here, Florine." Then she turned and was gone.

Florine stood there for a moment, taking everything in. The store was full of colors and textures and interesting clutter. She shut her eyes and took a deep breath. She could smell leather. She walked over to another aisle and this time she could smell scented soap and a familiar fragrance. She picked up a pretty bottle and took a big sniff of her favorite cologne she had used as a young girl before she graduated to the more expensive perfumes. For some odd reason it made her stomach feel queasy. She put the bottle down and quickly left that area. She could also smell some kind of smoked meat along with a dozen other aromas of things she couldn't identify… yet. She looked around again and planned to learn every nook and cranny in this store, from its warped wooden floors to the patterned tin tiles on the ceiling.

"Well, what do you think, Miss Locke?" George said as he walked up to her.

"I'm excited about working here," she said, "but I'm a bit nervous, too."

"After what I saw earlier, I think you're going to do a fine job around here," he said.

"You really think so?"

"Those combs have been sitting there for weeks."

"I don't know much about anything else in here, but I do know what the latest fashions are."

"Well, that's a start," he said. "Women are my biggest customers."

"Would you mind if I did some re-arranging?" she asked.

"Not at all, but just remember to keep things in the same general area—most customers like to know where to find things, and some ladies would get perturbed if I were to make too many changes too quickly."

Florine nodded. "I understand that. It's hard for my parents to accept any kind of change in their routines. I not only upset the apple cart, I pretty much destroyed it."

"Well, hopefully they'll come around," George said, sighing heavily. "I have some orders to tend to before we head home. Can we put off starting the training until tomorrow?"

"Yes, sir," said Florine. "In the meantime, I can dust some shelves if you'll loan me something to dust with."

George's mouth dropped open again, and Florine couldn't help but giggle. He almost ran across the store to retrieve several dust rags and a feather duster.

"That's a chore that is painfully ignored around here," he said, "primarily by me. France used to come in and dust for me every few days, but since the children have come, she doesn't have time anymore. I appreciate you offering to help in that capacity."

Florine knew that she never would have thought of that task if France hadn't mentioned it. But she patted herself on the back for paying attention to France's words of advice.

She held up the feather duster and turned around to the nearest shelves, feeling extremely capable in that moment… until she realized she had never dusted anything in her life other than herself with Poudre de L'Amour No. 1 dusting powder.

Chapter 17

Florine realized again how hungry she was when she walked through the door to the Samuels' home. The wonderful aroma of the stew permeated the house, and she couldn't wait to bite into a piece of Matilda's cornbread. Her stomach had felt queasy ever since she had sniffed that cologne back at the store, and she felt like she needed to eat something heavy to keep it down.

George brought in a low bench to set up in the corner of the dining room. Three of the younger children would sit on the floor using the bench as a table so there would be room for the guests at the big table. The big table was actually two tables pushed together that almost spanned the entire length of the dining room. France could have put some of the children in the kitchen or on the back porch to eat, which she usually did if they had familiar guests. Or the women would visit in the kitchen while the men and children ate first. But in this case she knew the children wanted to hear the conversations at dinner since they didn't have out-of-town visitors very often. And they all seemed to be in awe of the beautiful woman with the golden hair and fancy dress—everyone but Faith, who seemed to ignore her.

Florine stood in the door of the dining room watching Faith and three of the girls set the table. After a moment, Florine actually offered to help, but Faith looked coolly at her and declined, saying there wasn't enough room for another helper there.

Florine had a feeling her words meant more than setting the table. Faith seemed to be threatened by her presence. They had known each other for years, but Florine had never paid much attention to her before. She honestly didn't know Faith, probably because she had never made the effort to get to know her. Florine's focus had always been on her brother

Justin. She had never looked at Faith as a true sister to Justin, but rather a charitable case to be pitied for a moment and then ignored.

But she looked at her now. Florine realized for the first time how lovely Faith was. She had arranged her raven black hair neatly in a bun at the base of her neck. Her skin was a dark olive, like Jimmy's, and it was smooth and clear. Her smile towards the girls in the room was genuine and revealed straight, white teeth. Her eyes were as black as her hair, and seemed to speak even when her voice didn't. And the few times Florine caught Faith watching her, she knew she wasn't welcome there.

A pang of guilt shot through her. Why should she expect Faith to treat her any differently than she had treated her all those years? The tables were turned here, and Florine was in the weaker position. She wondered if Faith had guessed the reason she had shown up on their doorstep.

Florine realized with a start that she was now the outsider, and not only that, but an outsider with a moral failing. It suddenly felt very uncomfortable to be standing there, so she turned around and took a seat in the parlor to wait for dinner. Was it too late to try to develop a friendship with Faith? Florine wondered if she would even know how. She had never had a close friendship with a girl before. Girls were always rivals. But what was to compete for here? Her poor choices and their consequences had taken her out of the race. And she knew without a doubt that she would need the help of friends in the coming months.

She decided right then and there that she would learn how to make a friend of Faith.

Rune knocked on the front door of the house before coming into the parlor. He took a seat across from Florine. She could see splatters of paint on his clothes and smudges of white on his hands.

"Did you get it done?" she asked.

"Yes, ma'am," Rune said, "but it'll need to dry overnight. I've had to swear the boys to secrecy. Are you sure about this?"

Florine said she was.

"That means we're going to be here three more days, though," he said. "Your father's not going to be happy."

"Well, he'll get over it," she said. "Three days, you said?"

Rune nodded.

"That's perfect! I've been thinking about another idea for you."

"Uh-oh..."

"It'll help you pass the time while you're here, Rune."

George came in and sat down near Rune. Florine listened to what they were saying, but her head was full of ideas. She started to mention her plans to George, but at that moment France called everyone to supper.

A meal in that house with such a large family was a new experience for Florine. The children were well-behaved—even Caitlin, who sat by Florine and smiled shyly at her every so often. The only social blunder was when Florine and little Mac took a few bites before George said the blessing. But no one dressed them down for it.

The conversation was also different from what Florine was accustomed to. She was used to talking about her wardrobe, or the latest gossip, or how dry her skin was, and what was the best cream she could use for that. And there didn't seem to be any appropriate places to interject comments of that sort, so mostly she ate her food and listened quietly.

The Samuels family talked about the new kittens in the barn, and Zane lost her third tooth, and R. James's reading had greatly improved, according to Faith. He might even be promoted to the community school soon. The older children already attended it, but Faith taught the younger ones at home. France leaned over and whispered to Florine that R. James couldn't read when he first arrived, but he had made great strides.

France and George both bragged on Florine's sewing and organizational skills at the store. Florine found herself sitting up even straighter and feeling as proud as R. James did. And it made her believe she could do even more.

Midway through the meal, France asked everyone to go around the table and introduce themselves, starting with the youngest at the bench in the corner.

"Stand up so our guests can see you, Mac."

The little boy stood. "I'm Mac Samuel, and I'm four years old." He held up five fingers.

France reached over and gently tucked his thumb in. "Good job, Mac. You are such a big boy."

His grin stretched all the way to his dimples. And the next child stood—Florine recognized the little girl whose basket had been taken by Caitlin earlier. Her hair was a dusty ash brown and she had the biggest blue-gray eyes.

"I'm Emma Samuel, and I'm six," she said solemnly, following Mac's lead in giving his age.

"I'm Zane Samuel, and I'm six years old, too," said a little girl who looked like Mac.

France turned to Caitlin on her left, who had claimed the seat next to Florine. "Your turn, sweetheart."

Caitlin shook her head shyly.

Florine piped in, "But how will I ever know your name?"

Without hesitation the little girl looked up at Florine and said, "I'm Caitlin Murray, and I'm five."

France caught George's eye and raised her eyebrows slightly. George nodded and smiled.

"Very good, Caitlin!" France said, and then looked at Florine. "Now let's just continue going around the table."

"I'm Florine Locke from Waco, and I'm very happy to be here," she said.

"I'm Katherine, the oldest, and I'm thirteen years old."

"I'm Lorelle, and I'm eleven."

"I'm Faith Taylor, and I'm also very happy to be here."

"I'm Finn, and do I have to sit on the girls' side?"

"Yes—it's not going to hurt you this once, Finn," George said. "Now tell everyone how old you are."

"I'm almost nine."

"Thank you, sir, and I'm George Samuel, and I'm very proud of this good-looking bunch," he said, which made the girls blush and the boys snicker. "And we're very happy to have our guests here with us this evening."

"I'm Rune Bishop, and I appreciate your hospitality."

"I'm Matilda Bishop, and I'm not about to tell you my age."

Everyone laughed.

"And we have Mrs. Bishop to thank for this wonderful meal," France said. "What do you tell her, children?"

A chorus of 'thank you's' was directed towards Matilda.

"My goodness, most of it was already cooking before I helped, but thank you for letting me finish it for you," she responded. "It's been my pleasure. And we have a dessert, too. The girls helped me make it."

"It's a cake with real icing!!" Lorelle said.

The children clapped and acted so excited about dessert—like cake with icing wasn't a regular occurrence around here, Florine noticed.

France quieted them down so the introductions could continue.

"I'm R. James, and I'm nine years old."

"I'm K. James, and I'm ten and a half."

"I'm Joseph, and I'm next to the oldest."

The girl next to him waited a moment before saying, "And Joseph is twelve years old, and I'm Jenna, and I'm ten years old."

"My name is Annie Samuel, and I'm also ten years old, but we're not twins even though she *is* my sister," she felt compelled to explain to Florine, as if she might not understand the situation.

"Ten seems to be a popular number in this family," France said. "And I'm France Samuel, and I'm so happy to tell you that Florine will be living with us and helping us for a while."

The children seemed to be glad about that, especially Caitlin and the girls. The older ones chattered on about her pretty dress and hair and asked if they could see her other clothes. They seemed to be in awe of her.

Florine decided that maybe children weren't so irritating after all.

After the cake was served and eaten, each of the children took their plates and utensils to the kitchen. Faith and the older girls began to wash the dishes, and Matilda and the younger girls finished clearing off the table. George and Rune went outside with the older boys to feed the animals. Florine overheard Annie tell Matilda that the boys fed the horses and the chickens, but it was Joseph's job to milk Miss Clara.

"Who's Miss Clara?" she asked Lorelle, walking by with a handful of towels.

"She's our milk cow," Lorelle said. "Someone traded her for store supplies last year. She only tried to kick Joseph once before she got to know him. Nobody else can go near her." And then she walked into the kitchen to start drying dishes with Jenna.

France had disappeared with the four youngest children.

Florine noticed that everyone seemed to know what to do... everyone but Florine. The kitchen was too crowded to help. She had carried her plate in there along with the other children and stood there for a moment, hoping someone would tell her what to do. But she seemed to be more in the way than anything else, so she walked back into the dining room. The table was clear and everything in order, except for some of the chairs. She took her time going around the table pushing in each chair carefully like it was an important job requiring some skill.

She wondered how they knew all of this other stuff to do. She had never paid attention to those everyday chores before. Someone else had always taken care of those things.

Florine walked through the parlor and down the hall of the newer part of the house. She peeked into the bedroom she would be sharing with the three oldest girls. She was concerned that it only had two beds and four would be sleeping in there. Someone, probably Rune, had brought in her trunk and other belongings and set them just inside the door.

She needed to figure out a better sleeping arrangement—she couldn't sleep with a child. She needed her privacy. She never had to sleep in a bed with anyone before, that is, until Eustace came along. And guilt and condemnation crawled up and sat heavily on her shoulders again with those thoughts. Maybe God was punishing her by putting her on the same level as these orphans—these children that nobody wanted except for the Samuels. With a shocking thought, she realized she and her baby fit that description, too.

She stepped back in the hall, noticing a door to the back porch and two windows along the outside wall that gave light to the hall. She walked up to the barricaded stairs. The steps were built along the outside wall up to about eye level before turning and traveling up the adjacent wall to the second floor. The steps had no banister alongside them. She figured the chest of drawers and stacked crates were probably to keep the younger children from climbing on the steps.

Florine un-stacked the crates beside the stairs and walked up to the second floor, which had a closed door with a latch up high. Florine reached up to unlatch it and pushed the door open to peek inside. The long, narrow attic was lit by four dormer windows—two on each side of the room. The ceiling was the actual boards that held the roof. The floor above the older room at the far end was finished, but the floor to the newest section was open rafters to the room below except for a narrow path around the sides. She realized why the door was latched up high—this was a dangerous area for the children.

She walked along the board path to look out the closest window facing the back of the house and the barn. She could see Mr. Samuel and Rune talking and the two boys called James hauling armfuls of hay to the pen connected to the barn. Her two horses and another one she hadn't seen before walked up to the fence. She watched the Samuel horse flatten her ears and run off the other horses from the first bundle of hay the boys put over the fence. The other two horses yielded to her and were content to eat together at another pile of hay. Florine smiled, recognizing that her horses had yielded to the Samuel horse, who had quickly informed them who was in charge.

She turned and walked around the board trail to the finished far side of the room and back around to see a view of a neighboring house and further, the backs of the front street buildings in town. This definitely wasn't Waco, where she grew up, or even Galveston or Dallas—two bustling cities in which she would have willingly settled down with Eustace. But he always thought his luck would be better in the next town.

How did she end up in a place like this? Life moved much slower out here than what she was used to. More punishment from God, perhaps? Florine was convinced Brownwood was on the edge of civilization where culture and society had yet to find it. Before dinner, she overheard Mr. Samuel telling Rune that some members of John Wesley Hardin's gang had been lynched over in a nearby town called Comanche three years before. No one knew where Hardin disappeared to—he was still on the loose. And two years ago, the Ft. Worth to Brownwood stage had been robbed five times in a two month period. A shiver ran through her as she remembered how close she and Jimmy came to being robbed by those men a couple of weeks ago.

Florine thought that maybe it wasn't such a bad thing after all that new kittens seemed to be the most exciting event happening around here.

Chapter 18

The sun had long set, and everyone was already asleep by the time Florine finished her nightly routine—this time in the Samuel's kitchen. She had waited until everyone had gone to bed so she wouldn't have a dozen pair of eyes watching her every move. Afterwards, she tiptoed back to the bedroom and set the lamp on the table beside the bed. She pulled back the covers and crawled into bed, stretching unimpeded every which way. Then she looked over at the three sleeping girls in the bed across from hers and smiled to herself. Katherine and Lorelle had pinned their new cameo brooches to their nightgowns and Annie had fallen asleep clutching the delicate necklace and locket in her hand. Florine deemed the jewelry a fitting exchange for the comfort and luxury of a bed to herself.

She blew out the lamp with the memory fresh in her mind of her horses yielding to the dominant Samuel mare who managed to get her way earlier.

Not this time, she thought smugly to herself as she shut her eyes.

Early the next morning, shouts awakened Florine, and she rolled over to see the girls scurrying out of the room to find out what was going on outside the house. She figured her first plan was about to unfold, so she jumped up and grabbed her peignoir to cover herself before rushing outside. She wasn't about to miss this either.

Rune and the four older boys had pulled the funeral hearse from behind the barn to show it off to everyone. George and France were the last ones to step out on the back porch.

"What in the world is going on?" asked France, and then saw the funeral hearse with the grinning boys standing beside it, waiting for her response. "And what is this?"

"Well, now we know where the white paint went," George said to his wife, smiling.

They both looked at Florine for an explanation.

"You said you always had to borrow the neighbor's wagon to haul the children to church, so I thought you could use a wagon for yourself."

"A funeral hearse?" France couldn't help but say.

"Well, that's why I asked Rune to paint it," she said, "so it wouldn't look so much like one."

"But now it just looks like a white funeral hearse," said Finn.

Florine frowned at him.

"I can't wait 'til Charlie Smith sees this," he said proudly. "He'll want his daddy to get him one, too."

Then Florine couldn't help but smile at him.

"We can't take your wagon, Florine," said George. "How would Rune and Matilda get home?"

"They're taking the stage on Saturday," Florine said. "We've already bought the tickets so the wagon has to stay, and the horses, too."

The boys and the younger children were so excited and began climbing all over the hearse, but the older girls stood back with looks of disdain on their faces.

The Samuels tried to argue with Florine, but she wouldn't change her mind. She was determined to win this debate, too.

"Not many people would do what you've done for me, and my father doesn't want it," she said. "Just think of this as a down payment for my time spent here."

"What do you think, France?" George asked as he mulled over the proposition. "You know, I could use it to haul a lighter load of freight in addition to the wagon I have to contract out."

"Well, we wouldn't have to depend on Mr. Watson's wagon for church anymore, but for now, let's just say we're borrowing it from Florine while she's here," France said as she noticed the girls scowling at the hearse. "What's the matter, girls?"

"We're not riding in a wagon that's carried dead people," Katherine said.

Florine smiled. "That's exactly what I told Jimmy, but he assured me the wagon had never been used before he bought it."

"Jimmy bought the wagon?" Faith spoke up, suddenly interested with the mention of her brother.

Florine nodded. "In Fort Worth."

"But everyone will make fun of us," Jenna said, looking at her sisters.

"We'd rather walk, thank you," Annie said.

"Well, we'll discuss that later," said France. "We all need to get dressed and ready for the day. Breakfast is on the table. Come on, kids! Joseph and K. James—off the wagon! You're going to be late for school."

The Bishops were a godsend to the Samuels the next few days. Matilda took over the kitchen and fall garden, teaching Faith and the older girls how to cook new recipes with the same food they had been eating for weeks now, especially with the dried and canned vegetables from the summer garden. The girls churned butter and Matilda even showed them how to pickle boiled eggs.

With Mr. Samuel's permission, Rune started working on Florine's latest plan: completing the floor to the attic, which she figured would earn her the right to use the room. Rune said he would attach several boards running horizontally up the stairs for a temporary banister, too, until Mr. Samuel could put in a nicer one.

Florine spent her first morning at the store learning the tasks she would be responsible for. She didn't realize how much she enjoyed putting things in order and found plenty of work doing just that during those times Mr. Samuel was busy with customers. He found a pencil and paper for her to make a list of those items that were getting low in number and needed to be re-ordered soon.

After the first few customers left, word spread quickly around the town square about the beautiful new clerk at the Samuel's store. A number of folks drifted in *just looking,* they said when Florine asked if she could help them, and it wasn't the merchandise they were taking a gander at. But before several left, they had purchased something that Florine had convinced them they couldn't live without.

Mr. Samuel recognized another benefit of having her there—she was drawing customers in like honey draws flies.

The clock struck twelve noon, and Mr. Samuel motioned for Florine to come to the front of the store. They stepped outside and he locked the door, and they walked back to the house for the midday meal.

"Won't you miss customers during this time?" Florine asked.

"Everyone knows the store hours," he said. "They'll come back later."

As they walked up to the house, they could hear Rune hammering away in the attic. Mr. Samuel said he wanted to check on him, and headed around to the back of the house. Florine stepped into the parlor and breathed in. Something sure smelled good. Through a window, she could see Matilda outside in the garden with the little ones. She walked through the dining room and up to the kitchen door where she saw Faith and France standing in front of the stove. She drew up short of walking in when she heard her name mentioned, and stepped to one side of the door. They must not have heard her come in with all the hammering going on.

"You don't know the real Florine," Faith was saying. "She's putting on a show for you."

"What do you mean?" France asked. "How do you know this?"

Faith was quiet for a moment. "I just know."

"What did she do to you, Faith? Did she hurt your feelings?"

Florine heard only silence. Then she could hear sniffing, like Faith had started to weep. Her heart suddenly felt like a rock in her chest.

"What happened, honey?"

"Five years ago my mother made me participate in the Cotillion in Waco when I was fifteen—like it was my introduction to society, too," Faith said. "I guess she had my best interests at heart—she was always trying to get me involved in something or other. But she seemed to be blind to the fact that I wasn't welcome there."

She took a deep breath and exhaled. "I tried to tell her that, and that I wouldn't know a soul there, but Mom said that Florine would be there. Our families were friends, so she assumed Florine would take me under her wing, which was laughable."

"Why?"

"Florine was crowned queen that year, and when I approached her to say hello, she looked at me and acted like she didn't know who I was," Faith said. "She even denied knowing me to her friends and walked away, leaving me and my escort standing there alone, which was pretty much how I spent the entire evening after that. No one even asked me to dance, including my escort, who disappeared for the rest of the evening like he was ashamed to be seen with me after that encounter with the Cotillion queen."

"I'm so sorry, Faith," France said. "What did your mother say? Did she confront Florine?"

"I never told my mother about it," she said. "It would've broken her heart. She never knew it was the worst night of my life."

Florine felt sick to her stomach. She could remember everything about the Cotillion the year she was crowned queen; it was the best night of her life. But she barely remembered that Faith was even there. How could she have dismissed her and even the memory of it so easily when it had been so devastating to Faith?

Florine backed away from the door opening and bumped into the buffet before she turned and walked quickly back through the parlor and out the front door. She ran around to the side of the house and leaned up against the wall. She felt nauseous again and put her hand over her mouth. She stood there for a moment, breathing in deeply.

Everything had gone so well that day—Mr. Samuel seemed pleased with her work at the store so far. How could everything change so quickly? She knew Faith would never be her friend now. How could she after she had treated her so horribly? She figured Mrs. Samuel would probably change her mind about letting such a hateful person stay, and Florine knew she would have to tell Mr. Samuel how she had treated Faith. She slumped down to a sitting position, wrapped her arms around her legs, and leaned her head on her knees as she wept bitterly.

"There you are."

Florine looked up through her tears, surprised to see France, who sat down beside her against the house.

"How'd you know I was here?" Florine asked.

"I heard you in the dining room," she said.

"Did Faith…"

"No."

Florine sat there, waiting for the guillotine to drop.

"I knew something was wrong between you two," said France, "but I didn't know what it was until a few minutes ago."

"Are you going to send me away now?"

"Why would I do that?" France asked.

"Because now you know I'm a horrible person."

"You'd already told me something about that," France said.

"I did?"

"But you said it in a remorseful way, so I knew your conscience was working," France said. "And we all hurt each other at one time or other, intentionally or not. The important thing is to recognize when we've done something wrong and to try to make amends."

"I barely even remember Faith at the Cotillion that night—I was so focused on myself. How could I have been so cruel to her? I didn't even realize it until I heard her tell you about it. How can she ever forgive me?"

"I think now's as good a time as any to tell you what your middle name means," France said as she thought for a moment. "Mercy can mean compassion—especially from one in a higher position towards another in a lower position—like God is merciful towards us. Or like you should've shown Faith that night. Or it can mean kindness, like you can show Faith from now on. I think of forgiveness, too, when I think of mercy—like Faith showing you mercy for what you did to her back then."

"I don't think she'll ever forgive me," Florine said. "And I don't blame her."

"I think you underestimate Faith and the power of forgiveness," France said. "She's a Christian and has learned that unforgiveness will ultimately hurt her more than it will ever hurt you, so she'll come around eventually. Sometimes it takes time—even for a person as sweet as Faith."

"What can I do?"

"Ask her to forgive you, for starters," France said, "and then be a friend to her."

"I want to be her friend, but I'm not sure I know how."

"Well," France said as she gathered her thoughts, "being a friend to someone means getting to know them and... being thoughtful and earning their trust... and at times, putting their needs above your own. Ask God to help you; I ask His help all the time—especially for patience when these children push me to my limits."

"And you still love them even after they make you mad?"

"Of course, Florine—love shouldn't have conditions tacked onto it."

"What do you mean?"

"It means that I've *chosen* to love and care for them—no matter how they behave or what they say that may be contrary to what we usually think love is."

"I always thought love was a feeling."

"And it is, and it's a wonderful feeling, but love goes beyond a simple feeling," said France. "More important, love is a choice and a commitment because there'll be times in our lives when feelings will fail us," France explained. "Did you know that there have been times when I didn't *feel* love for George?"

Florine looked at her in surprise. "But you seem to have the perfect marriage."

"I've been so mad at George at times I could spit nails. And I certainly didn't feel love for him in those moments—I was just too angry," said France. "But I still loved him because I had made a commitment to love him—even during the times I thought he was acting like a scoundrel."

Florine looked away in thought.

France put her arm around her. "I know you'll figure out a way to work this out with Faith. I can already see the cogs turning in that smart head of yours."

Florine looked back at France and smiled. "Nobody's ever called me smart—pretty, yes, but never smart."

"Why can't a woman be both?"

Florine nodded and then paused. "Can I ask you something?"

"I think the correct term is *'May I'*, isn't it?" France said as Florine cringed. "And yes, you may."

"Sorry—I was hoping you missed that yesterday—my mother's old habits sure die hard," Florine said. "I love what you said about my middle name, though. Do you remember what I told you about my grandfather—about him saying how important names were?"

France nodded.

"Well, as of this moment, could you start calling me Mercy like he did? I'd like to try to live up to that name from now on."

"I like that idea," France said. "A new name for a new beginning. And names are important, but remember, it's not the name that will change you, Florine. It's the choices and actions you make that will do that. But from now on, you're Mercy to me."

Chapter 19

Jimmy slowed up to walk the stallion through town. He was pleased with the progress he had made training the horse over the past month. He knew that problems with a horse usually started with the rider, so he was careful not to let any bad habits develop. Jimmy had taken his time breaking the horse, and it had paid off. He knew this horse was worth even more money now than he had originally paid for him.

As he passed by Kimball's Mercantile, his sister Jenny came out the door to give him the mail to take home.

"You two make a striking pair, Jimmy," she said, smiling at him. "That is one heck of a horse."

"Thanks, sis," he said, pulling up and grinning back.

"You ever going to put a saddle on him?"

"Soon," Jimmy said, nodding. "He's a fast learner. He's getting to where he can almost anticipate my every move."

"I think people will come from all over to get a piece of his bloodline," she said.

"I think you're right," he said. "Do you think you can help me come up with some wording for the newspapers?"

"Sure," she said, "and by the way, you got a letter from Faith."

"Really?" he said as he thumbed through the stack.

"But so did Mom, so you aren't the only special one around here," she said, teasing him. "Let us know how she's doing, all right?"

Jimmy nodded and told her he would see her later. He rode the stallion up the road and around the house to the barn. He dismounted and walked the horse inside and set the mail on a work table before leading the horse to his pen. He stood there for a moment talking softly to the horse, rubbing his neck as he spoke.

His mother Julia stepped into the barn to get the mail—a routine they seemed to have established every Monday and Thursday. She paused to watch him take care of his newest possession. It never ceased to amaze her to watch Jimmy's skill with a horse. She wasn't sure where he learned all of that—he just seemed to instinctively know things about horses and could communicate with them in ways too subtle for her to catch.

He looked up and saw his mother watching him. She smiled and he smiled back at her. His mother was around fifty years old, but she was still a beautiful woman—tall and slender, and had those striking blue eyes—the same as his. Her hair had turned completely white years before—he couldn't remember her hair being any other color, but she could still turn heads walking down a street in Waco.

"That is a beautiful horse, Jimmy," she said. "And he seems to be responding so well to you. How'd you teach him to take to a bit so quickly?"

"Simple logic and lots of repetition," Jimmy said, "but he's smart. It didn't take him long to learn that doing what I ask him to do is more comfortable than not doing it. When he does something right, you reward him with a release of pressure."

"I must try that on your father sometime," Julia said, grinning. "Have you come up with a name for him yet?"

"Nope—nothing seems good enough for him," he said as he opened the gate and walked him into his pen.

"You'll come up with something fitting, I'm sure," she said, looking at the mail she was holding.

"And there's a letter from Faith in there," he said, which caused her to quickly flip through the stack to find it. "But she sent me one, too, so leave mine here."

"It's about time we got another letter from her," said Julia, comparing the two envelopes from Faith. "Looks like she had a little more to say to you, so that means we'll be talking later," she said as she set Jimmy's letter down and turned to head back to the house.

Jimmy brought Faith's letter unopened to the house and ran upstairs to the third floor. He walked down the hall and out onto the balcony above the front porch. He pulled up a comfortable chair and sat down, propped his boots on the neighboring chair and took in the view for a moment before turning his attention to Faith's letter. Getting a letter was a treat, and he planned to take his time. He carefully tore open the envelope and began to read.

Dearest Brother,

I hope this finds you well. I know you're home now because I know you found Florine. And the reason I know that is because she showed up on our doorstep about two weeks ago. But she doesn't go by the name "Florine" anymore. The day after she arrived, she asked us to start calling her by her middle name, "Mercy." She has been very nice to me and even apologized for hurting my feelings some years ago at the Cotillion in Waco. I'm surprised she even remembered that happened. She doesn't seem to be the same dreadful person we knew growing up.

At first I thought she was just play-acting and that her real self would eventually come through. But she caught the little ones playing with her fancy clothes one day, and she didn't scream at them like I thought she would. They had even spilled her Poudre de L'Amour No. 1 dusting powder on the floor, and I thought for sure that would put her over the brink. But she just turned and faced the wall for a moment—I think she was grinding her teeth—either that or she was praying. Then she turned around and calmly told the children that they shouldn't play with other people's things and asked them to help her pick everything up and put them neatly back like they'd found them.

But the thing that convinced me that she had really changed was the day that Rune and Matilda Bishop left to go back to Waco. Did you meet them when you took her home? Rune had finished putting in the floor in the attic room, which Mr. Samuel hadn't had time to finish yet. I thought Mercy had him finish it just so she would have her own room away from me and the children. She even put makeshift curtains in the attic windows. I was shocked to find out later that she had talked the older boys into carrying my bed and my belongings up there for me to have my own room.

The finished walls and ceiling haven't been added yet, which makes the room really long and cavernous-looking, although you can't stand upright along the sides except where the dormer windows are. But Mr. Samuel will get to it when he can find the time—hopefully before the cold weather arrives. I slept in the room just one night by myself before deciding that I would prefer to have company in such a large room, so I invited Mercy to share the bedroom with me. I feel like we've become friends, although I'm not ready to share my deepest thoughts and dreams with her like I do with you.

I'll tell you something funny that happened. We'd been having a lot of problems with Caitlin, the Samuel's newest child—a five-year-old girl whose father isn't able to take care of her at this time. But she's really taken to Mercy, for some odd reason. One day Caitlin didn't get her way about something and responded by the usual throwing herself on the floor and screaming. Well, Mercy just threw herself down on the floor beside her and started kicking and screaming even louder. I thought Mercy was acting like her old self for a moment. (smile)

Caitlin was so shocked, she stopped screaming and sat up and watched Mercy. Mercy finally stopped and looked at Caitlin and told her that her tantrums were not going to work—that she could scream louder and kick harder and last much longer than Caitlin ever could because she's had years of experience doing just that. Then they both started laughing at each other. And then we all laughed with them. And would you believe that Caitlin hasn't thrown a hissy fit since?

I love working for the Samuels. They are as nice as you said. I get to teach the four youngest children and R. James, who's nine years old and couldn't read when he first arrived last year. France had been working with him for quite a while before I arrived and continued to work with him, and he's doing so well now that we think he'll be able to start attending the community school with the other children soon. He's a bright boy and has worked so diligently to catch up to the others his age, and his pride won't be hurt now because of his inability to read.

We've all been working very hard, so I'm really glad Mercy is here to help. She works at the store in the mornings and helps with the sewing and a few other chores in the afternoons, although cooking isn't one of her fortes. (smile) She said you showed her how to make pancakes and gravy and camp bread, but she must've not paid enough attention. We had to throw away the first batch of pancakes she tried to make! And no one has had the courage to ask her to make the gravy or camp bread yet.

Several of the local families hosted a dance last Saturday night in the school building, and we all attended (along with most of the town and surrounding territory, I think). Mercy was the belle of the ball (as usual), and all the men seem enamored of her. But this time when the first couple of men asked her to dance, she agreed only if they would dance with me first. I felt embarrassed about that, but then for the rest of the evening I hardly sat down! And she didn't have to bribe anyone after the second man danced with me. I actually enjoyed myself immensely, and I'm looking forward to the next dance in three weeks.

I hope you will come visit soon. If you don't, you'd better write me back. Mercy knows I'm writing you a letter—she asked me to say hello and that she would like to see you, too, and maybe go horseback riding with you. Speaking of horses, did you get that high-priced stallion you were wanting?

She also said to tell you that she has decided to send her father the first installment of five dollars, and that you would know what that meant.

With much affection,
Your sister,
Faith

Have you learned that verse I gave you? It definitely works. I know without a doubt that God led me here. And you had something to do with that, too!

Jimmy smiled as he carefully folded the pages of the letter. He would enjoy reading it again later. He was surprised and pleased to hear about Florine, or Mercy, as she called herself now—especially that she was treating Faith with respect. And friendship between them? That was even better.

He thought about the 'first installment,' knowing that Mercy had decided to keep her baby. He also knew without a doubt that Mr. Locke would not take that news well.

But Jimmy was happy for her, even though he knew the road ahead wasn't going to be easy. And for some reason, the thought of Mercy dancing with every man in town didn't set too well with him. He decided he just might have to pay them a visit soon.

Chapter 20

Saturday was the bigger of the two laundry days of the week. They rotated washing the bed sheets each Saturday by bedrooms, so each bed had its sheets washed once a month, but the bulk of the laundry was the mountain of clothes. Faith hung the last bed sheet along with the other whites on the line and had picked up the empty basket when she saw the horse and rider pull up at the barn. She shielded her eyes from the sun to get a better look as the man dismounted. When recognition set in, she let out a scream, threw the basket down and ran towards the barn.

France stepped out of the kitchen just in time to see Faith throw herself in the arms of a man standing near the barn. Then she watched as they walked arm in arm inside, leading the horse.

"Who in the world?" she said aloud as she dried her hands with the dish towel and stepped down off the porch.

Dinner would just have to wait a minute, she thought as she walked toward the barn. What man would Faith be that forward with? She didn't think she had a beau back in her hometown, but maybe she had acquired one here since the last dance. Then she stopped in mid-step and smiled, realizing who it was. She turned around and walked quickly back to the house, knowing she would be receiving company soon. She needed to walk through and make everything presentable—starting with the kitchen.

"Katherine, we'll finish ironing later—help me straighten up the kitchen. Do we still have some apple fritters left? I'll put on a pot of coffee. Lorelle and Annie—make sure the dining room and parlor are picked up. Jenna, clean off the porch—it won't take long. Maybe I should fix a pie—no, I don't have time."

"Who's coming, Mother?" Katherine asked.

Mercy's Face

"He's already here," France said as she filled the coffee pot.

"Who's here?"

"Jimmy!!" she said. "Jimmy Taylor's here!."

Katherine looked down at her sweat-stained blouse and looked up at France with a horrified expression. "I have to go change!"

She heard a flurry of "Me, too's!" in the dining room and on the porch and laughed out loud when she heard a stampede of footsteps abandon their posts. She couldn't get angry at them. The girls were all enamored with Jimmy Taylor and wanted to put their best foot forward in front of him. She guessed a little bit of herself felt the same way.

France finished straightening up the kitchen and walked through the dining room to glance at her reflection in the mirror above the buffet. She straightened the fly-away strands of hair as best as she could and had just untied the apron around her waist when she heard laughter and footsteps on the back porch.

Faith led her brother into the kitchen, and France met them at the dining room door.

"Look who's here, France!" said Faith excitedly.

"Will wonders never cease," she said, smiling. "How in the world are you, Jimmy?"

She walked over and gave him a big hug. "I'm so glad to see you!"

About that time, four young ladies, freshly primped, came stumbling into the kitchen to line up for hugs, too. Jimmy obliged, but had to be reminded of a couple of their names again.

Jimmy looked around and asked where the rest of the multitude was.

France told him that the little ones were probably in the barn playing with the kittens—their usual habitat when they weren't doing chores. The older boys were helping harvest hay on Mr. Watson's place outside of town. She said he would pay them mostly with hay for the Samuel's livestock at the end of the season, but Mr. Watson usually gave them two bits apiece for their help each week until he was finished haying. They had been working for several weeks after school during the weekdays and most all day Saturdays, she chattered on.

"And Mr. Samuel?" Jimmy asked.

"He's down at the store," France said. "Did you know we have three other stores in town now? George has had to work even harder since he's experiencing some serious competition for the first time. But Mercy's made a huge difference working down there. She even talked him into leaving the store open at noontime—she stays there while he comes home to eat, and then she comes home after he goes back. He's quite impressed with her; in fact we all are with her abilities."

"Except for her cooking," Lorelle said as she crinkled up her nose.

"Well, we haven't given her much of a chance to practice," Faith said, defending her.

France looked at the clock. "I'd better finish dinner—George will be here in a little bit. He's probably started walking home already."

"I think I'll just head that way and meet him," Jimmy said.

"He'll be so glad to see you, Jimmy," said France. "I think he was hoping you could work with our old mare the next time you came through. He just hasn't had time, and the kids want to ride her. But we haven't let them yet because we're afraid she might try to pitch them off. It's been so long since she's been ridden—we just mainly use her to pull the buggy, and that isn't that often any more. I'm afraid she's gotten spoiled to doing little or nothing."

"Except eat," said Faith. "She's really good at that."

"I'll be glad to work with her," he said. "Now, if you'll excuse me, ladies, I'm going to head to the store. I'll see you later, Faith."

They all watched him walk through the dining room, and the younger girls followed to watch him walk through the parlor. He opened the front door and donned his hat as he stepped through it. He turned and winked at the girls before shutting the door to the sound of giggling.

France brought them back to the present. "Come on girls—Mr. Samuel is going to be disappointed if we don't have his dinner on the table for him," she said. "But I think Jimmy will buy us a little time."

"Hey!" Katherine said. "He's come just in time for the dance tonight! Do you think he'll dance with us, Faith?"

"He doesn't care too much for dancing, but I just might be able to talk him into it," she said.

* * *

The postmaster witnessed Mr. Samuel greet a stranger outside his door. He overheard them share the usual questions and comments of health and work and family. Then the conversation shifted.

"Where is she?" the tall, dark-skinned man asked Mr. Samuel.

"Inside—I can hardly get her out of there to come home," he said. "Go on in—I know she'll be surprised to see you."

"I'll see you after lunch, then," the stranger said, and the two men parted ways.

The postmaster made a mental note of the name, *Jimmy Taylor*. It sounded familiar for some reason.

* * *

Jimmy stepped inside the door of the Samuel's store and looked around, remembering the first time he was here with his brother Justin, Allie, and his grandmother two years before. The smells were the same, but the store seemed different for some reason.

He smiled when he saw the reason standing on a stool down the first aisle rearranging the dust on the shelves with a fierce determination. He almost chuckled out loud when he realized he was witnessing Florine Locke actually doing some honest labor. She looked good—no, she looked better than good. She had filled out a little and looked much healthier than the last time he'd seen her when she was so scrawny and pale. He had to remind himself that she was in a family way, because she sure didn't show it. Her blonde hair was braided and sat atop her head like a crown. He wondered what it would feel like to let it down and run his fingers through it.

He shook the thought clear of his head and walked over to the counter and rang the little hand bell.

Florine turned at the sound and saw she had a customer standing at the counter up front.

"I'll be right with you," she said in a friendly manner as she climbed down from the stool.

She walked briskly up to the back of the tall man and said, "May I help you, sir?"

Jimmy turned and looked at her with those blue eyes.

"Hello, Florine."

He heard a sharp intake of breath, and she just looked at his face for a moment. Then she smiled at him—her eyes first, then the mouth followed, and this time it took *his* breath away. He knew she was pretty, but he couldn't remember her being this beautiful.

"I hoped you would come, Jimmy Taylor," she said as she stepped up to hug him. "And it's *Mercy* now. I left the old Florine back in Waco."

"Well, Mercy sakes, it sure is good to see you," he said teasingly as he wrapped his arms around her and held on for what had to be an entirely improper length of time, but he didn't care. She didn't seem to mind either, and besides, she smelled so good.

Unfettered now, he breathed in deeply and allowed his mind to be filled with her for the first time.

Chapter 21

Everyone knew something was different in the house with Jimmy there. He sat between Mercy and Faith at supper, and he began by giving them equal attention, but after a while, he couldn't keep his eyes off of Mercy.

After supper they all scattered to get ready for the dance. Saturdays were not only laundry days, but it was bath day, too—a *sit in the tub* bath for everyone in the Samuel household. But no one was allowed to sit and soak for any length of time. The girls used a tub in the kitchen while France filled a tub on the porch for the boys since the weather was still warm. She draped a sheet across the corner by the door to the new addition hall so the boys could finish getting dressed in their bedroom. She assigned George and Jimmy to oversee that operation, and insisted that they make sure the boys scrubbed behind their ears and all their cracks and crevices. And still, George and Jimmy were the first to show up in the parlor ready to go.

France shooed them out onto the front porch, though, when the girls had to make a dash to the bedrooms to finish getting ready.

Mercy and France dressed the youngest children while Faith worked on the older girls' hair. France and Mercy were the last to get ready, and Faith helped arrange their hair, too. The three walked out on the porch to the anxious throng insisting they get going—that the dance had already started. The older children ran on ahead of the adults, who walked slower with the younger children.

After a couple of blocks, they could hear the fiddle music drifting down the street ahead of them, and they met and greeted other townsfolk walking that way, too.

"Do you dance, Jimmy?" Mercy asked.

"Slow ones," he said. "And the waltz, if it isn't too fast."

Mercy smiled. "Then you'll dance the first waltz with me."

"Will you dance with me, brother?" Faith asked Jimmy as they walked through the entrance foyer into the largest room of the school house.

"Maybe," he said, teasing her.

"Then save one for me," she called out as a short, red-headed man grabbed her hand and pulled her onto the dance floor to line up for the Virginia reel.

Another man grabbed Mercy's arm to complete the line

Jimmy walked over to the corner with George and France, who introduced him to several people along the way. The Samuel kids scattered—Joseph and the older girls chose to dance in a children's reel to one side; the other boys found friends to play with, which really was the only reason they wanted to come.

France held little Mac's hand until she found out where the women were taking turns watching the babies and youngest children in a side room. She took Mac over there and assured Ruth Crain and the others that she would be back to relieve someone later.

Jimmy watched as Mercy turned heads all over the dance floor. She wore a full, red skirt with a matching jacket trimmed in black velvet. It wasn't long before she shed the jacket to reveal a beautiful white lace blouse and black sash fitted just above her waist. He tried to watch what was going on around him, but his eyes kept drifting back to her.

He wasn't the only one mesmerized by Mercy. He overheard several comments by men and women alike about how beautiful she was. One young lady fussed to her friend that her own beau couldn't seem to keep his eyes off of Mercy's face.

Jimmy missed finding her during the first slow dance, so he looked around and grabbed Katherine to dance with her.

Katherine's face was flushed the entire time as she worried about stepping on his toes.

Jimmy noticed a few annoyed looks and glares directed his way, but he was used to that.

Several more vigorous dances later, the fiddler finally played a waltz, and Mercy declined several offers as she walked across the room to find Jimmy. But he was watching her and met her halfway across the dance floor. The music had already started as he swept her in his arms and began turning around the room.

Mercy threw her head back and laughed with delight as they twirled around the dance floor. Every eye in the room was on the handsome couple waltzing so gracefully.

Then he stepped on her foot, and she almost fell.

"Dang it," he said as he grabbed her to keep her from falling. "I'm a little rusty."

Mercy was laughing so hard she could barely get going again. A thought fleetingly passed through her mind that not too long ago she would have been mortified to have made such a mistake on the dance floor. But it didn't seem to bother her now as long as she was with Jimmy.

They managed to get through the waltz without any more major stumbles. Mercy suggested they get a cup of punch and step outside to catch their breath.

They walked around to the side of the building in the light of the windows and came upon a small porch towards the back. Mercy looked around for a place to sit and was about to give up when Jimmy pulled out his kerchief and spread it on the top of the steps for her.

"Thank you, kind sir," she said as she sat down to catch her breath and sip her punch. "You know, I still have those kerchiefs you bought for me in Fort Worth."

"You certainly put them to good use on that trip," he said, teasing her.

"I was such a crybaby—I'm surprised you could stand to be around me," she said. "But I assure you, I'm in much better control of my emotions now."

"Well, you had good reason to cry," he said, noticing several men walking around the building towards them.

"Can you believe it's been two months?" she said, looking at his face. "I'm so glad you're here, Jimmy Taylor."

"So Jim Taylor's your name?" one of the men asked.

Mercy turned to acknowledge some of the men she had danced with earlier. She stood up to make the introductions.

"Hello," she said. "Uh, yes, this is Jimmy Taylor, my friend from Waco. Jimmy, this is Silas and Hubert, and I'm sorry I haven't learned your last names yet." She turned to face the third man and said, "And this is Jed Crawford. His father runs the post office next to the Samuels' store."

Jimmy held out his hand. No one took it. He dropped it by his side and knew he wasn't facing the welcoming committee.

Mercy was shocked at their blatant disregard of social propriety. "Where are your manners, gentlemen?!"

"Are you sure he's from Waco?" the one called Silas said.

"No, he's actually not from Waco, but I figured you hadn't heard of the small town he's from," she said.

"I can't believe you'd have the nerve to show your face around here after what you've done," Jed said.

"I don't know what you're talking about," Jimmy said.

Mercy looked at Jimmy and back at the men. She didn't know how they would know about Jimmy's past, but she felt obligated to defend him.

"He's not a kidnapper, no matter what you've heard," she said. "Well, actually it started out that way, but everything turned out all right."

"Mercy, you're not helping," Jimmy said exasperatedly.

"Kidnapping, too?" Silas said. "What are you doing with this man, Mercy? Don't you know who he is?"

"I know exactly who he is, and I think this conversation's over," Mercy said as she turned to Jimmy. "Let's go back inside."

The men blocked their path.

"You're not going anywhere, Taylor, except to jail, where you belong," Jed said as he reached for him.

Jimmy pushed Mercy out of the way before he swung at Jed with a jaw-crunching blow. The other two jumped in the fray, and Jimmy ducked and tackled one of them.

Mercy could not believe what was happening. She turned and started screaming and pounding on the locked door. No one could hear her over the music and noise of the dance since that particular door didn't open directly into the big room. She pulled up her skirt and ran around to the front of the school and inside to find some help.

George was dancing with France when he saw Mercy come running into the room crying. He stopped dancing and pulled France to the side to meet the distraught woman.

"Mercy! What's wrong?!" he said, grabbing her by the shoulders.

By then, the song had stopped, and everyone turned to look at the hysterical woman in George Samuel's arms.

He could only make out the words, 'hurting Jimmy' and 'outside,' which said enough, so he turned to several men and told them to come

Mercy's Face

outside with him.

Mercy tried to follow, but France wouldn't let her.

"Let George handle this," she said as she tried to comfort Mercy. "What happened, honey? Who's trying to hurt Jimmy?"

Faith came up and heard Jimmy's name mentioned and ran outside before France could stop her.

"Come on," France said, "We'd better go get Faith."

Someone over by the window yelled 'fight!' and most of the dance emptied out of the building behind them.

By the time France and Mercy rounded the corner, the older men had just broken up the fight. France could hear her husband's voice above the ruckus. He was angry, and that wasn't like George.

The women quickly walked up to find him standing in front of Jimmy. The light from the school windows showed his face was bleeding from a cut above his eye. Faith stood beside him, looking like she was ready to take on the whole lot of them.

"What are you boys doing?" George was yelling. "This man is a guest in my home and in our town, and this is how you treat him? I thought your parents taught you better than that." He was about to remind them that all men were created equal, but Silas interrupted him.

"But he's Jim Taylor!" he said, wiping his bloody nose with his sleeve.

Gasps and murmurs rumbled through the crowd.

It finally dawned on George that they weren't mistreating Jimmy because of his skin color. They assumed he was the same Jim Taylor who associated with the Hardin gang several years before and was still on the run. A local man had been killed by Hardin over in Comanche, and everyone was still heartsick and angry about that. Anything and anyone connected to Hardin was fair game to punish, and these boys thought they were doing the town a big favor.

"No, no, no!" George said progressively louder when he could see the crowd beginning to sound angry. "This isn't that Jim Taylor—the criminal. That Jim Taylor is older and besides, do you think he'd be stupid enough to show up at a dance anywhere in this part of Texas where everyone, including me, would like to send him to meet his Maker, preferably at the end of a rope?"

No one said anything for a moment.

Mercy walked over to the porch steps to retrieve Jimmy's handkerchief, and stopped and stared angrily at the three young men who had confronted and attacked Jimmy.

"How could you?" she said, and then her angry expression melted into blistering disappointment.

Silas dropped his head and the other two looked away to avoid Mercy glaring at them. They honestly thought they had acted bravely coming to her rescue earlier, but now they felt like fools.

Mercy turned and walked over to Jimmy to gently wipe the blood off his face.

George asked the boys if they had anything to say for themselves.

Jed stepped up and mumbled an apology to Jimmy, and Silas and Hubert nodded in agreement behind him. Jed's father also came up and apologized, admitting that he had inadvertently put the idea in his son's head earlier.

The fiddle music started up again, and the crowd began to disperse and move back inside.

George pulled France aside and said that he would rather round up the children and go home, but he couldn't just yet. As a businessman and leader in the community, he felt that it was important that they stay and show that there was no ill will towards the misunderstanding that had taken place. But Jimmy was ready to call it an evening, and Faith and Mercy chose to go home with him, too.

Faith and Jimmy waited outside while Mercy went back to retrieve her jacket, and they said their goodnights to the Samuels. George and France went back inside where they outwardly smiled and visited and even danced a few more dances that evening. But on the inside, they were heartsick over what had happened to Jimmy.

The trio started walking back to the Samuel house. Faith reached over and clasped her brother's left hand, and a moment later, Mercy slipped her hand into Jimmy's right. Little was spoken on the way home, but much was said in those gestures.

The girls gathered some extra blankets and a feather pillow and made Jimmy a comfortable bed out in the barn, and each of them hugged him good night.

Later in bed, Faith and Mercy were still wide awake from the shock of the incident earlier. The lamp burned bright to keep the darkness at bay.

"I've never seen men fight like that," Mercy said. "It was terrifying."

"You've never seen a fight before?"

"Oh, I've seen men argue and talk big, sometimes to the point of slapping at each other, but most of the boys and men I've been around wouldn't want to get their clothes dirty. I'd heard of men fighting in the gambling houses, but until tonight, I'd never witnessed physical violence in person," she said, and then looked at Faith. "And you have?"

"That wasn't the first fight Jimmy's been in," she said. "He's been picked on all of his life, although tonight was different."

"Why's that?"

"He's never been mistaken for one of the Hardin gang before," Faith said. "I can't wait to write Mother about this one."

"Well, I have to say that you looked like you were ready to whip all of them yourself, if need be," Mercy said, smiling. "That took a lot of courage, Faith."

"Not that I could've done any good, but I'd have given it my best if I had to," she said. "If you had a brother or sister, Mercy, you'd feel the same way."

"You think so?"

"There's something about family—I've seen Justin and Jimmy fight like cats and dogs, but if anybody from the outside tried to hurt one of them, they would defend each other to the death."

"And they'd do the same for you, too," Mercy said, envying her at that moment.

Faith nodded her head.

"What if they'd caught him someplace by himself?"

"They might've really hurt him," said Faith, "but before they were through, Jimmy would've made them regret tangling with him."

Mercy shut her eyes, remembering what it felt like wrapped in his strong arms. "He *is* tough," she said.

Faith was quiet for a moment.

"But his heart isn't, Mercy," she said softly. "Please don't hurt him."

Chapter 22

Everyone in the Samuel household gathered out back of the house to load up for church the following morning, taking both the white hearse and the buggy. Everyone was concerned about Jimmy. His face showed that he had been in a pretty good fight. He was moving a little slow, too. But Jimmy set everyone at ease with his enthusiastic reunion with the funeral hearse. He even insisted on driving it for old times' sake. The older girls didn't hesitate to ride in it this time, but Mercy won the coveted seat beside him.

Jimmy was impressed when he learned that she had come up with the idea of giving the funeral hearse to the Samuels to use, but France reminded everyone anew that it was only on loan. And after hearing it called *funeral hearse* for the fourteenth time, she came up with the idea of renaming it *Mercy's wagon* from then on so the rest of the town wouldn't think they all had completely lost their minds.

"This wagon's for the living," she said, "not the dead."

After church, George and Joseph unhitched the horses from Mercy's wagon and led them to the big pen. Jimmy unhitched the Samuel's mare from the buggy and led her into the barn. He tied her to a post and took a rag and started rubbing her down. He told George he would work with all of the horses, but especially her over the next two days.

George told him they called her Boomer—short for Boomerang. He said if they didn't tie the buggy reins securely to something when they got to where they were going, she would get loose and head back to the barn—without her passengers.

"It only took a couple of long walks home to learn to tie those reins tighter," he said as he patted the horse's neck.

"Well, at least she's old and fat and too lazy to pitch now," Jimmy said. "I don't think she'll give the kids much trouble, but I'll teach them a few things about riding and handling a horse this afternoon and the next few evenings after school. And I'll show them how to rub her down and get her used to them being around her. She'll look forward to the kids coming when she knows there's something in it for her."

"Rub her down?" George said. "I don't think I've ever rubbed down any horse before, much less Boomer. She just might have a heart attack with the shock of it."

Jimmy chuckled. "Well, a brush works better, but I didn't see one around here. Most of our horses don't get that kind of treatment either, but I make the exception when I'm working with a horse and trying to get her used to me touching her."

After the second round of lessons on Monday evening, Mercy took a glass of water to Jimmy in the barn.

"Thanks," he said, downing half of it and setting it on the corner post of the pen. He rolled his stiff neck and then continued to rub oil into the dry leather on the neglected saddle.

Mercy reached over and started to rub his neck before she realized how forward she was being with him. She quickly pulled back.

"I'm sorry," she said. "I used to rub my daddy's neck sometimes…"

"No… that was nice… thanks," he said glancing her way. "I could get used to that."

"What's your secret in training a horse?" asked Mercy, changing the subject as she walked around to face him.

"I think you already know," said Jimmy.

"I do?"

Jimmy nodded. "It's like any kind of relationship, it takes time—spending a lot of time getting to know her…" he looked up at her before finishing, "…the horse—her character, her intelligence, her behavior—and learning to communicate with her."

"Like the time I spent getting Rogue used to me," she said, "and bringing him treats."

Jimmy smiled and nodded. He reached over and grabbed the glass of water, downing the rest of it and handing it to her.

"Thanks for the water."

"You're welcome."

She watched him for a while as he patiently worked new life into the dry, stiff saddle that had been neglected for too long.

"Your eye's looking much better," she said. "That was big of you to walk up and shake Silas's hand at church yesterday. I think everyone was impressed."

"Yeah, it's taken me years, but I've finally learned it's better for my health to not hang onto anger," he said, looking up at her again, "and it was a close companion to me for years."

"I know I gave you good reason to get angry on a number of occasions," she said, smiling coyly. "But I'm trying to let go of a lot of things, too."

He nodded. "You've done good, Mercy. I'm proud of you."

"And thank you for doing this for the kids," she said. "I know George and France really appreciate it."

"Well, if they could get a hold of a couple more saddles, they could ride all three horses," said Jimmy, setting down the rag. "Now are you ready for your lesson?"

"My lesson?"

"Faith's letter said something about you wanting to go riding with me," he said.

"It's been a while, but I haven't forgotten how," said Mercy. "In fact, why don't you ride Boomer, and I'll ride Brave."

"Not in your condition, you won't," he said and looked around. "Does anybody know, other than the Samuels?"

Mercy shook her head. "Except for your sister. She figured it out not long after I arrived; otherwise why else would someone like me show up in a place like this? The other children are so used to adding new members to the family, they haven't even questioned it. I guess they think I'm just the newest hired help," she said, giggling. "Who would've ever guessed that Florine Locke would be in gainful employment today?"

"Life can change fast, can't it?" Jimmy said. "I hear you're doing a good job down at the store, too. How'd you know all that stuff?"

She shrugged her shoulders. "I really don't know that much. But it seemed pretty easy to sell things—especially those things that I'm very familiar with."

"I heard you can be awfully persuasive," he said. "George says his business has been booming since you started working there."

Mercy actually blushed from the praise. "And I didn't realize how much I enjoyed arranging things and putting things in some semblance of order, like… it's the one part of my life that I've been able to make right when everything else seems to be out of control," she said as she looked at him. "That probably makes no sense to you, does it?"

"I know exactly what you're talking about, but for me, it's working with horses."

"And you definitely have a gift there," she said. "I've really enjoyed working at the store, but I won't be able to work there much longer."

"Aren't you feeling all right?"

Mercy nodded her head. "I feel fine, but it'll cause an uproar in town when it becomes obvious that I'm a woman of loose morals, and I don't want to do anything that will hurt Mr. Samuel's business. Did you know the town has three other stores now?"

Jimmy nodded his head. "How do you know everyone will react that way? Maybe they'll be more forgiving."

Mercy looked uncomfortable all of a sudden and looked away. "They won't be any more forgiving than I was when that happened to someone in Waco, and we could be vicious."

She looked back at Jimmy and said, "What do people say—you reap what you sow? Or turnabout is fair play? I don't deserve one bit of concession for my behavior with the way I acted towards others in the same situation."

"Well, I think you're being too hard on yourself," he said. "My family forgave me, although they didn't let me off the hook. I just wish I'd had the chance to make it up to Allie's family before they went back to Dalton. But their faith had a lot to do with forgiving me."

"My family and circle of acquaintances are quite different from yours," said Mercy. "We went to church when it was profitable to do so—around election time or Christmas when we felt charitable, but especially at Easter to show off our new dresses. It had little to do with faith, and everything to do with appearances."

"But people can change, Mercy," Jimmy said, meeting her eyes, and then glancing at her lips.

Nothing was spoken for a moment. She knew something *had* changed between them. And the look in his eyes told her he wanted to kiss her.

But he didn't.

She decided that maybe he was just a little shy. She waited a moment longer, then leaned toward him, shutting her eyes.

139

"Well, we don't have much daylight left—can we go riding tomorrow?"

Her eyes fluttered open to see Jimmy walking away from her.

At breakfast the next morning everyone noticed that Mercy didn't sit in her usual seat next to Jimmy. Katherine scooted over beside Jimmy when she saw Mercy sitting on the opposite side of the table. That bumped Finn back to the girls' side, and he was none too happy about it. And it was the same for lunch and supper that evening.

The conversation at dinner was much the same as usual. It was Emma's turn to lose a tooth—her second, and Caitlin, not to be left out, was absolutely sure she had a loose one. The kittens were getting big, and they would soon need to find new homes for some of them.

But George had the biggest news of the day.

"Jimmy's agreed to drive Mercy's wagon to Fort Worth with the other freight wagon tomorrow," George said. "That means we'll be able to get twice the supplies in half the time."

"Thank you for doing this, Jimmy," France said. "That ought to give George an edge over his competitors."

"He's going to take Joseph with him to start training him to drive the team," said George as he looked at Joseph. "And before too long, he'll have that job."

Joseph sat up a little straighter and couldn't have looked more proud.

"But that's too dangerous right now for a young boy to do by himself," France said, alarmed. "Remember what happened with the stage line on that same route a while back?

"I was working a man's job at his age, France," George said. "And those robberies took place several years ago. And besides, Joseph won't be alone—Roeder always takes an extra armed man with him."

"But remember, it's Mercy's wagon—not ours," France argued. "And you won't always have use of it, so you shouldn't be counting on having it for Joseph to use."

"The wagon's yours, France," said Mercy, but regretted saying it when she saw France's face.

She wasn't sure if France was about to cry or yell.

But instead, her voice quivered only slightly when she looked at her oldest son and said, "I'm sorry, Joseph, but you're not ready to do a man's job just yet."

She looked at George and said, "Would you all please excuse me."

And she left the table before the meal was over.

Everyone was silent. That had never happened before. It unnerved them to witness a crack in the rock of the family. The children had never seen their mother upset like this. Annie spoke first.

"What's wrong with Momma?" she asked.

"Is she mad at Joseph?" K. James asked.

"Kids, your mother's all right," George said, "and no, she's not mad at Joseph. I guess she's just a little upset with me. Most mothers have sixteen or seventeen years to get used to the idea that they'll have to let go of their children eventually, and for most parents, they're ready by then."

He winked at Finn and continued.

"I want you to know that you made France the happiest woman alive when each of you came to live with us. She's wanted to be a mother for longer than all of you have been in this world, but remember, no matter how old you are, she's only been a mother less than two years. Some of you have a head start on growing up because you're older, but I think Momma's just not ready to start thinking about letting you grow up and leave yet. She's still getting used to the idea of being your mother, and she absolutely loves it. She just needs some time to remember that you won't stay children for very long."

"But she'll always be our mother, whether we're here or not," Katherine said.

"You're right, KK," George said. "Why don't you go find her and tell her that."

The dining room immediately emptied of children, and Mercy and Faith followed. They found France at the sewing table in her bedroom, but she hadn't been able to make one decent stitch due to the tears that kept filling her eyes and spilling over.

She was startled to see the door fly open and a passel of children running into her room calling for their momma. And she cried even harder when they took turns hugging her and telling her they loved her and that she would always be their mother.

But she smiled through her tears, wondering how in the world her heart could be broken and yet completely whole at the same time around these children... her children.

Chapter 23

After everyone came back and finished supper, Faith and Mercy insisted that France relax for the rest of the evening—that they would take care of everything. George, Jimmy and the boys fed the animals—their evening chores. Faith and the older girls washed the dishes while Mercy bathed the little ones and put them to bed. They said their nightly prayers, and Emma and Zane rolled over and shut their eyes. Mac fell asleep in no time next to Caitlin, but she was wide awake.

"Do you want me to rub your back?" Mercy asked her.

Caitlin nodded and rolled over as Mercy sat on the edge of her bed and began rubbing and lightly scratching her back.

"Mercy?"

"What, sweetie?"

"I called her Momma, but she isn't my real momma," Caitlin said quietly. "I just didn't want her to be sad."

"That was very kind of you, Caitlin," said Mercy. "Did you know that France didn't give birth to any of the children here?"

Caitlin turned to look at Mercy and shook her head, no. "Where did their mommas go?"

"The same place where your momma is," Mercy said gently. "And they all loved their mothers just like you loved yours. But since they couldn't be with their mothers, God knew the next-best place for them would be right here with Mr. and Mrs. Samuel."

Caitlin nodded. "But I miss my daddy."

"I know you do, and I miss my daddy, too."

"You have a daddy?"

Mercy nodded.

"Where is he?"

"We're kind of far apart right now," Mercy said. "But I'm hoping we'll be together again one of these days."

"Me, too."

"Do you know where your daddy is?"

Caitlin shrugged her shoulders. "But he told me he'd come back for me."

"Then I bet he will one of these days," Mercy said. "And now you need to go to sleep, little girl."

She pulled the sheet up to Caitlin's chin and leaned over to kiss her forehead. Before sitting up, Mercy looked her in the eyes and whispered, "You know what?"

Caitlin shook her head.

"If I ever have a little girl, I hope she'll be just like you," Mercy said, smiling.

Caitlin grinned and whispered, "Me, too."

Mercy walked upstairs to gather her toiletries and wait until the kitchen cleared out before she went downstairs to start her nightly routine. It didn't take nearly as long to complete now since perfection had moved quite a ways down her list of priorities.

She met Faith coming up the stairs and wished her a good night. The house was quiet when she walked into the kitchen and closed the door behind her. She pulled the curtains across the window and pumped enough water to fill half of the bowl in the dry sink.

She sat down and unlaced her shoes, and stood to disrobe. She dipped her lavender soap and washrag in the water and began her bath. She smiled, thinking how things had changed so much in her life. It was simpler, and harder, and fuller somehow.

She looked at the pittance of water in the bowl and recalled the distant memory of taking a full sit-in-the-tub bath almost every day. But now that luxury only happened once a week—and in a small tub at that. But someone would have a full time job just filling and emptying the tub if this large family took soaking baths every day. She looked at the water again with a new appreciation.

Mercy patted herself dry and used her diminishing assortment of creams sparingly. She tried to get the last little flecks of Poudre de

L'Amour No. 1 out of the blue glass jar onto the puff to dust her neck. She had planned to ask Mr. Samuel to special order it for her… until she looked up how much it cost. And she knew without a doubt now that she would need to save every cent to pay back her father the money she owed him.

She sniffed the puff one last time and smiled, remembering the reason she started to buy it in the first place. The box said it was a love potion. She had used it for years, and it had yet to prove that claim. But she loved the fragrance and would miss using it.

Mercy reached down and touched her rounded tummy and thought about the life it held. Several weeks before she had begun to feel a fluttering down there, and she felt sure it was the baby… her baby. The past month had also convinced her that she could learn to be a good mother. She was surrounded by folks that would help her, too, and that made all the difference in the world. She knew it would be next to impossible to raise this baby by herself.

She pulled her nightgown over her head and slipped on her robe before gathering up her toiletries and clothes. She leaned over to blow out the lamp when she remembered she hadn't thrown out her bath water. She set down her things when a light knock on the door startled her.

"Who's there?" she asked.

"It's me, Jimmy."

Mercy walked over to the door and opened it a crack.

"What do you want, Jimmy?"

He pushed the door open and stepped inside.

"Just you."

He grabbed her arm and pulled her to him and kissed her before she could say otherwise.

She tried to push him away… only for a moment, then she couldn't help but give into him.

Jimmy shut the door with his foot and kissed her again. Then he said he needed to talk to her.

Mercy could hardly catch her breath, but asked him how he knew she was in there.

"I could smell you."

"What?"

"Nobody around here smells like you… or was it your Poudre de L'Amour No. 1 calling to me?"

Mercy leaned back and her mouth dropped open thinking for a split second that the stuff really worked... before she realized Jimmy was teasing her again. Then she couldn't help but giggle.

"How did you know about that?"

"Faith told me in her letter that the kids got into your powder and spilled it, but that you handled the situation very... calmly, I think was the word she used to describe you."

"I almost went through the roof before I caught myself," she said. "But I used the last of that dusting powder tonight, so I'll smell like everyone else around here before too long."

"You do smell good," he said as picked up her hair and buried his nose in it. "I love your hair."

"Hey, I'm supposed to be upset with you," she said pulling away to stand by the table.

"I came here to apologize for last night," he said. "I didn't mean to embarrass you."

"Why did you walk away from me?" Mercy asked. "I thought you wanted to kiss me."

"I did, but there's more to it than that."

"More to it?" she said. "Don't you want me?"

"I think I answered that question when you opened the door a minute ago," Jimmy said. "I'm just not sure where this is going, but when I get back from Fort Worth, I want us to talk about it, all right?"

Mercy nodded and smiled, suddenly feeling secure and warm with the thought that he desired her. And as she looked at him, she knew within herself that the feeling was mutual. Her voice changed as she sauntered closer to him.

"So we don't have to talk right now?" she said.

Jimmy shook his head slowly as she pressed her body close to his. It felt like she was on fire. He wrapped his arms around her and kissed her again...hard this time.

Her hands began to touch him.

He couldn't catch his breath all of a sudden, and he couldn't get close enough to her.

"I want you, Jimmy," she whispered in his ear. "Take me to the barn."

The barn? Hell, the kitchen would do just fine, Jimmy thought. He couldn't even think straight anymore.

"No one will know," she whispered again, kissing his neck. "You want me, too, don't you?"

"Lord, help me, but I want you so bad I can hardly stand it," he whispered back, trembling as he started to raise her nightgown.

"It's badly," she corrected him, kissing the other side of his neck.

Jimmy suddenly pulled back as if she had slapped him. He looked her in the face.

"No, it's *bad*, Florine, and we can't do this," he said before walking—no, running out of the kitchen.

He called me Florine, she thought to herself, and with a shock, she realized he was right. The old Florine had returned, if only for a moment, and something inside her went dark.

What was she doing—throwing herself at him like that? She stood there for a moment, feeling a deep ache in the pit of her stomach. The tears came as she picked up the bowl of bath water and walked out the open door to pitch it. She looked sadly towards the barn, but it was too dark to see anything.

Jimmy stood in the shadow just inside the barn… watching her… still wanting her fiercely. He saw her head drop, and he almost called out to her before he caught himself. He watched her turn around and go back inside.

Mercy placed the bowl in the sink and gathered up her things again, blew out the lamp, and walked through the darkness towards her room.

Chapter 24

Mercy slept fitfully that night. She woke up well before sun-up and decided to just get up and get dressed for the day. She couldn't face Jimmy at breakfast anyway, so she decided to head down to the store and get some work done before it opened. She knew her time there was running short, and she still had so many projects to finish. She wrote a quick note of apology, folded it up tight, and wrote Jimmy's name on it. Then she wrote another note asking Faith to give Jimmy's note to him before he left for Fort Worth.

Mercy found France already awake reading her Bible and drinking a cup of coffee in the kitchen.

"Will wonders never cease," she said. "Good morning, Mercy! I think this is a first for you."

"Good morning," she answered as she looked at the clock on the shelf and saw that the time was 4:30.

"Morning, my foot, France—this is still the middle of the night!" she said. "Do you get up this early every day?'

France chuckled. "No, most days I sleep until five. I've just had a lot on my mind and couldn't go back to sleep."

"Me, too," Mercy said under her breath as she scrounged around to find a bite to eat. She lifted a towel over a bowl to find a couple of day-old biscuits and brought one to the table to spoon some honey on it.

"I'll be making some fresh ones in a little bit if you can wait."

"This is fine—I'm in a hurry," Mercy explained. "I just thought I'd go on down to the store and get some work done."

"This early?"

"I didn't sleep well last night either."

"Everything all right, honey?"

"Yes, of course!" she said a little too fast. Then her shoulders slumped and she set down the biscuit. "Or, no…"

She rubbed her puffy eyes, hoping she wouldn't start crying again.

"What is it, sweetie?"

Mercy took a deep breath and said, "I messed up last night, and I don't want to face Jimmy this morning."

"What happened?"

"I'm too ashamed to talk about it."

"You know you can tell me anything, honey."

Mercy nodded and tried to think of a tactful way to broach the subject. "Let's just say the old Florine made an appearance last night."

"What do you mean?"

"Well, she opened the door to Jimmy in more ways than one."

"And what did Jimmy do?"

"I could tell he wanted to, but he backed off at the last second," she said. "I should've been strong, but last night I wanted him so badly that I would've let him go as far as he wanted. But I used to never be that way, France. I was never forward with a man like that. I didn't even know what… those kinds of feeling were, but they were so powerful last night, and things got out of hand so fast—almost like a fire out of control."

"I didn't know how that felt either until after I married George," France explained. "Certain feelings wake up in our bodies after we've been with a man, and they can be powerful. I think that's why God intended for us to wait until after marriage to have that kind of relationship with a man because once those feelings are awakened, they're harder to keep under control—especially so for a man."

"Well, Jimmy was the only one that showed any kind of restraint last night. He didn't walk away from me—he ran. I guess he probably hates me now."

France smiled. "He doesn't hate you, honey. In fact, I think it's quite the opposite. I'm sure it took every bit of willpower for him to walk away from you last night. But he did the right thing."

"But how can I face him after the way I acted?"

"Are you going to see him before he leaves?"

Mercy shook her head. "I can't right now, but I left a note for him, and I'm hoping we can talk when he gets back."

"How do you feel about *him*, Mercy?"

She looked down before answering. "I'd just about decided I would be living my life alone, but after the past couple of days, I can imagine being with him."

"Have you thought about the ramifications with your father if you made a life with Jimmy?"

"Well, my father will probably disown me anyway because I plan to keep my baby," said Mercy.

"I had a feeling you would," France said as she reached over and hugged her. "And we'll continue to pray for your father—that he'll come around. You know we'll do anything we can to help, right?"

Mercy nodded. "I'm so glad Jimmy sent me your way. I'm going to repay you somehow."

"You owe us nothing, girl!" France said. "You've definitely earned your keep around here and especially at the store, and Mercy, look at the time! I'd better go find you a key so you can be on your way, and I can get those biscuits started."

Mercy pulled the hood of her cape over her head as she stepped off the porch and headed toward the town square. She breathed in the cool, dry air as she walked along. She had never liked the darkness, but this time she felt no fear even though it was still night. Stars filled the night, and although the full moon sat low in the western sky, it still shone bright enough to illuminate everything about her, even casting shadows behind every object. Mercy watched her own shadow keeping company with every step she took.

But she jumped again when Sentry greeted her atop the overhang at the corner of the furniture store.

"You should be sleeping like everybody else, you little sneak," she scolded him. "You'd better be glad this isn't a hotel, or someone would've cooked you a long time ago."

She walked across the street and passed the post office to the front of the Samuel's store. She paused to unlock the door, and locked it again behind her after she entered. She found the coal oil lamp on the front counter and lit it, carrying it to the back of the store where she stopped and stared at the beautiful Stuart Singer sewing machine she had recently come to know very well.

Mercy had convinced Mr. Samuel to order one, even though he was sure no one in the area could afford to pay forty-five dollars for a sewing machine. Mercy said she was positive she could talk someone into buying it eventually. But before that happened, she wanted to use it herself and asked Mr. Samuel to not tell his wife about it just yet.

She had seen one of these machines at her seamstress's house in Waco. She recalled how quickly Mrs. Thomas could sew a fashionable dress, which meant she only had to wait a matter of days rather than weeks to get a new dress. And that was the extent of any interest she had in sewing at the time. But after spending hours resizing and mending the hand-me-down clothes by hand for the Samuel children this past month, thoughts of acquiring a machine to do the same work in a fraction of the time became foremost in her mind.

The machine had arrived only a few days before, along with a boxful of patterns. After reading the manual through several times, Mercy learned how to coordinate the pedal and wheel to sew forward and backward stitches. She had brought some of her fanciest dresses that she knew she had outgrown even though an occasion hadn't arisen in this small town that afforded her the opportunity to wear clothes such as these. And she knew, too, that the future held little or no possibility of that situation changing.

Mercy had no idea how much fabric went into her dresses until she began taking them apart. She planned to sew a new item of clothing for each child for Christmas, which was about six weeks away. Combining the nice material from her dresses with a washed muslin or calico would stretch the expensive material far. She held up a simple muslin frock, her first attempt from yesterday. She planned to make this for all of the girls except the eldest, Lorelle and Katherine. They would each receive a waisted skirt. But all of the girls would get a blouse made of the materials from her dresses.

She hadn't decided what she would make for Faith and France; she might even give each of them one of her other dresses. She had brought enough outfits to wear two weeks straight without laundering anything, and that amount seemed decadent compared to the few outfits the children had to wear. France and Faith probably had only a half a dozen dresses between them.

For the boys and Mr. Samuel, she would attempt to make each of them a new shirt, and possibly for Jimmy, too. But she wanted to do more for him. She would have to think about another gift for him—meaningful and inexpensive.

Mercy's Face

Mercy pinned another pattern piece to the muslin and started to cut around it. She couldn't ever remember feeling this excited about giving gifts before—much less making them. She felt such a sense of accomplishment, and she hoped she could keep it a secret.

Mr. Samuel came in at his usual time and walked to the back of the store to check on Mercy. She couldn't stand it—she had to tell somebody her latest plan. He was surprised and very pleased with her efforts. He even told her he would contribute the material for the boys' shirts since her dress materials were a little too pretty for *his* boys to wear.

About mid-morning, George told Mercy to cover the front while he went out in the back alley to meet with Mr. Roeder, the freight driver.

"And send Joseph and Jimmy around back when they get here," he said over his shoulder. "We need to load some empty barrels and crates."

Mercy's heart sank. She was hoping to avoid Jimmy that morning. She began to mentally rehearse some words of greeting, then wondered if she should just apologize first and then tell him good morning. She stood in front of the window watching for the hearse.

Two men walked into the store and began to look around. One of them stepped up to the counter and asked Mercy where the tobacco was. She turned to face him, and her heart stopped when she recognized him.

It was the man called Hank—one of the men who had tried to rob her and Jimmy on the road to Waco.

Chapter 25

Mercy stammered, "Pardon me?"

She was unsure if she should scream or run. But her legs wouldn't move.

He stared at her for a moment, but didn't recognize her.

"The tobacco—where do you keep it?"

"I'm not sure," she said and turned around to face the shelves behind her, trying to keep from panicking, and trying to remember where Mr. Samuel kept the tobacco.

"Well, here it is," the man said, looking through the glass at the items under the counter.

She turned around and slid the counter door to one side.

"Damn, is Grant tobacco all you got?"

"I guess so," said Mercy, trying to keep her voice from shaking. "We're running low… on a few things."

"I guess it'll have to do then, and give me some papers while you're down there," he said as he stared at her again as he set some money down on the counter. "Have we met before?"

"Have you ever been to Brownwood before?" she managed to ask shakily, handing him the tobacco and rolling papers before picking up the money.

"No."

"Then I'm sure we haven't met," she lied, handing him his change.

He looked her up and down again, and Mercy held her breath.

"Come on, Ethan," he said over his shoulder. "We need to go."

The other man looked around the store like he was watching for someone, and then gave up and walked out with Hank.

Mercy backed up to a stool and sat down before her shaking legs collapsed with her.

What is he doing here? she thought to herself. She took several deep breaths and put her hand to her forehead trying to think what she should do.

Mr. Samuel! She stood and ran to the back of the store, through the office and out the back door.

Mr. Samuel was talking to a couple of men beside a large wagon and a six-horse team. He turned when he heard something hit the door and saw an ashen-faced Mercy running towards him.

"What is it, Mercy?"

"They're here," she said, trying to catch her breath, "in Brownwood. They're here!"

"Slow down, Mercy, calm down! Who's here?"

"The men who almost robbed me and Jimmy, I mean Jimmy and me after we left Fort Worth—the same men who robbed the stagecoach we should've been on, but we missed it, and they shot a man, and now they're here, Mr. Samuel, and I know they're going to do something bad!"

"Are these the same men you turned in the information to the Rangers about?"

Mercy nodded frantically.

"Oh, dear Lord," he said. "But he didn't recognize you?"

Mercy shook her head, no. "But he kept looking at me like he knew me from somewhere."

"I'll go talk to the sheriff," George said. "Maximus, would you and Red watch the store—I'd lock it up, but I'm afraid if they're still out front and planning something, anything out of the ordinary would warn them. And take your guns. If they do remember Mercy, they'll be back."

The two men went to the wagon and grabbed their weapons.

"How many were there, Mercy?"

"There were only two in the store, but there were four that day on the road."

He told the men heading into the store, "Be on your guard, Max—there may be four of them."

"Listen to me, Mercy, I want you to go home, but don't go out the front," he said. "Just walk down this alley and around the corner. Tell France what you told me, and y'all make sure the little ones are inside and lock the doors. If you see Jimmy on the way—tell him what's going on, and he'll take you home and come back and help. I'll be home as soon as I can."

She started to cry.

He put his arm around her and told her that she shouldn't worry—that they were going to get them.

"I know," she said. "But please be careful, Mr. Samuel."

"Now go on home," he said. "We'll be fine. Tell France I'll be fine."

George watched Florine walk quickly down the alley and out of sight before he ran the opposite direction. He wasn't even sure what these men looked like, but he knew most everyone in town and would easily recognize four strange men on the street. He knew Jimmy could help with that, too, and hoped he would get there soon.

Then it occurred to him that these men could just as easily recognize Jimmy and shoot him on sight. He needed to find the sheriff—and fast.

* * *

Mercy quickly crossed the road and stayed close to the wall as she walked along the front of the furniture store. She could see the usual activity around the square, but didn't see Hank. Sentry squawked at her on the corner, but this time she didn't even hear him. Her heart continued to race as she walked away from the square.

She didn't see Mercy's wagon sitting empty in front of the Samuel's store in the middle of the block behind her.

She didn't see Hank standing in front of the boot shop staring at the odd-looking white hearse.

His eyes widened as he recalled a humiliating ruse and failed robbery attempt on another hearse a while back… a black hearse and a beautiful blonde.

A rooster crowed at the corner of the square, and Hank turned toward the sound to see the comely blonde-headed store clerk walking quickly away from the area.

And the pieces of his memory fell into place.

"Well, I'll be damned," he said under his breath. "What in the hell is she doing here?"

"What'd you say?" Ethan asked.

"Wait here for Cullen," said Hank, flicking his cigarette butt to the ground and walking off. "Tell him not to do anything until I get back."

"But I told you, I need to go see my girl."

Hank turned around. "You're not going anywhere until you tell Cullen we have a little snag in our plans."

"What snag?!" he asked. "And what plans?"

"Just tell him I'm fixing a problem, and I'll be right back."

He walked quickly to the corner and around it to see the woman about a block away. He followed slowly on the opposite side of the street for another block, and watched her run up to a rock house and go inside. He looked around and walked across the street and through the neighbor's yard and from that vantage, he could see a barn behind the rock house. He circled around it, staying out of sight, and climbed over the rail fence behind the barn. He found a door in the middle of one of the smaller pens. Once inside, he walked to the front of the barn near the open big door and stood just out of sight, watching the house.

He pulled a paper out and began to roll another smoke as he contemplated how he was going to fix this problem.

A cat walked up to rub on his leg, followed by a couple of playful kittens. He kicked the cat away and lit his smoke.

He never saw the little girl scoot out of sight in the corner of the barn.

He took a couple more drags on his cigarette and flicked it away when he heard the door slam from the back of the house. He smiled slightly when he saw who was running toward the barn… running toward him.

This is going to be easy, he thought to himself.

Chapter 26

George approached the sheriff's office in the courthouse from the east side of the square. He walked around to the door on the north side and found Sheriff Gideon sitting at his desk drinking coffee with one of his deputies. George told him that several wanted men had just been in his store, and he was concerned that they intended to do harm in town. He told him that Mercy was almost robbed by these same men before she came to Brownwood, and she found out later that the stage line between Fort Worth and Waco had been robbed and a man shot by these same men.

The sheriff searched through a stack of papers and found a notice confirming the stage robbery that had taken place south of Fort Worth several months before and the information on the four men being sought. He asked George if Mercy was sure that these were the same men. George told him that she was the actual witness who turned in the detailed information about them on the piece of paper he held in his hand.

"Did you see them yourself?"

"No."

"Do you know where they might be?"

George shook his head and walked over to the west window to look outside. The sheriff followed.

"I figure if they're going to attempt to rob something, it'll be the bank," George said, looking toward the bank building across the street at the northwest corner.

The sheriff's eyes wandered from the bank at one end of the street to the other, and stopped on four men standing in front of the boot shop a couple of doors down from the bank.

"There—do you see them?"

"That has to be them—I've never seen those men before," George said.

The sheriff told his deputy to round up whatever men he could find around the square and have them come to the back of the courthouse armed—but to be careful about it so not to raise any suspicion. He said to tell them that a possible bank robbery could happen at any moment, and he needed their help.

George continued to watch the men, who seemed to be getting more agitated by the minute.

"I think it's going to happen soon, Sheriff," he said. "We need to do something quick. I've seen several women and children enter the bank in the past few minutes. We can't let those men go in there. No telling who they'll hurt."

"If they start moving, we'll go," the sheriff said. "But until then, we'll wait for a couple of men to show up, and that'll even the odds. I don't want anyone to get killed today, George."

The sheriff threw a key ring to George and told him to take off his apron and arm himself. George had just unlocked the gun safe when Jimmy and Joseph walked in the door.

* * *

Mercy slammed the front door behind her and tried to figure out a way to lock it. It looked like a board could be placed across it as a barrier, but there was nothing in sight that looked like it fit.

"France!" she yelled. "How can I lock this door?"

Faith walked around the corner from the dining room.

"What's the matter, Mercy?"

"I have to lock this door," she said, breathlessly, leaning her back against the door. "We could be in danger."

Faith's eyes widened. She stepped back into the dining room and told the four little ones to go to their bedroom—that she would be there in a little bit. France came from the kitchen and asked what was going on.

Once the children had left the room, Faith tried to get Mercy to come into the kitchen, but she wouldn't step away from the door until Faith propped a chair underneath the knob.

They led her into the kitchen and seated her at the table.

"Let me fix you a cup of tea, and you can tell us what is going on," France said.

"Remember those stage robbers I told you about?" Mercy asked.

"The ones that almost robbed you and Jimmy?" Faith asked.

Mercy nodded. ""They're here," she said. "They're in town."

"Here in Brownwood?" France asked. "How do you know?"

"They were in the store," she said, "or two of them were."

"Oh, dear Lord," France said as she sat down. "Did they see you?"

Mercy nodded. "The one named Hank did, but he didn't recognize me, even though he asked if we'd met before. I'm afraid he might remember me, though," she said and then realized something. "Where's Jimmy?"

"Honey, you should've met him on the road when you were coming home—he left just a little while ago."

"I didn't see him. But what if they see him and recognize him?" Mercy asked. "And he's driving the hearse, too."

France put her hand to her mouth when she thought about the danger Jimmy was in. "Where was George?" she asked.

"He was out back talking to the freight drivers, and I went to tell him after those men left. Mr. Samuel told me to come straight home, and he went to the sheriff's office to report it."

"What were they going to do?"

"I think they were going to try to arrest them," Mercy said, "before anything happened."

"There may be a gunfight," France said. "Faith, go get the children and bring them to the kitchen. We're only two blocks away, and I don't want any of us on that side of the house until this is over with."

Faith left the room to go get the children. In a moment she was back with Emma, Zane, and Mac.

"But you told her she could go play with the kittens when she finished writing her letters," Emma was explaining, "and she finished them."

"Except her *Z* is backwards," said Zane. "It looks like an *S*."

"Caitlin's gone to the barn again," Faith said, exasperatedly. "I'll go get her."

"No, she'll probably hide from you." Mercy stood and walked to the door. "I'll be right back."

She ran down the steps and across the yard.

* * *

Two men, each carrying a pair of boots, walked across the street towards the boot shop. Several others visited casually as they walked along the boardwalk toward the four strangers.

One of the strangers turned and recognized George carrying one of the pairs of boots.

"Mr. Samuel?" he said.

"Ethan? What are you doing here?" George asked him.

The sheriff dropped the pair of boots he was holding, and in its place was a drawn gun. By then, four other men followed suit and surrounded the strangers.

"Cullen!" the sheriff called out to the four men.

The four men were shocked to see they were surrounded by guns.

"What's going on?" Ethan asked Mr. Samuel.

"Which one of you is Cullen?" the sheriff asked.

Cullen looked at the sheriff, but his face registered no recognition of that name.

"You must be mistaken, Sheriff," he said. "There's nobody here by that name."

"Hank, you'd better help him change his mind," the sheriff said again, hoping to draw someone out.

No one responded.

"But Hank's not..." Ethan started to say, but Cullen told him to shut up.

"I don't know why you have your sights set on us," Cullen said calmly. "We haven't done anything."

Sheriff Gideon told them they were under arrest and told them to put their hands up while his deputy and another man relieved them of their weapons. Cullen declared their innocence—insisting again that they hadn't done anything wrong, and demanded that they be released. The sheriff told them that the arrest was based on prior charges, and they again declare their innocence—that they'd been mistaken for some other men. The sheriff called Cullen again by his name, and Cullen answered before he caught himself.

How did they know? Cullen thought to himself. He realized that somebody had to have recognized them and looked around for a familiar face. He stopped on a dark-skinned man with light blue eyes. And he remembered.

"You!" Cullen said. "It was you!"

Jimmy glared back at him.

George confronted Ethan. "Why are you running with these men—don't you know what they've done?"

"Mr. Samuel," Ethan said, "I honestly don't know anything about these men. I swear it!"

"The information said *four* men, George," the sheriff said.

"I'm really disappointed in you, Ethan," said George. "I know you were going through some hard times, but I thought you had better sense than this."

"I met up with these men outside of Fort Worth only a week ago," he said. "I told them I was on my way here, and they asked me about Brownwood and decided to come along."

"What did you tell them about Brownwood?"

"That my girl was here, and that it was a good town with good people..." he paused as he turned around and looked at Cullen, "...and you asked me if it was big enough for a bank—that you needed a safe place to deposit some money. And I told you it had a bank—a fairly new bank."

"Shut up, Ethan," Cullen said.

Ethan looked over their heads to the Pecan Valley Bank a few doors down.

"Were y'all planning to rob this bank, Cullen?" Ethan asked and then shook his head. "I think I just led the foxes into the hen house." He looked back at Mr. Samuel and swore again that he knew nothing about their plan.

Jimmy looked around, realizing they were short one man—the one called Hank.

"Where's Hank?" he asked.

"He told me he had to fix a problem," said Ethan, "and he walked down the street and turned right at the corner."

Jimmy's heart stopped when he saw where Hank was headed—towards the Samuel house. He started running just about the time someone down the street hollered, "FIRE!!"

Chapter 27

The smoke billowed high in the sky by the time Jimmy came tearing around the rock house. The barn was an inferno—fueled by the new hay the boys had earned from Mr. Watson.

It was beyond saving.

Jimmy saw France and Faith clinging to each other and sobbing hysterically beside the pump. Two pails, one empty and one full, sat at their feet. Jimmy saw the little ones huddled on the porch crying.

Jimmy ran up to the women, and threw his arms around Faith, relieved to see his sister was all right. France's face was grief-stricken.

"We tried, Jimmy, but it was too big, too fast," said Faith. "We don't know what happened!"

"Where's Mercy?"

France turned away and fell to her knees with her face in her hands.

Faith sobbed, "We heard her screaming, Jimmy—Mercy and Caitlin were inside, but we couldn't get to them."

"No!!" Jimmy screamed, and started to run towards the barn.

Faith grabbed his arm. "No, Jimmy—you can't—it's too hot! We tried!"

"No!" He said, frustrated at her attempt to stop him. "Let me go!"

She held on even tighter.

"Look at France, Jimmy!" Faith said. "She tried to go in there, but it's just too hot!"

Jimmy looked at France, still weeping with her face covered. He walked over and knelt down in front of her and gently pulled her hands away from her face. Her eyebrows and hair were singed, and her face was red and blistered.

"I tried, sweetie," she said, sobbing. "I tried."

Jimmy pulled her to him and broke down. Faith knelt down and laid her head on his back and wept with them.

George and Ethan came running around the house, along with a group of townspeople—most were carrying buckets.

"France!!" George yelled.

Jimmy stood and helped France to her feet. She fell into her husband's arms and tried to tell him about Caitlin and Mercy.

"Oh, no, no, no…" was all George could say.

"Caitlin is in there?!" Ethan asked.

Faith nodded sadly, wondering who this stranger was.

"My baby!" he cried with an anguished voice. "Not my baby girl!!" Then he turned around looking for someone. "That buzzard Hank killed my baby!" He started to walk away from the group.

"Ethan!" George yelled at him, but Ethan kept walking.

The townsfolk were filling their buckets as fast as they could to put out the small grass fires started by flying embers. They knew the barn was lost, but they could at least save the house and the neighboring places from going up in flames, too.

"The horses!" Jimmy said, running towards the big pen. Through the smoke, he could see the horses at the farthest corner. But then something else caught his eye—something small walking towards him.

It was Caitlin!

He was over the fence in two seconds. He turned and hollered over his shoulder at the others as he ran to Caitlin and swept her up in his arms. She reeked of smoke and was sopping wet and shaking like a leaf as she cried, but otherwise seemed all right. She wrapped her arms around his neck and held on for dear life.

"I am so glad to see you, little girl," Jimmy said, holding her tight. "Where's Mercy?"

Caitlin pointed towards the barn, but Jimmy couldn't see anything but smoke and flames.

Jimmy ran to the fence and passed her across to George's waiting arms. France and Faith wept with relief this time as they walked with George carrying her back to the house.

Jimmy ran back towards the side of the barn where the smaller pens were attached. The smoke was so thick he couldn't see more than two feet in front of him. He started coughing so he pulled his handkerchief over his face, but his eyes watered so badly he might as well have been blindfolded.

He dropped to the ground and began to crawl back and forth across the pens. The heat coming off the burning barn was so hot he could hardly stand it.

"Lord, please help me! Please don't let her die!" he said aloud. He began to call out Mercy's name as he crawled.

He heard a faint moan and a muffled cough to his right and turned to follow the sound. He almost crawled right over her before he realized he had found her. She lay in a crumpled heap underneath a wet horse blanket. He threw the heavy blanket aside and grabbed her around the chest and crawled, dragging her under the fence and away from the smoke and out into the open air on the far side of the pen.

He stayed on his hands and knees for a moment coughing and trying to catch his breath. He was relieved to hear she was breathing when another moan escaped her lips. He carefully rolled her over to try to revive her, but almost stopped breathing himself when he saw her face. It was beyond recognition. Her lip and nose were bloody; her right eye was swollen almost shut; her left forehead and the side of her face were burned. The skin looked raw and partly peeled away. Her left shoulder was also burned—most of her blouse on that side had burned away. But her hair and the rest of her clothes were wet like Caitlin's.

"Mercy," he finally said. "Mercy, can you hear me?"

Another moan.

"I've got you," Jimmy said. "You just hang on, you hear? You're going to be all right."

Jimmy picked her up and walked across the pen through the smoke until he was in sight of the house. Several men climbed over the fence and ran to meet him and tried to take Mercy from him, but he wouldn't let them. They walked with him to the far gate and opened it for him, and Faith and the Samuels met him and walked with him back to the house.

France took one look at Mercy's face and said, "George, send someone for Dr. Hood... and to tell him to come quick."

George ran ahead and told Mr. Watson to go fetch the doctor.

Ethan sat on the porch holding Caitlin in his arms as Jimmy carried Mercy up the steps and into the house.

Caitlin began to cry.

"It's okay, Caitlin," Ethan said. "Jimmy found Mercy."

But Caitlin kept crying.

"Why are you crying, baby?" Ethan asked her. "You helped him find Mercy."

She just buried her face in her father's chest and held onto him for a while.

After the shudders left, she finally whispered, "They're all gone, Daddy."

"What's gone, honey?"

"The kittens," she said, "…and Mercy's face."

Chapter 28

France led Jimmy to the bedroom closest to the Samuels' room and watched him gently lay Mercy on the bed. She told Faith to put some water on to boil and then turned back to Jimmy.

"Thank God she's still alive," she said, wiping the tears from her face. She leaned over the bed to take a good look at Mercy's face and shoulder. "Dear Lord in heaven, how did this happen?"

"Hank did this," Jimmy said angrily.

"She was so frightened when she got here," France said. "She told us he was in the store, but that he didn't recognize her. How did he know she would be here?"

"Ethan said he saw her on the street and followed her here."

"And I sure didn't expect Caitlin's father to show up today," she said.

"I thought he was one of the four men at first," Jimmy said. "In fact, we all did. I could only recall Cullen and Hank since they did all the talking that day."

France began to remove Mercy's shoes. "I thought her whole face was burned, but the left side looks like she's been beaten."

"When I find that son of a...," he stopped and caught himself. "I'm sorry, France. I'd wait and help out here, but I don't want the trail to get cold."

"Jimmy, let the sheriff handle that," said France. "He's a dangerous man, and you could get yourself killed."

"The sheriff's got his hands full right now," he said, "but I won't go by myself."

"That's good," she said. "Maybe they can help you keep a cool head about this."

"Yeah," he said, looking at Mercy. "I'm sure he'll help me deal with Hank."

Jimmy walked outside and asked Caitlin's father to go with him.

Ethan was more than ready. He had almost taken off by himself after Hank before he heard someone hollering that Caitlin had been found.

But before they left, Jimmy needed to ask Caitlin what had happened in the barn.

She told him she was playing with the kittens when a man came in through the side door in the pens. She said he looked scary so she hid behind the corn bin.

"What did he do, Caitlin?"

"He stood by the big door and smoked a cigarette," she said, "like you used to do, Daddy, and then Mercy came in, and he grabbed her and called her a name that wasn't her name."

"Can you remember anything else?"

Caitlin nodded and her lip began to quiver.

"He said that she owed him something, and then he dragged her to the back of the barn, and I saw her hit him, and he started hitting her back, and he knocked her down."

A tear rolled down her cheek. "I wanted to help her, but I was scared."

"You did the right thing, baby," Ethan said. "That man would've hurt you, too."

"Then there was fire everywhere and he ran away and Mercy got up and started calling my name, and I ... I couldn't move—the fire was everywhere, but she found me."

"How did you get out of the barn?" Jimmy asked.

"The front was all on fire, and all of the hay up high was burning, and Mercy put me in the water trough and she got the horse blanket wet, too, and she put it around me and carried me out through the pens. Fire was falling everywhere, and she started screaming and then she fell on me. I couldn't breathe and I couldn't hardly get her off of me. But then I got out and she wouldn't wake up and I put the blanket on her, and... then I found you," she said, looking at Jimmy.

"You probably saved her life putting that wet blanket on her, Caitlin," Jimmy said.

A man carrying a black bag came running around the house, and Jimmy took him inside. Then he found Faith and told her that he and

Ethan were leaving for a little while and to be sure and watch Caitlin. She followed Jimmy out to the porch and watched Ethan try to explain to Caitlin why he was leaving. They had to pry her arms off of his neck.

"It's just for a little while, baby," he said. "Then Daddy'll be right back."

The two men walked quickly away from the hysterical little girl towards the pen with the horses.

"It tears me up to see her crying like that," Ethan said, "but we can't let Hank get away with this."

Most of the townsfolk had gathered either to watch the fire or to take part in the water line filling buckets at the pump. They let the barn continue to burn itself out, but had to keep putting out grass fires and burning fence rails and posts. They had saved the buggy earlier by pulling it further away from the barn. The canvas top had burned, though, and would have to be replaced.

Jimmy stopped before they got to the fence. "What am I doing? I don't even have a saddle or a bridle for my horse anymore," he said, looking over at the burning barn.

"I've got a horse, and I know where there are some extra ones that won't be needed for a while," said Ethan. "And I'm sure Hank headed there first. We ought to be able to pick up his trail easily."

"Let's go," Jimmy said, and they started running back toward the town square.

Ethan's and the outlaws' horses were still tied to hitching posts at the side of the bank out of view of the courthouse and sheriff's office. Between the near-bank robbery and the fire, no one had thought to round up the arrested men's horses.

"Do you think we need to tell the sheriff?" Ethan asked.

Jimmy shook his head. "We don't have time. We'll just bring Hank back here to join his friends."

"What if he puts up a fight?"

"Then he may not be sitting up in his saddle when we ride back into town," Jimmy said grimly.

Jimmy studied the tracks where the horses were tied. Then he looked at the remaining horses' feet.

"His horse has thrown a shoe," he said. "That'll make it easy for us to spot his tracks."

They mounted their horses and followed the tracks north, but Jimmy pulled up after half a mile or so.

"That's odd," he said, looking down. "He stopped here, but then he turned east."

They followed the trail past several more houses, and Jimmy pulled up again, looking down at the tracks. Then he looked up.

The tracks were headed back to town.

"He's gone back," Jimmy said, his forehead furrowed in thought.

"You don't think he'd try to bust his friends out, do you?" Ethan asked.

"What better time to try when most of the town is distracted by a fire," said Jimmy.

"Maybe that just occurred to him right along here."

Jimmy nodded. "And he doesn't know anybody's looking for him just yet either. He probably figures he's got the upper hand."

They headed back at a trot towards the town square until they were within a block of it, then slowed to a walk. They found Hank's horse tied to a post in the alley behind the newspaper printing office. They dismounted and tied their horses nearby.

Jimmy whispered to Ethan to go through the back door of the newspaper office to make sure Hank wasn't hiding out in there.

"I'll take the front," he said.

Jimmy pulled his revolver and walked quietly to the corner at the front of the building facing the courthouse and jail. He found several cigarette butts on the ground. He figured Hank had stopped to think about a plan of action. The square was eerily quiet and looked abandoned. Jimmy could smell the smoke in the air. He had a good view of the front of the courthouse. The jail cells were on the east side of the first floor, but they had very small windows with bars across them about nine feet up—no escape by that route.

The door to the sheriff's office faced Jimmy. A number of tall trees surrounded the courthouse, blocking part of the view. Hank was nowhere in sight.

Where are you, Hank? Jimmy thought to himself as he scanned the square. *What are you planning?*

He thought about what he would do if he wanted to break someone out of jail. Several scenarios came to mind—he could bust in the front door of the sheriff's office with guns blazing, but then he had no idea how many men were guarding his friends. He could be shot before he took one step inside.

Hank really needed some help—another gun. But the only ones that could help him were behind bars in the jail. But what if…

Ethan suddenly stepped out of the door of the newspaper office and pointed up towards the second floor. Jimmy looked up and then looked questioningly back at Ethan.

"It's Hank!" he whispered. "I can see him up a tree on the east side. What in the hell is he doing in a tree?! He can't break them out of those little windows."

"He's trying to arm someone on the inside," Jimmy said, "to do some damage before he goes in through the front. Go out the back and down the alley to the sheriff's office from the other side of the square so Hank can't see you. Tell the sheriff what he's up to. Hurry—Hank probably knows he doesn't have much time before everyone comes back."

Jimmy planned to wait until the sheriff or a deputy showed up, but he saw Hank working his way across the limb towards the window.

He couldn't wait any longer—Hank would have a pistol to them in less than a minute. Jimmy walked quickly and silently across the street. He could see Hank about six feet up in the tree, standing on a limb. He had tied a rope up above him and was trying to lean out as far as he could towards one of the tiny, barred windows near the ceiling of the jail cell. He had tied a kerchief around a pistol and his hand was within two feet of the window. The end of the rope dangled near the ground.

Jimmy saw his chance. He leaped at the rope, grabbed it and jerked it as hard as he could to one side, throwing Hank off balance.

"What the…" Hank said as he lost his grip on the gun and dropped it as he tried to catch himself.

He didn't.

Hank fell out of the tree and landed hard on his shoulder, and immediately started hollering in pain. Jimmy kicked the fallen pistol out of the way and stripped Hank of his other gun.

"Hurts, doesn't it," Jimmy said as he rolled him over with his boot. "Get up," he said. "We've got some talking to do."

"We don't have anything to talk about," Hank said, moaning.

"I'm referring to you beating a defenseless woman and leaving her to die in the fire you set," Jimmy said.

"I didn't set any fire," he said. "I didn't have anything to do with that. And you don't have any proof either."

"We have a witness, Hank, and she told us everything," said Jimmy, "and what were the words you used—that she owed you something?"

Hank looked shocked. "But how would you know that? I heard her screaming…"

Jimmy grabbed him by the front of his shirt and jerked him to his feet. He reared back to punch him when the sheriff and Ethan ran around the corner with guns drawn.

"Thank God, you're here, Sheriff," Hank said. "This man was fixing to assault me."

"He was?" the sheriff said, stepping up to separate them.

"I'm under the protection of the law now, you half-breed," said Hank. "Get your hands off of me."

"He beat a woman, Sheriff," said Jimmy, "and left her to die in that fire back there."

"Was she your girl, pretty boy?" Hank taunted him from behind the sheriff. "Well, she and I had some fun before you got there."

Jimmy lunged at him, and Ethan grabbed him in a bear hug.

The sheriff glared at Hank. "Some fun, huh? We don't allow anyone to abuse our womenfolk around here." He calmly pulled out his pocket watch and looked at it.

"I think I'm going to stand over here by this tree and look at my watch for about a minute," he said as he turned to Jimmy. "And for that one minute, Taylor… he's all yours."

Jimmy smiled, but it wasn't a friendly smile.

"But, Sheriff!!" Hank said before Jimmy punched him in the jaw.

Jimmy's left jab bloodied his nose.

True to a coward, Hank turned and tried to run. Ethan blocked his path and pushed him back towards Jimmy. He started swinging blindly, but Jimmy was too fast for him.

"I know you know how to hit," Jimmy said, punching him in the gut this time, "especially a woman half your size. Does it make you feel like a big man to beat a woman?"

Hank was doubled over, trying to catch his breath.

"I just pushed her around a bit," he said, gasping.

"You pushed her around a bit?" Jimmy asked, and hit him in the eye. "Like this? Is that what you call fun?"

"I didn't mean that," Hank said. "I didn't have time for that—the fire was too fast."

Jimmy punched him again.

"Why are you defending her?" said Hank. "You ought to know what kind of woman she is."

"You don't even know her."

"Y'all were the talk of the town in Fort Worth—the woman had quite a reputation around there. And we found out you weren't even carrying a body in that casket wagon. You were just running away. No telling how much money we could've gotten off of you that day, except Cullen stopped us in respect for the dead."

"SHUT UP, HANK!!" a voice hollered from the jail cell.

Jimmy knocked him to the ground this time.

Hank wiped the blood off his mouth with the back of his hand. "It's been more than a minute, Sheriff," he said.

The sheriff tapped his watch. "It has?" He held it to his ear. "I think my watch has stopped."

Jimmy reached down to pull Hank back up on his feet when Hank cowered and scooted back against the wall of the courthouse.

"Mercy! I'm asking for mercy," he pleaded, covering his head with his arms.

Jimmy froze for a moment, and then let him go.

"I bet you didn't even know that's her name."

Hank just lay there. The sheriff walked up beside Jimmy.

"Her name's Mercy," Jimmy said, looking at Hank. "But you sure didn't show her any, did you."

The sheriff reached down and pulled Hank to his feet.

"I think it's about time you joined your friends, Hank," he said, and then turned to Jimmy and Ethan. "I appreciate your help, boys. I think this conversation I just heard is going to be a big help when we stand before the judge."

"Thanks for your *time*, sir," said Jimmy, almost smiling.

"It was my pleasure, son," said Sheriff Gideon as he led Hank away.

Chapter 29

The calendar changed for Mercy and the Samuels the day of the fire. Days were counted from that event: the first day after the fire... the second... the third.

Time slowed to a crawl—the pain was responsible for that. And when Mercy wasn't crying in pain, she moaned, even in her fitful sleep. The sounds turned to screams every time they tried to clean her wounds.

Dr. Hood had told France that was a good sign. She didn't understand why pain could be a good sign, but he explained that the worst kind of burns caused little pain because the nerves were dead. If Mercy was feeling pain, then some of her nerves still functioned in her shoulder and face.

The doctor told France to keep the burned areas clean and to try to remove as much of the peeling skin as possible to keep infection down. He also instructed her to force Mercy to drink a lot of liquids, but that her jaw might be broken, which would make it hard to get her to drink anything.

And within five minutes of examining Mercy, the doctor knew her secret, too.

"No one knows, Dr. Hood," France said.

"She hid it well," he said, "and you know her secret's safe with me, but it won't be long now before it's obvious to everyone else. Half the boys in town will be heartbroken, you know."

France nodded. "I know she'll be shunned, but she'll always be welcome in our home. Can you tell how far along she is?"

"I'd figure around five months," he said as he started packing his bag. "Well, watch her close the next few days. The baby seems to be fine now, but Mercy's wounds are serious, and the pain and shock to her system might affect the pregnancy. I'll come by again tomorrow and check on her."

During the first night France found herself humming quietly at times to keep herself awake sitting beside Mercy's bed.

"Sing…the words," Mercy struggled to say.

France began to sing.

> "When peace like a river, attendeth my way,
> When sorrows like sea billows roll;
> Whatever my lot, Thou has taught me to say,
> It is well, it is well with my soul.
>
> It is well, with my soul,
> It is well, with my soul,
> It is well, it is well with my soul."

"More…" Mercy whispered.

"That's the only verse I know of that song—it's pretty new, but I know others," she said, noticing the music seemed to soothe Mercy's spirit.

> "He leadeth me: 0 blessed thought,
> 0 words with heavenly comfort fraught,
> Whate'er I do, where'er I be,
> Still 'tis God's hand that leadeth me."

Before the night was over, France had sung most every song she knew, including *My Country 'Tis of Thee* and *The Battle Hymn of the Republic*.

France and Faith were exhausted by day two. Sleep had become a rare commodity in the Samuel household. They all suffered with Mercy. The older children could see the toll the care of Mercy was taking on their mother, and began taking over the care of the younger ones. Katherine and Lorelle made a big pot of stew for supper that first night. By the next day, though, most of the town had heard of the attack on Mercy and had started bringing food and offers of help in any way. The older girls took over as hosts and accepted the prepared dishes. Annie and Jenna did most of the dishwashing and straightening up, although France still insisted on handling the lye and boiling the bedding and bandages they had to wash and re-use on Mercy.

George went back to the store for part of the day just to send Mr. Roeder and his partner on to Fort Worth with their freight wagon. Ethan volunteered to take Mercy's wagon so Jimmy and Joseph could stay behind to mend the fences around the pens and start cleaning up the charred remains of the barn, or at least the parts that weren't still smoldering. That's what Jimmy had told them, which was the truth, but the real reason was that he didn't want to leave Mercy so soon after the attack.

Joseph showed K. James how to milk the cow, and he proudly took over that duty. Miss Clara didn't seem to mind either as long as she had something to eat in front of her. Mr. Watson had brought by a wagon full of hay to tide them over for a while.

Another good thing that happened in the couple of days after the fire was that the momma cat showed up on the porch with two of her kittens—a little singed around the ears, but healthy otherwise. Caitlin and the other children were ecstatic.

Jimmy took his turn sitting with Mercy several hours at a time during the day and even at night so France and Faith could get a few hours of sleep. Mercy held his hand, and she gripped it hard when the pain became unbearable. Jimmy told France he wasn't about to sing like she did, though, because it would do Mercy more harm than good. Instead, he talked to her about training horses when she needed to be distracted.

On day three, they left the burns uncovered for a while because peeling them off to change them caused Mercy such agony.

France asked her if she wanted them to contact her parents, but Mercy made her promise that they wouldn't.

"I've made my choice," she said raggedly. "And I choose my baby."

Later, Caitlin slipped into Mercy's room and whispered something to France.

France walked the little girl up to the side of the bed and told Mercy that Caitlin wanted to tell her something that would cheer her up. France said she would be right back and stepped out of the room.

Mercy's Face

Mercy turned her head and tried to smile at Caitlin standing there, but her face still felt swollen and stiff, and only one side of her mouth seemed to move as it should.

Caitlin stared wide-eyed at Mercy for a moment, and then told her about the cats.

"That *is* good news," she said through her teeth, trying to speak with minimal movement to her jaw.

Mercy looked beyond the little girl and noticed for the first time a bed sheet draped over the dresser mirror beside the bed.

"Does my face look scary to you, Caitlin?" Mercy asked.

Caitlin shook her head, no. "I know what you look like under there," she said. "Does it hurt?"

"Yes."

"But it'll get better, right?"

"Yes, sweetie," Mercy said and paused as she looked again at the covered dresser. "Caitlin, could you do something for me?"

The little girl nodded.

"Could you pull that sheet off the dresser behind you?"

Caitlin turned around and grabbed a hold of the sheet and pulled it off the mirror.

Mercy sat up stiffly and leaned over to take a look.

Jimmy was hammering on the fence when he heard the screams again, but this time they sounded different. He ran toward the house. He knew the wound-cleaning screams. He remembered how her angry screams sounded when he first met her in Fort Worth. These weren't either of those. He ran up the porch and into the door by the bedrooms. He stopped a few feet inside her room, trying to catch his breath.

He watched as France tried to calm her down, but Mercy became even more hysterical and tried to pull the bedding over her face when she saw Jimmy. He knew the movement had to have caused tremendous pain in her injured shoulder, but she seemed to be more concerned that he not see her rather than avoid the pain.

"Shut the door!" she tried to scream. "Don't let him see me!"

Jimmy stood there confused. "But I've already seen you, Mercy. Why are you so upset?"

"Get out!!" she yelled. "France, make him get out."

Chapter 30

France walked to the door and stepped out, shutting it behind her.

"What in the hell is wrong with her?" Jimmy asked.

"Come with me," she said as she took him by the arm and walked him through the parlor.

Faith sat on the settee trying to comfort Caitlin, who was still upset from Mercy's outburst.

Zane, Emma, and Mac sat wide-eyed at the big table in the dining room.

"Keep working, kids," she said. "Faith and Caitlin will be right back."

France led Jimmy to the kitchen, shut the door behind them, and told him to sit down. She put the coffee pot on to boil.

"I don't understand, France," he said. "I've been with her ever since the fire—why is she shutting me out all of a sudden?"

"She asked Caitlin to remove the sheet from the dresser mirror," France explained. "I knew we should've taken it out of the room when we moved the other bed. Mercy saw her face in the mirror for the first time."

"But she knew she was hurt—she had to have known her face wouldn't look the same."

"She didn't know how bad it was, Jimmy, until she saw it."

"She's acting more like her old self again," he said.

"We all have certain parts of ourselves that we're not particularly proud of," said France. "Some people can turn their lives around in the snap of a finger—some encounters with God can do that. But with most of us, it's a life-long process of God chipping away at our rough spots, changing those things about us that need changing. And most change usually happens in the difficult times of our lives. That's when I've had to lean on God the most, and He's gotten me through them. Mercy hasn't learned that yet."

"I learned some of that during my time with Allie," said Jimmy.

"And time has taught me that if I didn't learn the lesson God intended for me to learn, he'll bring it back around again until I do. When you invited Jesus into your life, did you completely change overnight, or has it been a process for you?"

Jimmy thought for a moment. "I'd have to say it was a big turning point for me, but since then, it's definitely been a process. I still have a long ways to go. Didn't I just say 'hell' in front of you a minute ago? Sorry about that."

France snickered and lowered her voice. "I've even said it myself a time or two when no one was around."

"Mrs. Samuel! I thought you were purt near close to perfect," he said.

"Don't you dare tell George otherwise," said France as she grabbed two cups from the cupboard, "because he thinks I am. But that's part of Mercy's problem. Her face has been her perfection—her greatest strength all her life."

"But she's more than that now," said Jimmy. "She's changed, or at least I thought she had."

"Mercy's come a long way, but you're seeing some of her rough edges still. She may have to deal with the loss of what's always been most important to her—her looks. And, heaven forbid, if her face is badly scarred from this, will that affect how you feel about her?"

Jimmy shook his head. "For years I couldn't stand to be around her when everything about her physically was perfect. But she's actually grown a heart since I found her in Fort Worth—especially since she's been here."

"Humility has a way of doing that," said France, stirring a pot of beans on the stove. "Her circumstances have definitely put her in a life-changing position, which can either make her stronger, or it can destroy her if she lets it."

"I can't stand the thought of her avoiding me just because of a few scars," he said.

"Then be patient with her, Jimmy," said France as she poured him a cup of coffee. "Give her some time and some space, and I'm sure she'll eventually come around."

"I hope you're right," he said.

They heard George come in the front door for lunch, and France realized she hadn't finished making the cornbread yet. She grabbed the bowl that already held the dry ingredients. She asked Jimmy to add some more wood to the stove while she broke the eggs and poured the milk in the bowl. She could hear George talking with Faith and the children as she frantically stirred. Then she wiped the inside of a cast iron skillet with some bacon grease and dumped the batter in it.

Jimmy grinned watching her frenetic work.

"Perfect, huh?" he teased.

France shushed him as she slid the skillet into the oven and shut the door just as George came walking into the kitchen.

"I'm hungry!" he said as he hugged his wife. "What's for lunch?"

"Ellen Watson brought us a baked ham and a big pot of beans, my darling," said France, kissing his cheek, "but the cornbread's not quite ready."

She smiled slyly and winked at Jimmy.

He almost laughed out loud. He enjoyed watching France and George together. They reminded him of the way his parents acted around each other—still very much in love after all these years.

"How's Mercy doing?" asked George, placing several envelopes on the table.

"We've had a little set-back today," said France.

"What happened?"

"She saw her face in the mirror, and she didn't take it very well."

"Oh, dear," George said. "I'm sorry to hear that. But speaking of faces, there's a certain man sitting in the county jail right now with a banged up face. The whole town is talking about what you did to Hank, Jimmy. I just wish I could've been there to get in a lick or two myself for what he did to Mercy."

"What are you talking about, George?" France said and turned to Jimmy. "What did you do, Jimmy?"

"Nothing," he said and then admitted, "or… maybe that's another rough spot I need to work on."

"Got a confession out of him, France, and he wasn't even trying," George said proudly. "By the way, do you think Mercy's up to reading a letter from her father?"

"Oh, my," France said as she picked up the long, expensive-looking

Mercy's Face

envelope. "I don't know—it's probably not good news. I don't know if you knew, Jimmy, but she sent her first payment to her father a couple of weeks ago. She told me it wasn't much, but it was enough to inform him of her intentions. He's probably fit to be tied about her decision."

"You'd better read it first then," said Jimmy, "so you can decide if she's strong enough to handle it."

France opened the envelope carefully and pulled out several folded pieces of paper.

"This looks like some kind of legal document," she said as she read it silently to herself. She looked at the second page and gasped. "I don't believe this! There's no way Mercy can deal with this right now."

"What is it, France?"

"Mr. Locke has given his daughter until the end of the year to pay her debt unless she signs this paper giving up all rights to her baby," she said. "Then he'll forgive the debt and remove the charges."

"There's no way she can come up with that amount of money," said George. "What if she refuses?"

"It says that a warrant for her arrest will be issued in January," said France. "Surely he's just bluffing—he's her father!"

"He's trying to force her hand," said Jimmy.

"You don't think he'd follow through with it, do you?" France asked him. "I've never heard of a father doing such."

"I don't know," he said. "He's probably convinced she can't refuse this demand. Langston's a hard man to deal with when it comes to business—especially if he wants something. If Mercy gives up her child and the mistake goes away, Mr. Locke probably thinks they can go on as if nothing's happened."

"So Mercy really has no choice in the matter," said France. "We can't tell her this, George—not right now."

"We'll think of something, honey," he said, "even if it means hiding her or sending her away."

"How can she go anywhere in her condition?" said France. "Where would we send her? And who'll help her when the baby comes and afterwards?"

Jimmy was quiet as he listened to their exchange. Then he asked Mr. Samuel where he could buy another saddle. George told him about one of the liveries in town and asked what he was planning to do.

"Don't worry about Mr. Locke's threat," he said. "I'll take care of him. Just take care of Mercy and don't even tell her about the letter. She doesn't need to know."

"Where are you going?" George asked.

"Home."

"Now?"

Jimmy nodded. "And eventually to see Langston Locke."

He shook George's hand and apologized for not being able to stay around to help rebuild the barn.

"We can handle it," he said. "But we sure hate to see you go, Jimmy." George sniffed the air and looked at the stove. "Do I smell something burning?"

France handed him a dish towel and told him to check the cornbread while she followed Jimmy outside.

Jimmy walked toward the pen where his horse was.

"I probably have the oven way too hot," she said, as if Jimmy was concerned about the cornbread. "Let me pack you something to eat, Jimmy."

He declined, saying he would get something at the store after he outfitted his horse. He made France promise to not tell Mercy about the letter—that he would take care of it.

"How in the world are you going to take care of it?" she said and then paused. "You're not going to threaten Mercy's father, are you?"

"Knowing Mr. Locke and the influence he has in that town, threatening him would probably land me in jail," he said. "That's one lesson the Lord won't have to repeat with me."

Jimmy stopped at the corner gate and whistled at Brave. His horse trotted towards him.

And suddenly France knew what he was going to do.

Chapter 31

"You're going to sell your stud horse to pay her debt!"

Jimmy wouldn't look at her, much less answer her. But she could see his jaw working.

"Oh, Jimmy," she said. "That's your dream."

Brave stuck his head over the fence, and Jimmy started rubbing his face and neck.

"How'd you know about him?" he asked.

"Faith told me—she said you bought the horse with the money Mr. Locke paid you for bringing Mercy home."

"Ironic, isn't it," said Jimmy, smiling ruefully. He turned to her. "Promise me you won't tell her, France."

"You have to tell her!" she said.

"No, I don't," he said. "When she's ready to let me back in, I want everything to be right. I don't want her doing anything because she thinks she owes me."

He opened the gate and slipped a simple rope bridle on Brave.

"But I'll have to wait until a couple of weeks before the deadline to take the horse to Langston," he said. "He's not ready yet. I need more time to work with him."

He led Brave out the gate, and shut it behind him.

"I'm sorry I can't wait until after school to tell the kids goodbye," he said. "Can you do that for me?"

France nodded. "We're all going to miss you, Jimmy... especially Mercy."

"Tell her I'll be back by Christmas," he said, "when I come to take Faith home for a visit."

"I will." France smiled as she opened her arms to hug him. "We've sure gotten used to you being around here."

"I think this is a good time to do what you said earlier—give Mercy some time and space," he said. "I'll walk you back to the house—I just realized Faith will kill me if I don't tell her goodbye."

"So now I can pack up some food for you?"

"Yeah," he said, smiling. "You're worse than my mother, but she's purt near perfect, too… like you."

"Just keep that thought, and we'll get along fine," said France. "Are you going to tell Mercy goodbye?"

Jimmy shook his head, no. "You tell her for me."

France wrapped up some ham and bread while Jimmy said goodbye to his sister and the little ones. Then she and Faith walked him outside and hugged him goodbye again.

France went to Mercy's room to tell her Jimmy was leaving.

"He is?" she said, surprised, and then caught herself. "Well, that's probably for the best."

"It's not either, and you know it," said France. "He said he'll be back by Christmas."

"That long?"

France nodded. "Are you going to be all right?"

"Yes."

"Well, I need to feed the babies, honey," she said. "I'll bring you some broth in a little bit."

Mercy nodded her head.

As soon as France left the room, Mercy slowly got out of bed and went to the window. She could see Jimmy walking down the road leading Brave. She put her hand against the pane as the tears came quietly this time.

"Goodbye, Jimmy," she said softly.

She watched Jimmy pause in his steps, but this time he turned around.

He couldn't see Mercy's face in the window, but he knew she was there. He could see her slender hand on the pane. He raised his own to say goodbye and turned and walked away.

Mercy watched until she could no longer see him, and crawled back into bed and pulled the covers over her head again as the deep sobs came.

* * *

France woke with a start in the middle of the night. She reached over and poked her husband.

"George!"

"What?!" he said sleepily.

"Something just occurred to me," she said. "How in the world did Mr. Locke know where to send the letter?"

"Oh, my gosh," George said. "Why didn't I catch that?"

"He knows exactly where Mercy is," said France.

"Well, he's not going to take her without a fight," George said firmly.

"I seem to recall not so very long ago that you doubted our decision to let Mercy come stay with us," said France. "You thought she would be a big burden."

"Well, now that I think about all that's happened lately... "

France elbowed him.

"No, you were right again, honey," he said. "I'm glad she's come into our lives—problems and all. We've grown to love her, haven't we?"

* * *

On day five Mercy sat in a chair looking out the window while France changed her bedding.

"I've been thinking," said Mercy.

"Mercy Locke has actually been thinking?" France teased.

"I think God is punishing me," she said.

"Why do you think that?"

"Well, for breaking his laws—for living in sin," she said. "I'm not sure I can even go to heaven now—is that possible after what I've done?"

"Now maybe if you lived in Old Testament times when man was living under the law that might have been the case. But we live in the age of grace, thank the Lord, and our righteousness before Him isn't based on what we do or don't do other than accept his Son."

"I don't understand—what about the ten commandments?" Mercy said. "They're pretty clear."

"Honey, if our going to heaven was based on us not breaking any of those commandments, none of us would get there."

"Well, then why did he set them up in the first place?"

"God is serious about us living right, and when you think about it, that's just plain healthier for us. Man can be awfully depraved without some kind of rules to go by—look at all the laws we have today to try to keep people in line," France said. "But after Jesus came, He turned man's outward appearance of piety and religious ceremony into an inward relationship with Him. The Bible says He wrote his laws on our hearts, and that's what God looks at—our thoughts, our motives. We might fool others into thinking we're good, but we can never fool God."

"What do you mean by an inward thing?"

France thought for a moment as she fluffed a pillow.

"Well, have you ever done something only because someone was around that made you do it?"

Mercy nodded. "Like eating collard greens?"

France laughed. "Exactly! And why did they make you eat collard greens?"

"I guess they're supposed to be good for me."

"But would you still eat them if no one was there to make you?"

Mercy shook her head, no.

"That's an example of the outward thing or the law when someone or something outside of you forces you to do the right thing," France said. "But the inward thing is when *you* recognize that collard greens are good for you and eat them because it's the right thing to do—not because someone else forced you to eat them. Does that make sense?"

"Does this mean I have to start eating collard greens from now on?" Mercy asked.

France put her hands on her hips and shook her head.

"I'm just kidding, France," said Mercy. "I think I understand what you mean."

"Well, that has to do with trying to live the way God wants us to live," said France. "Now get back in bed and I'll try to explain what the Bible says about going to heaven. That's based on what Jesus did for us. Remember in the Old Testament how the Jews always had to make sacrifices to pay for their sins?"

"I'm not much of a Bible scholar," said Mercy, "but I do remember I didn't like that part of the Bible. It's too harsh and bloody."

"Well, whether we like it or not, the Lord decided in the beginning that the shedding of blood was the only means of forgiving the sins man committed," France explained. "But those sacrifices were outward acts of repentance. Man's heart could have been as black as that charred barn out there as he went through the motions of making a sacrifice to take the place of him paying for his own sins."

"But his heart didn't change," Mercy said.

"Right, so the old covenant was good, but it was impossible for man to live perfect, sinless lives," France said, "so that's why God sent his Son to be the perfect and the last sacrifice for mankind. Otherwise, we'd still have to be going through ceremonial sacrifices to atone for our sins."

"So if keeping the commandments and being good enough doesn't get us to heaven, what does?"

"Inviting Jesus into your heart," France said.

"That sounds too simple," Mercy said.

"That part is simple, but the hard part is trying to live for Him—doing the right thing because you know in your heart it's the right thing to do."

"The inward thing again," Mercy said. "How do you do it?"

"Well, it took me years, but I finally learned that God loves me more than I can ever imagine, and He knows what's best for me. After years of doing things my way and making lots of mistakes, I've gotten to where I'm afraid to take a step without Him. I trust Him now in every part of my life."

"I can't believe you've made many mistakes," said Mercy.

"We all have, sweetie," France said. "No one's perfect."

"I thought I was," she said, "but not any more."

"There's so much more to you than your face, Mercy," said France. "When are you going to learn that?"

"But if I can't stand to look at myself in a mirror, I'm sure others will feel the same way."

"No, we don't," said France, tucking her in and walking to the door.

"Why don't you?"

"Because when I look at you, Mercy, I see your potential, and I see your heart, and it's getting more beautiful every day."

And Mercy smiled as tears filled her eyes.

On day seven, Mercy insisted she be moved back up to her and Faith's room. She said her face and shoulder could heal just as quickly up there as it could downstairs, and she told France that she needn't have to check on her as often—that she was perfectly capable of helping herself.

The Samuels' steady stream of visitors bringing gifts of food and supplies the first few days had begun to dwindle after a week as everyone settled back into their old routines.

Mercy had gotten to know many of the people in town from working at the Samuels' store, but she allowed none of the visitors to see her. Her face had begun to heal, although it was obvious she would have some scars. But she realized hiding from the public because of her scars also postponed the inevitable scandal when everyone learned of her *other* condition. She wasn't ready to take on the mantle of *fallen woman* just yet.

George brought the sewing machine and all of her assortment of materials home from the store—temporarily, he said, and set it up in Mercy's room upstairs. She was overjoyed to have something to do to pass the time.

She only had a little more than a month to finish making her Christmas gifts for the family. She also realized she could start making baby clothes up in her room with no one the wiser. That would have been impossible to do at the store.

On day nine, a package arrived from Jimmy. France was surprised to find it contained an odd-looking plant. His short note said it was called aloe vera, and that it was good for healing burns. France began to use it on Mercy's face and shoulder.

By day seventeen, Mercy had finished sewing all of the children's clothes for Christmas, as well as the shirts for George and Jimmy. She set aside two of her dresses to give as gifts—a deep purple and lavender taffeta for Faith, and an elegant dark green wool jacket and skirt for France. She thought it would look pretty with her auburn hair.

She took apart several more dresses and re-made them into several large blouses and a skirt that had a waistline which could be let out as she continued to grow. And grow, she did. She couldn't fit into any of her other, close-fitting dresses now. She began working on a hip-length sacque to wear around the house as the days became shorter and cooler. She remembered seeing expectant mothers around Waco wearing fashionable sacques to be discreet about *their* conditions.

Mercy rarely came out of her room, even preferring to take her meals upstairs. Katherine and Lorelle suspected her condition but didn't dare voice it aloud. Joseph and the rest of the children just thought she was still 'sick.' But Mercy continued her nightly routine, going to the kitchen to bathe after everyone had gone to bed.

Mercy's Face

Late in the evening on day twenty four, Mercy's back began to hurt. Mercy didn't say anything to France, thinking she must have just wrenched it somehow.

But around daybreak the following morning, the cramping started, and Mercy knew what that meant. She used to feel it every month, but this was more severe. She asked Faith to go get France.

France came into her room and saw the fear in Mercy's face.

"What is it, sweetie?" she asked. "Did you have a bad dream?"

Mercy barely shook her head. "I'm hurting."

"What do you mean?"

"It's hurting down here, France," she said, putting her hands on her lower abdomen.

Chapter 32

The baby came just before noon—a boy, and France couldn't stop crying, knowing he wouldn't live but a short time. Mercy insisted on seeing him and holding him, though. France quickly wiped his little face. He was so small, she could easily wrap him in a dish towel.

The doctor stepped out of the room to give Mercy a few moments with her baby.

"He's so tiny," Mercy said as tears streamed down her face, "but already so perfect." She looked up at France. "He has my hair—look at all that fuzz on him. But he's beautiful, right?"

France could only nod, she was weeping so hard. She leaned her head down and kissed Mercy's head. Her heart ached for her.

"He's real, isn't he?" Mercy asked.

France nodded.

"But no one will ever know he existed," she said, looking at his little face. "I can't stand the thought of that, France. I want him to know that I loved him so much that I would've given up everything for him."

"We know, honey," said France, "and we'll never forget that."

After a few minutes, the baby lay still in Mercy's arms.

"He's gone, Mercy," France said. "Let me and George take care of him."

Mercy shook her head, and the anguish began. "I don't think I can let him go, France. I don't know what to do now. He was my future; he was my dream."

The doctor and George came back in the room. George walked over by the window and wiped his eyes.

"I promise we'll take good care of him, honey," said France. "And we know what you're going through, Mercy. George and I have been through this before."

Mercy looked up at her.

"Three times," said France.

"I'm so sorry, France," said Mercy. "I didn't know."

And they wept again together. Mercy lifted the tiny bundle to her face and kissed his head. Then she handed him to France.

"I was going to name him Langston," she said to the Samuels as they walked out the door.

They could hear Dr. Hood's soothing voice speaking over Mercy's low, mournful cries.

"I've never heard her cry like that before," France said as she paused on the landing.

George looked at her sadly and put his arm around her.

"What?" she asked.

He shook his head as if it were nothing, but he recognized the same involuntary sounds of deepest grief his wife made after the loss of each one of their babies.

France waited until they were in the parlor before she said, "Bless her heart—she named her baby after her father, and yet she doesn't even know what he almost did to her. We're going to have to tell her eventually, George. She can't go back home without knowing."

"And we need to get word to Jimmy, too," George said. "I just hope it's not too late."

When they got to the kitchen, George and France worked without speaking, shedding more tears as they performed the heartrending job that needed to be done. They said a prayer together and held each other for a moment before George left the house with the small wooden box he had brought from the store.

Later, France went back upstairs to check on Mercy. She opened the door halfway and saw her lying there with her eyes shut, still swollen from crying. France started to close the door.

"Don't leave," Mercy said. "I'm not asleep."

France came in and pulled a chair up to her bed.

"I've been thinking again," Mercy said, hoping for a teasing remark from France.

Instead France just smiled sadly and reached over and grasped Mercy's hand.

"Nothing has ever hurt this bad before, France," Mercy said. "But it's a different kind of hurt—inside rather than outside like the burns. How did you make it through without losing your mind?"

"George will tell you I almost did," France said. "But I learned to lean on the Lord—from minute to minute at first, then hour to hour, then eventually day to day."

"Did you name your babies?" Mercy asked.

"I had Hannah's name picked out before she came," France said. "But after we lost her, I refused to name any others, thinking it wouldn't hurt as bad if I lost them. But I was wrong; it hurt just as much."

"I'm so sorry," Mercy said.

"Well, God has a way of turning ashes to beauty, if we just let him," she said. "I never would've had these twelve precious children if I'd had my own three. And you know, I probably would have never met *you* either."

"Pray for me, France," Mercy whispered. "I feel like I've fallen in a deep well, and I don't know if I can get out."

France prayed with her. Then she made Mercy scoot over, and she crawled into bed with her, putting her arm around her as if she were a little child.

"I want to tell you about a woman who wrote the words to a song that's helped me so much when I think about where my babies are right now," said France. "Her name is Fanny Crosby, and a doctor's error blinded her when she was just a baby. But she didn't let that tragic mistake destroy her or make her bitter about her circumstances. Instead, she's written hundreds of beautiful hymns, and this one always heals my heart."

France began to sing softly.

> "Safe in the arms of Jesus,
> Safe on His gentle breast,
> There by His love o'ershaded,
> Sweetly my soul shall rest.
> Hark! 'tis the voice of angels
> Borne in a song to me,
> Over the fields of glory
> Over the jasper sea.

Mercy's Face

> Safe in the arms of Jesus,
> Safe from corroding care,
> Safe from the world's temptations,
> Sin cannot harm me there.
> Free from the blight of sorrow,
> Free from my doubts and fears;
> Only a few more trials,
> Only a few more tears!
>
> Jesus, my heart's dear refuge,
> Jesus has died for me;
> Firm on the Rock of Ages
> Ever my trust shall be.
> Here let me wait with patience,
> Wait till the night is o'er;
> Wait till I see the morning
> Break on the golden shore."

France held Mercy until she fell asleep, and then kissed her head softly and slipped out of bed. She stood there, looking down at Mercy's face. Everything had healed well except the most severe burns on the side of her forehead and cheek. And she knew her shoulder would always be scarred. But she was still beautiful, and France thought even more so than the first day she met her. But she knew, too, that she was looking at her through a prism of love.

The calendar started over again for Mercy on the day she lost her baby, but she was the only one who marked those days off in her mind.

She slept through most of days one and two, and thought she had found an easy way to endure the pain. But the nightmare began all over again every time she woke up. When she tried to sleep through day three, she found she just couldn't. She got up and looked through her sewing box of finished clothes.

Her hands came across the few baby gowns she had finished, and she stared at them for a moment before putting them deep in her trunk. She didn't cry this time—she felt like she was bone dry from all the crying she had done the past month.

She looked at the latest basket of hand-me-downs and pulled out a couple of pieces to mend. Then she hemmed the sacque she had started, and ate a little of the supper Faith had brought up to her. Faith sat with her a while and told her what the rest of the children had been up to that day. Emma and Caitlin had drawn pictures of the cats to help cheer her up. Mercy smiled at the funny pictures, which looked nothing at all like cats.

Mercy knew Faith would be writing home soon, and she asked her not to say anything to Jimmy about the baby. She wanted to be the one to tell him when he came back.

Later, Mercy bid Faith goodnight and gathered up her toiletries and sat at the top of the stairs until she was sure everyone had gone to bed before she tiptoed downstairs to take her bath.

She hadn't left her room since...

She stopped that train of thought. She had to look forward, not to the past and the agony of what could have been. That was all behind her now.

She walked into the kitchen and found a tub of water waiting for her—cold, but the tea kettle was still hot.

And it wasn't even Saturday.

She smiled.

"Bless you, France," she said, touched by her thoughtfulness. "How did you know?"

But she had no idea France had done the same thing the night before, hoping she was ready for it.

Mercy put another log in the stove and stepped out of her clothes. She poured the hot water into the tub and set the kettle back on the stove. She stirred the water with her hand before she stepped into the tub and sat down. She shut her eyes for a moment and remembered her bath tub at home—it was so big she could lean back and stretch her legs out straight. She chuckled when she pictured herself at that moment sitting in a tub with her knees almost up around her ears.

But it felt so good to sit there and soak for a little while. She took the washcloth and dipped it in the water and squeezed it above her, letting the water run off her scarred face onto her shoulder, and onto her stomach. She did it again... and again... and again.

And she knew the healing had begun.

Chapter 33

Jimmy turned every head on the street in Waco as he rode his stallion through town. He thought about the last time he had visited the Locke mansion with Florine. His world had never been the same since.

Christmas would come in a week, and Jimmy knew Langston Locke had to be worried. His deadline was only two weeks away, and he had heard no word from his daughter yet. On the ride from Brownwood, it had also dawned on Jimmy that Langston knew where Mercy was. He figured he must have really pressed hard on Matilda or Rune to get that information.

That sounded like Langston.

After Jimmy arrived home in Grace, he said little to his parents about Mercy, other than she had changed… a lot. He knew he would eventually tell them more about Mercy and what had happened to her, but he wasn't ready just yet.

When Jimmy immediately went back to working with his stallion, his family figured everything was back to normal.

After a couple of weeks, he sent word to Langston in Waco that he would meet with him on December seventeenth to resolve the issue with his daughter. But until then he still needed more time to train the horse— he wasn't ready to give him up just yet. Jimmy wanted no doubts in anyone's mind that the horse he was giving Langston was worth more than the debt his daughter owed.

He rode up to the back of the Lockes' mansion just after twelve noon. He tied the horse to the grandiose hitching post and walked up the steps to the back porch. He could see Matilda working in the kitchen, and was glad to see she was still employed. He waved at her when she looked up, and she dropped her spoon and came to the back door.

"Mr. Taylor!" she said, smiling. "How good it is to see you!"

"It's Jimmy, Matilda," he said, and he leaned over to hug the older woman. "And it sure is good to see you, too."

She looked beyond him to the horse stamping impatiently.

"My, what a beautiful horse," she said. "Looks like you've done very well for yourself. Come on inside—it's a little chilly today."

"I need to see Mr. Locke," he said. "He should be expecting me."

"Are you sure?" she asked. "He didn't ask me to set an extra plate for dinner."

"It's not a social call, and it won't take long," Jimmy said. "I've come to talk to him about Mercy… Florine."

"Is she all right?" Matilda asked quietly.

"Well, she should be by now, but that's a long story."

"He knows where she is, Jimmy," Matilda said. "He told me Rune would never work in this town again if I didn't tell him. I prayed that he'd leave her be, though."

"Well, he won't bother her after today," he said. "Could you tell him I'm here?"

Matilda nodded and stepped back inside.

Jimmy walked back to his horse and started rubbing his neck.

"I doubt I'll ever have the likes of you in my hands again, boy," he said. "But I'll have some of your offspring next year—maybe one will turn out like you."

The door slammed, and Langston walked out on the porch.

"What do you want, Taylor?"

Jimmy turned to face him.

"I want you leave Mercy alone."

"Mercy? So she's going by her middle name now," he said. "I never cared much for my mother-in-law's name. And who are you to tell me what I can or cannot do with my own daughter?"

"What kind of father would threaten to have his own daughter arrested if she didn't do exactly what he wanted?"

"How do you know about that?" he said. "That's none of your business either."

"Well, I've made it my business, and I have a proposition for you," Jimmy said. "You can take this horse to cover Mercy's debt, and I guarantee he's worth considerably more than that amount. Or I can sell him and give you what Mercy owes and keep the difference."

"I don't want your horse," Langston said. "I want my daughter back."

"Don't you realize what you're doing is just driving her further away from you?"

"She's not thinking clearly," he said. "But she'll eventually realize that I'm right, and she'll understand that I've had her best interests at heart all along."

"Do you honestly believe that?" Jimmy asked. "Or is it *your* interests you're so concerned about?"

"She's throwing her life away," Langston said. "I can't let her do that. I won't let her do that."

Jimmy pulled a paper from his pocket and walked over and handed it to Langston.

"What's this?" he asked.

"It's a statement saying that Mercy's debt to you has been paid."

"I won't sign that," he said. "Get out of here."

"So you're serious about arresting your daughter?"

"No, of course not," he said. "I just want her to come home and forget all this ever happened."

"So you plan to hold this debt over her for the rest of her life?"

Langston just glared at him.

"Well, I happen to know some of my father's friends here in Waco who would be very interested to see the letter you sent Mercy," Jimmy said. "And why you sent it."

"You wouldn't dare," Langston said. "I just told you I wouldn't follow through with it."

"But the debt will always be there as leverage between you two, won't it?" Jimmy said. "You'll never get your daughter back this way. I know her—she's just as stubborn as you are. Now sign it or I talk."

Langston looked at the horse, and then he looked at Jimmy, and he knew he wasn't bluffing. He turned around and stomped into the house and after a couple of minutes he came back and threw the paper at Jimmy.

"Damn it, Taylor, you're making a big mistake crossing me," he said.

"I'm not crossing you, Mr. Locke, and I hope you'll understand that some day," Jimmy said as he turned to walk away.

Jimmy's brother-in-law Marcus waited for him in his freight wagon in front of the house.

"Well, has he got a name?" Langston said gruffly.
Jimmy stopped and looked at his horse, possibly for the last time. "I think *Redeemer* would be a fitting name."

Chapter 34

"Come on," France said to Mercy after supper. "I want to show you something."

She led Mercy towards the front door, and Mercy pulled back.

"We're going outside?"

"There's very little daylight left—it'll be dark soon—nobody will see you," France said.

But Mercy ran back and grabbed a shawl to drape over her head.

France walked Mercy down the road to the cemetery—to the large Samuel plot. A tall gravestone with the Samuel name stood in the center of the grassy expanse.

"George is very big on pomp," France said, pointing to the monument. "He wants to make sure the Samuels are remembered for centuries to come."

"Why did you bring me here?" Mercy asked.

"George did something for me," she said, "and for you, too, that I want to show you."

She took Mercy's arm and walked her to the back of the family headstone.

"We're so fortunate to have a good mason in town," she said. "He built our house; he built this monument, and he finished inscribing these letters for us earlier today.

Mercy read the inscription, "Safe in the arms of Jesus," and saw several names listed beneath it. She continued reading aloud, "Hannah Samuel..." and turned to France. "These are your babies. You named them."

France smiled as tears filled her eyes. "I thought it was about time I named the rest of them." She nodded toward the headstone and said, "Keep reading, honey."

Mercy turned back and read aloud, "Jacob Samuel… Eleanor Samuel, and …" she paused and just stared for a moment. Then she knelt down and ran her fingers across the last name as she read, "Langston Samuel."

"He's here?" she said quietly, looking at France.

France knelt down beside her and nodded, putting her arm around her.

"With yours?" she asked.

"Yes."

"Where?"

"They're all right here close to the Samuel name."

Mercy reached for her and they held each other as they wept again.

"Oh, France! I can't think of a more fitting name for him to have," said Mercy. "And he was real—he existed—his name is right here for all to see." She brushed her hand across it again.

"He won't be forgotten now," France said.

They stood together, still with arms linked, and then started to walk back to the house. Mercy looked around the plot.

"I can't tell that the ground has even been disturbed—no more than where weeds have been chopped and cleared out."

"George was discreet," France said. "No one will know this baby was anyone's other than mine, so you can pick up your life where you left off, if you choose to, Mercy."

"You know that will never happen with my face now."

"That's entirely up to you," said France, and then paused. "Why are you pushing Jimmy away? You know he loves you."

"How could he? I look repulsive."

"It doesn't bother anyone else but you—you're making a mountain out of a molehill."

"The scars will never go away—I can't show my face again in Waco."

France started to disagree with her, but stopped and shook her head in frustration. They'd already had this talk too many times.

"But I'll never forget what you and Mr. Samuel did for me today," she said. "And I appreciate Mr. Samuel bringing the sewing machine to the house. I wouldn't want to scare the customers away."

France stopped walking and sighed impatiently. "All right, Florine

Mercy Locke. I have had just about enough of this self-denigrating talk. Don't you know that even with a scarred face, you're still prettier than any woman in this town?!"

Mercy turned and stared at her. That sounded like a compliment, but France sounded mad when she said it. She had never acted upset with her before.

"I'm sorry, France..." was all she could think to say.

"You are so much more than those scars on your face—when is that going to sink into that stubborn head of yours? You are alive, and you're smart, and you are so talented, but you're letting your scars lock you away from life and from people and from love. Jimmy loves *you*—who you are on the inside. And I'm sure he's more than satisfied with what's on the outside, too, but that's secondary to him. You know that, don't you?"

Mercy shook her head, no. She hadn't let herself entertain that thought ever since Jimmy walked away that day. And with her history with Eustace, she now felt even more like damaged goods—both inside and out.

France turned and faced the other way, fighting a battle within herself. She took a deep breath and turned around.

"I'm going to do something I've never done before," she said. "I'm going to break a promise I made not long ago."

"What are you talking about?"

"You received a letter from your father a couple of days after the fire," France began.

"He knows where I am?" Mercy asked. "But I sent the payment with Faith's letter to be mailed from Grace."

"Well, he found out somehow, although it didn't occur to us at first, and I'm sorry I opened the letter without asking your permission. But you were in no condition to read anything, and I was contemplating getting ahold of your parents anyway with everything that had happened."

"You didn't, though, did you?" Mercy asked, alarmed.

France shook her head, no. "But the letter said that you had until the end of the year to pay the debt you owed your father if you didn't give up your baby, or he was going to file charges on you."

"What?!" she said. "The end of the year? But that's only two weeks away."

"We're not sure if he would've followed through with it, Mercy, but we didn't want to take that chance."

"I guess I don't have to worry about that now," she said bitterly. "But then, maybe I still do because I don't think I can even think about going home now."

"Jimmy made me promise not to tell you, but…" France said, pausing again.

"What, France? —tell me!"

"He said he was going to pay your debt, Mercy," she said, "he was going to give his stallion to your father in return for a signed statement that said you owed him nothing so your debt would be clear."

"Oh, no, France," Mercy gasped. "That horse was his dream—how could he do that?"

"I think it's obvious to everyone but you."

"We have to stop him!" she said. "He's giving away his horse for nothing! Do you think it's too late?"

"He told me he needed to train the horse a while longer—that he'd take him to your father right before he came back to Brownwood for Christmas," France said. "We mailed him a letter the day after…," she stopped herself. "We sent it six days ago, but I don't know if it got there in time."

Mercy's face fell.

"I didn't tell you this to upset you, Mercy," she said. "I only told you because I wanted you to know how deeply Jimmy cares for you. But you have to promise me that you won't tell him that I told you, or we're both going to be in big trouble. He didn't want you to know this because he didn't want you to feel like you owed him your affection."

France paused, watching Mercy's face. "What are you thinking?"

Mercy looked at her and said, "I'm not sure."

"Did I just make a huge mistake telling you this?" France asked.

Chapter 35

Jimmy rode into Brownwood in mid-afternoon on Christmas Eve. He had sent his gifts for the Samuel family ahead by stage the week before and hoped they had arrived.

He walked his horse on past the rock house and around the back. He smiled when he saw the new barn—it looked finished from what he could see. Kids swarmed around it like bees. He could see Boomer in one of the pens closest to the barn. The other two horses were in the back pen. Miss Clara was staked in a grassy lot on the other side of the barn.

Caitlin spotted Jimmy first and screamed with delight. Jimmy dismounted, leading Brave the rest of the way, and found himself surrounded by most of the children. Katherine and Faith came running out of the kitchen. George and Ethan stood in the door to the hay loft up high and laughed at Jimmy's predicament.

Joseph shook Jimmy's hand and took the reins to lead Brave to the barn.

"When can we go riding again, Jimmy?" Lorelle asked.

"We've been practicing all week with Mercy," said K. James.

"You have?" Jimmy said as he looked around for her.

"Will you kids let me hug my own brother?" Faith said, pushing her way through the wiggling mass.

Jimmy grinned at his sister, the person he was closest to in this world.

"Merry Christmas, sis," he said as he hugged her tight. "It sure is good to see you. Mom and Dad and everyone send their love and said they can't wait for you to get home."

"You were cutting it pretty close, brother," she said. "We were all getting worried you weren't going to make it."

"Everyone doing all right?" he asked, glancing at the house again.

"Everyone's doing fine," she said, smiling, knowing he was asking about Mercy.

Someone pulled on his pants leg. Jimmy looked down to see little Mac.

"Come see the barn," he said. "I helped make it."

"You did not," Finn said to him.

"I did, too!"

"Well, let's go see it," said Jimmy, picking up Mac.

By then George and Ethan walked up and shook Jimmy's hand and were just as anxious as the children to show off the new barn.

"Half the town helped us frame it and get it in the dry," said George. "We've been finishing the inside on our own, and we're just about there."

George walked him around and showed him every detail. He said it was paid off, too, between the community's donations and the reward the stage line gave for the capture of the men who had robbed several of their stagecoaches.

"There was a reward?" Jimmy asked.

"Two hundred dollars," Ethan said. "And they gave it to Mercy, but she insisted that George use it to rebuild his barn."

"We were even able to buy saddles and blankets and bridles for the horses," he said. "The children have been riding them a lot this past week. We told them it was part of their Christmas."

Lorelle walked up to them and said, "Momma says you'd better bring Jimmy to the house so she can tell him hello or else."

"Or else what?" George asked.

"Or else some pies are going to burn while she comes out here. She can't leave the kitchen while things are cooking," Lorelle explained.

"She's working herself to death on Christmas dinner in there," said George. "But it's going to be good. Leave your stuff here—we even built a separate room for guests to bunk in."

George opened the door to a room built in the corner of the barn. It already had a couple of beds and a woodstove.

"Go on inside the house, Jimmy. You can join us out here later."

As Jimmy turned around, he noticed Ethan watching Faith playing with the little ones. And he didn't like the way he was looking at her. Faith looked up and glanced at Jimmy as he walked towards her, but her eyes looked beyond him at Ethan.

And she was looking at Ethan the same way he was looking at her. He wasn't sure if he liked that either.

"A lot's happened since I've been here," he said to his sister as he passed by and glanced back towards Ethan.

Faith blushed and smiled shyly.

He saw that Joseph had brought Boomer into the barn and was saddling her.

"Going riding?" he asked, feeling pleased with himself to see how comfortable the kids were around the horses now.

Joseph smiled and nodded.

He walked on past him toward the house. He thought he saw a movement in the window upstairs, and watched for Mercy's face to appear as he walked.

It didn't.

Instead of going up on the porch, he walked around the house and slipped in the front door. Something sure smelled good. He crept silently through the parlor and dining room and into the kitchen.

Katherine stood at the table putting a crust in a pie pan and looked up with a start to see Jimmy standing in the kitchen. He put his finger to his lips to keep her quiet. She grinned and looked over at her mother.

France was standing at the window holding a flour-dusted rolling pin.

"Now where did that boy go?" she asked, looking one direction and then the other.

Jimmy snuck up behind her and grabbed her from behind. She let out a holler and almost cold-cocked him with the rolling pin before she realized who it was.

"Jimmy Taylor!" she scolded him. "You should never walk up behind an armed woman!" she said, laughing as she hugged him. "It's about time you got here! I thought we were going to have to send out a posse for you."

"Did you get the packages?" he asked.

"Yes, and the kids are so excited about them," she said. "They're wrapped beautifully—did you do all that yourself?"

Jimmy snickered. "Are you kidding? I can't even tie a bowtie. My sister and her husband own a general store, too, and she helped me pick out everything and then wrapped them for me. So if y'all don't like your gifts, it's her fault."

"Did George tell you we'll be opening the presents tonight?"

"No, but that's fine with me."

"And we'll have the first of two Christmas dinners," France said. "We didn't have much of a Thanksgiving this year with everything that's happened, so we're going to make up for it this holiday."

"I'll do my part," he said. "In fact, if you need a taste tester right now, I'd be glad to volunteer."

"Have you eaten yet?"

"Not since this morning."

"Well, sit down and let me fix you something to tide you over," said France.

Jimmy glanced back towards the dining room before he sat down and watched Katherine pour an apple mixture into the crust. She added some spoons of butter on top before covering it with another crust. She pinched the edges together and started fluting them around the pie.

"That looks good," he said to her.

Katherine smiled as her cheeks blushed with the praise.

"Did you know apple's one of my favorite pies?" he asked her.

She nodded. "Momma told me."

"You remembered?" he said to France.

"Of course I remember how you and your brother went on and on about my apple pie," she said as she set a plate of roast and potatoes in front of him. "And it's George's favorite, too. That's the third one Katherine's made today. We had a good apple crop this year—half the cellar's full of dried apples."

"And we have pumpkin, pecan, and sweet potato pies, too," Katherine said proudly. "Lorelle helped with those."

Jimmy dug hungrily into the food. Every once in a while he glanced toward the dining room door. He finished eating and carried his plate and fork to the sink.

"That was good—thanks," he said.

"Did you get our letter, Jimmy?" she said quietly beside him.

He nodded, yes.

"So you know?" she asked.

He nodded again.

"Katherine, honey," she said. "Would you go to the cellar and bring me some more potatoes? Tell *Joseph* to help you."

"I think Joseph's gone riding," Jimmy said to Katherine as he pinched off another piece of bread. "You need me to help?"

"No, no—I've got it," said Katherine as she wiped her hands on a towel and walked out the back door.

"Did the letter get to you in time?" France asked. "We were so worried you would lose your horse for nothing."

"I took Langston the horse anyway," said Jimmy.

"Oh, Jimmy... why?!"

"He said he would never arrest his daughter—he was just trying to force her to come home without the baby," he said. "But I know Langston—he'll always hold that debt over her head."

"I'm so sorry, honey."

"I'm not," Jimmy said. "She's worth it."

France smiled. "I didn't know such chivalry still existed."

"How's she doing?" he asked.

"She's doing very well... finally," said France. "She even went to church with us Sunday. She's become quite the seamstress—stays up in that room sewing on that machine all day long. She even rigged one of her fancy hats with a netting that covers the scars. She won't leave the house without it on."

She watched as he glanced toward the dining room again.

"And she knows you're here, Jimmy."

"Is she avoiding me?" he asked. "Won't she even come out of her room?"

"She's been expecting you."

France walked over to the food cabinet and pulled out a folded piece of paper and handed it to him.

"She left this here for you."

Jimmy's heart sank as he looked at the paper.

"She couldn't even speak to me in person?" he asked.

"She had her reasons," said France.

Jimmy was afraid he knew what those reasons were. With the loss of the baby and no one the wiser about it, Mercy—no, Florine could now step right back into her life as she once knew it—before Eustace and Fort Worth.

She could go on with her life... without him.

Chapter 36

Jimmy's hand shook as he unfolded the note. His eyes blurred trying to read the one sentence on the page. His forehead furrowed as he read it a second time.

"Do you need an interpreter, honey?" France said, grinning.

The note simply said, *I'm ready for my riding lesson, Mercy.*

Jimmy looked up in surprise. Then he walked to the back door and stepped out on the porch just in time to see a streak of blonde hair fly by the house... on *his* horse.

France walked up beside him. He stood there with his mouth open, still holding the note.

"She took my horse!" he said.

"Well, then maybe you ought to go after her," said France.

"I can't run that fast," he said as his heart started to pound.

France doubled over laughing. "Has your brain gone completely soft, boy?" she asked. "Go to the barn—Joseph should have Boomer saddled and waiting for you by now. Mercy's been waiting days for you to get here."

"And I have to ride Boomer?" he said dejectedly. "I think I *can* run faster than that horse."

"Get going," France said, pushing him off the porch. "I hope you can find her. Do you want me to tell you where she's headed?"

"No, I'll find her," he said over his shoulder. He ran to the barn to get Boomer.

Mercy's Face

Jimmy followed Brave's tracks into the town square and completely around it before they continued to head east.

"You're playing with me, Mercy," he said.

But he loved the chase.

On the edge of town he pulled up when he saw Brave tied to a tree. Mercy had come to Pecan Bayou. He dismounted and led Boomer slowly up to Brave, who was happily eating tufts of grass around the base of the tree.

"Traitor," he said to the horse.

He looked around for Mercy. The trees grew big along here. He tied Boomer to another tree and walked down by the water.

He stopped when he saw her. She had stepped out to face him from behind the massive trunk of a pecan tree. She wore a riding skirt and a fitted jacket to match. Her hair was down—it made her look younger, and a handsome hat sat cock-eyed on her head with some kind of netting pulled over the side of her face.

She looked beautiful.

"I told you I could ride him," she said.

"I'm impressed," he said. "But I'm surprised he let you."

"He and I got to know each other the last time you were here," she said. "Did you know he loves dried apples?"

Jimmy smiled. "You're spoiling him."

"I thought you'd never get here, Jimmy Taylor," she said as she ran into his arms.

He caught her and held on tight. Then he kissed her, but his nose got tangled in the netting. He leaned back and started to pull the hat off. She tried to stop him, but he took her hands in his and shook his head. He placed them on his chest and held one hand over them as he reached up with his other hand and untied the ribbon under her chin.

"Please don't, Jimmy," she said.

He never took his eyes off of hers as he gently pulled the hat away from her head and let it drop to the ground. She tried to turn away, but he wouldn't let her. He leaned down and kissed her scarred forehead, her flawed cheek, and her perfect lips.

"Don't ever shut me out or hide from me again, Mercy," he whispered.

"But I don't want you to see me this way," she said.

He leaned back and looked at her scars. Then he smiled.

That made her mad. "What's so funny?"

"You think you're scary to look at now?" he said. "Don't you realize you were more frightening to me back in Fort Worth when your face was perfect?"

"But..."

"I love you, Mercy," he said. "Don't you know that by now?"

He kissed her again, and she believed him.

And for a moment... for the first time in a long time... she forgot about her face.

Chapter 37

Jimmy and Mercy stood and talked for a while. Then they walked and talked for a while. Jimmy didn't know how to bring up the loss of the baby, but he didn't have to. Mercy told him that the Samuels had adopted one more child this month—hers, and had given him their name. Jimmy held her as she cried again and told him it was the hardest thing she had ever gone through. But she said the pain had begun to lessen each day.

They talked about the new barn, and she told him about the sewing machine and all she had accomplished with it, and that she had taught Faith how to use it. She told him she had been riding Boomer with the children and the other horses all week in anticipation of his arrival.

"I've worn this riding skirt for the past three days thinking you'd be here any minute," she laughed. "Joseph, France, and Katherine were in on it, too. And Faith knew, of course."

"What's going on with Ethan?" he said.

"He was able to hire on with the sawmill," she said, "so he's going to be around for a while. He hasn't got a place to live yet—you're his bunkmate in the barn, by the way. But eventually he's going to build a home here and have Caitlin live with him again."

"I thought the Samuels had adopted Caitlin," Jimmy said.

Mercy shook her head. "They were just keeping her until Ethan could get on his feet—he was traveling around laying tracks for the railroad, but he knew he couldn't take Caitlin with him any time soon with that kind of job."

"Where's he from?" Jimmy asked, wanting to know more about him since Ethan was interested in his sister.

"Mostly Fort Worth, and everywhere else he could find work," she said. "He has no other family, and he thought he was going to have to put Caitlin in an orphanage until he heard about the Samuels."

"That was fortunate for him," Jimmy said, "and especially for Caitlin, wasn't it."

Mercy nodded. "And even after he gets a place to live, Caitlin will stay with the Samuels during the day until she goes to school next year, unless she has a new mother by then."

"Faith?" Jimmy said, shocked.

Mercy nodded.

"I don't think I'm ready for this," he said.

"Well, don't say anything to her about him," she said. "She hasn't shared anything with me yet, other than she thinks he's nice, but we've all noticed the way they look at each other."

"It's getting late—we probably need to get back," said Jimmy.

She retrieved her hat and they walked arm in arm back to the horses.

But only Brave stood where they had left them.

Jimmy looked around—Boomer was nowhere in sight.

"Dadgummit," he said as he walked around the area. "I thought I tied those reins tight."

Mercy laughed out loud. "Looks like you're out of luck, feller."

She untied Brave's reins and mounted him.

"I don't think so," he said.

He whistled at Brave. The horse walked over to him.

"Hey!" Mercy said, grinning.

"Good boy," he said, rubbing his face. Then he whispered loudly, "That makes up for earlier."

Mercy giggled at him talking to his horse.

Jimmy looked up at her. "You can't get rid of me that easily," he said, teasingly.

He climbed up behind her and slipped his left hand around her waist and took the reins with his right.

"Take your time," she said as she settled back against him for the slow walk home.

After supper France wouldn't let anyone open gifts until the dining table was cleared and the dishes were washed. George told Jimmy and Ethan that was like trying to hold back a cat from a trapped, wiggling mouse. The little ones sat as close to the presents as they could get without touching them. For R. James, Finn, Zane, and Mac, this was their first real Christmas, and amazement and excitement were written all over their faces.

The kitchen and dining room were cleaned in record time, and everyone found a spot in the parlor, packed to overflowing with people and a mountain of gifts around the Christmas tree. The tree was a cut cedar and its aroma filled the room. Mercy said if she shut her eyes, it made her feel like she had just opened her cedar chest back home.

The children had spent hours making decorations for the tree: paper stars, strings of apples and cinnamon, strands of popcorn and red berries. Lorelle had made the mistake of picking and stringing chili petin peppers, and her fingers still burned from that effort. Last year the tree had candles, but this year France wouldn't allow candles on the tree for fear of another fire.

The older children passed out the gifts, most of them wrapped in newsprint and tied with string. The children anxiously waited until George gave the go-ahead to open the presents. France told them to save the paper from Jimmy's gifts so they could re-use it for school.

The adults laughed as they watched the children tear into their gifts. Each of them received new socks and warm hats from the Samuels, as well as socks filled with nuts and hard candy. Faith bought each of the children a pair of mittens or gloves, depending on their age.

Everyone marveled at the new clothes Mercy had made with the even more amazing sewing machine. France told George he was not allowed to take the machine back to the store.

But Jimmy's gifts drew the biggest cheers because there was absolutely nothing practical about them. All of the girls except for the two eldest received dolls. Katherine and Lorelle each received a hair brush, comb, and hair ribbons. Joseph was speechless when he opened his box to find the engine for a model train. Jimmy told him it actually ran with a spring-wound motor and showed him where to wind it up. Each of the other boys received a different train car. Mac's was the caboose.

George couldn't stand it—he ripped opened his gift from Jimmy and discovered he had the wooden tracks for the train. He let out a loud whoop.

"Brownwood finally has its first train!" he said. "Let's go set it up on the table, boys!"

"On my dining table?" France said, quickly jumping up.

George and Ethan led the boys as well as Emma, Zane, and Caitlin—not wanting to miss out—into the dining room, and France threw herself in front of the table to put a stop to it. She shooed them out onto the porch before coming back to the parlor fussing, but it was a friendly fuss.

"Sorry, France," said Jimmy.

"That must have cost you a fortune!" she said.

"My sister let me have it at a good price, and she let me work most of it off," he said. "I'll have to tell her she made some good choices, though. Have you opened your gift yet? I'm curious to find out what I got you."

France picked up the small box from Jimmy. "It'd better not have anything to do with trains," she said threateningly.

She smiled as she pulled her gift out of the box—a ribbon bookmark with a tiny angel dangling at the end of it.

"I love it, Jimmy," she said. "And I have just the book to put it in. Thank your sister for me."

"Actually, I did pick that one out myself," he whispered to Mercy, "and yours, too. Go on, open it."

"Open your gifts first," she said. "They're not much, but I know they're something you can use."

Jimmy untied the string around the larger gift and held up a blue shirt.

"You made this yourself?" Jimmy asked.

Mercy nodded. "To match your eyes," she said.

"It's really nice," he said. "I'll be proud to wear it."

"Open the other one," she said.

He opened the smaller gift to find a horse brush. He looked at it and held it up.

"She got me a hairbrush, ladies," he said. "I'm sure I need it."

"It's for your horses, silly."

"Well, like I said earlier, you're spoiling Brave."

"It's for your stallion, too," she said quietly. "I promise."

Jimmy looked at her with questioning eyes and glanced at France, but said nothing.

France frowned at Mercy and quickly changed the subject. "Open yours now, Mercy."

She carefully removed the paper and smiled when she saw a familiar box. "Poudre de L'Amour No. 1 dusting powder," she said to the girls in the room and then turned back to Jimmy. "You're really good at this, Jimmy. Thank you."

"Well, show us the inside," he said.

"Everybody knows what the inside looks like," she said, opening the box and pulling out the powder puff and the pretty blue glass container. "See?"

She held up the glass jar and then put it back inside the box, set the powder puff on top of it, and patted the ring down so she could close the box lid. She stopped… and lifted the lid back up and stared at the ring tied to the ribbon on top of the powder puff. She looked up at Jimmy.

"I don't remember my other powder puff having a ring attached to it," she said.

"Well, the deal is if you don't accept the ring, you can't keep the powder," he said. "Sorry."

She sat quietly for a moment, looking at Jimmy.

"How did you know that I've needed this powder for quite some time?" she asked.

"Well, you told me—" he started to say when she interrupted him.

"And how did you know that I would love this powder enough to accept this ring?"

"Well, I was really hoping… you… would —" and he finally realized she wasn't talking about the powder.

"Well, I absolutely do love this powder," she said looking at his face. "So I guess I'll have to keep the ring."

Jimmy couldn't help it; he leaned over and kissed her softly—right on the mouth in front of everyone.

France and the girls held their breath as they watched Mercy slip the ring on her finger and hold it out for all to see. All they could see was the puff. Lorelle giggled.

"It's perfect, don't you think?" Mercy said, teasingly. "I've always wanted a big ring."

"Well, that way everybody'll know you're taken—they can't miss seeing *that* ring," he said, smiling.

She turned back to Jimmy. "Does this mean you're asking me to marry you?"

"Does this mean you're saying yes?" Jimmy asked.

Mercy smiled and nodded.

Chapter 38

The day after Christmas was a happy and sad day in the Samuel household. Everyone was happy about Jimmy and Mercy's engagement. But Jimmy had also come to escort his sister back home for a visit with her family in Grace right after Christmas. So that meant she would be gone for several weeks. Jimmy asked Mercy to come home with them, too. She didn't hesitate—she couldn't stand the thought of being separated from him again, and she knew they needed to tell their families the news. He said he would follow the stage, riding Brave home.

Mercy's trunk was half empty now, so Faith packed most of her belongings in it to save space. Ethan hitched up the horses to Mercy's wagon to haul the trunk to the hotel where they would catch the stage. But that worked out all right since all of the children wanted to go, too. Ethan and Faith took charge of rounding up the children, so France said she and Mercy would walk to the store to meet Mr. Samuel and head over to the hotel from there.

Mercy tied the hat ribbon under her chin and pulled the net down over half of her face. She and France stepped outside and walked the two blocks to the town square. Several women greeted them in front of the post office and even hugged Mercy, saying they were so glad she was doing well, and that they had missed seeing her in the store. Their response took Mercy by surprise—she had avoided people for so long, she assumed they would treat her the same way. But she felt like they were treating her as a friend, and it felt good.

She and France stepped into the store, and Mercy took one more pass through the aisles of the place she had become so familiar with the past few months. Back at the front, she closed her eyes and breathed in the smells, hoping she would never forget them. Then she and France walked back outside with George.

"I'm going to miss this place, Mr. Samuel."

"This place is certainly going to miss you, Mercy," he said as he locked the door and turned to escort the ladies down the street.

"I think Katherine and Joseph would be wonderful helpers down here," said Mercy. "And even Lorelle. You have a ready-made workforce in your household."

"You're right," he said. "I've been thinking that myself."

They walked along the board walk for a few moments in silence. A boisterous wagon came up the street, and all of the occupants hollered and waved at Mercy and the Samuels.

"I wonder who those rowdy kids belong to," said George.

"Why, I've never seen them before in my life," France teased.

Mercy looked at France's face. She was looking at her children with such pride and love.

"They're something else, aren't they?"

Mercy nodded as she watched the wagon pass by. Faith held Caitlin as she sat beside Ethan, and they looked so happy and... normal, as if they were already a family.

"Looks like the stage is here," said George.

"Already?" Mercy said. She didn't realize until that moment how hard saying goodbye would be.

They walked across the street to join the rest of the family. Jimmy had gone ahead to take care of the tickets and was trying to tell the children goodbye. Faith and Mercy started telling them goodbye, too, and couldn't remember who they had hugged and who they hadn't. It was chaos.

George whistled loudly and got everyone's attention. He lined up everyone that was staying and told the three who were leaving to go down the line—that way no one would miss getting a hug.

George and France stood at the end of the line. Mercy hugged George and thanked him for teaching her how to do some good, honest work.

"Nobody from Waco would ever believe I can do something useful," she said, laughing. "But it sure feels good to know I can do most anything I set my mind to."

"That's right, honey," France said. "And don't you forget it."

Mercy looked into the face of the woman who had taught her so much these past few months. She hugged her tight, and whispered in her ear.

"I've never had as good a friend as you've been to me," she said. "Why do I feel like I'm saying goodbye forever?"

"Miles mean nothing between friends," said France. "And I know we'll see each other again."

"You know you're invited to the wedding, don't you?" she said.

"Yes, honey, but between the store and these kids, I doubt George and I can go anywhere for a while. We have our hands about as full as they can get."

"The Lord couldn't have put these children in better hands than yours. And me, too, for that matter. I'll never forget what you've done for me."

"No more than what you've done for us, honey," said France. "Promise me you'll write and tell me all about your wedding and everything, all right?"

Mercy nodded. "I'll be thinking of you that day."

France hugged her tight again. "Me, too."

Jimmy shook George's hand and told him he would always stop by if he was within twenty miles of Brownwood.

"You'd better," said George.

Jimmy hugged France and whispered, "You're an angel, you know that?"

"You picked out that book mark, didn't you," she said.

Jimmy just grinned.

"Say hello to Nah-kay for me," said France. "I think about your grandmother every so often."

Jimmy helped Mercy onto the stage and turned to talk to the stage drivers. Mercy saw Ethan steal a quick kiss from Faith before helping her onto the stage and was glad Jimmy was distracted at that moment. Faith caught Mercy watching from the seat and blushed.

"We have some talking to do on this trip, Faith," said Mercy, smiling.

Two portly men climbed onto the stage and sat on the opposite side, completely filling the seat. One of them said he hoped that would be all the passengers traveling that day so they would get to stretch out a little, and especially to use the bench in the middle to prop their feet on.

"Did you know they only allow us fifteen inches per person in these coaches?" the shorter one said.

"My left cheek is bigger than fifteen inches," the other commented laughingly, and then acknowledged the ladies present. "Pardon my crudity, ladies."

Faith and Mercy nodded their heads, trying not to laugh.

One of the stage drivers stood by the open door and loudly informed the passengers of the rules. They couldn't see his mouth for the massive moustache perched above it, and it moved only slightly when he talked.

"Rule number one: If I ask you to get out and walk, I would advise you to do so and not grumble about it.

"Rule number two: If the horses get away from us, I would advise you not to jump or you could seriously hurt yourself. The horses will eventually get tired and slow down.

"Rule number three: Smoking and spitting on the windward side of the coach is discouraged."

Mercy raised her hand.

"Yes, ma'am?"

"Not that I'd ever spit, but what is the windward side?"

"It's the side that the wind is blowing from," he said. "Need I explain further, ma'am?"

Mercy shook her head and tried to keep a straight face. She could see Jimmy turn around and face the other way.

"Rule number four: Drinking spirits is allowed, but passengers are expected to share."

Faith snickered and covered her face with her hanky as if she had sneezed.

"Bless you. Rule number five: Swearing is not allowed, and neither is sleeping on your neighbor's shoulder.

"Rule number six: Travelers should not point out where murders have occurred on this road, especially when *delicate* passengers are aboard.

"And Rule number seven: Greasing one's hair is discouraged because dust will stick to it."

Jimmy walked over to Mercy's wagon and acted like he was laughing at something the children said. Ethan was grinning at Faith.

"Are there any questions about the rules?" the driver asked.

"No, sir," they all said.

"Then let's get on the road," the moustache said, and climbed up the side of the stagecoach.

George counted heads to make sure all of the kids were back on Mercy's wagon before he let the stagecoach leave.

The Samuels knew they would see Jimmy and Faith back here in a few weeks, but with pasted-on smiles and heavy hearts, they watched Mercy leave Brownwood, probably for good.

Chapter 39

After they arrived in Waco, they decided that Faith would wait at the stage stop hotel to meet her father who would arrive from Grace with a buggy to take them home while Jimmy and Mercy left to talk to Mr. and Mrs. Locke. They had made their wedding plans during the overnight stays on the trip home. Mercy dreaded the confrontation ahead, but she wasn't afraid anymore. She had decided if her father wanted her in his life, he would have to accept Jimmy.

Jimmy told Mercy he could rent a buggy from the livery for the trip to her parents' home, but she told him that wasn't necessary. She quickly changed into her riding skirt at the hotel, and they rode Brave through town, drawing quite a few stares from the townsfolk. Mercy recognized most of them, but tried to keep looking straight ahead. For only the second time in her life that she could recall, she didn't want to be noticed.

"You can't help but draw attention to yourself, can you," Jimmy teased.

"I don't mean to," said Mercy. "Do you think they're staring at my face?"

"I'm sure of it," he said.

She reached up to pull the veil down further on the side of her face. Jimmy noted the gesture and caught her hand.

"No one can see your scars with that contraption on your head," he said. "I'm sure they're staring at their beautiful Cotillion queen returning home in a very unladylike fashion."

"I can't think of a better place to be than your arms," she said quietly, leaning back against him.

Jimmy walked his horse up the drive to the Locke's house. He noticed Mercy staring intently at the mansion.

"Are you all right?" he asked.

Mercy nodded.

"I hope you realize we're not going to be living in as big a house as what you're used to," he said.

She was quiet for a moment, and then sighed.

"This house is big and beautiful and decorated with the finest of things, but I feel like I'm looking at a lifeless shell," she said. "After what I've been through, it all seems so vain and meaningless—which could very well describe my life before I met you."

But then she turned and her eyes lit up. "I would love to have a home just like the Samuels," she said. "Not too big and not too little—with plenty of room for children."

"So you don't mind being around children now?"

Mercy shook her head, no, and whispered into the side of his neck, "Especially if they're yours."

Jimmy smiled and kissed her forehead. He pulled up at the back of the house and dismounted. Mercy lifted her leg over the saddle and reached for Jimmy's shoulders as he grabbed her by the waist to help her down. He let her down slowly and gently this time, taking in the feel of her.

"Are you ready?" he asked, finally letting her go.

She nodded and slipped her hand into his. They walked up to the back porch and could see Matilda through the window. She turned when she heard the footsteps and ran to meet them at the door. She hugged Mercy and immediately realized something wasn't right. She pulled back and looked down and then up at her face.

"I'm so sorry, Florine," she said, but Mercy just grabbed her again and held on tight.

"Me, too," she whispered. "But I'll be all right."

Matilda hugged Jimmy, too, and thanked him for bringing Florine home safely.

"I'm not home yet, Matilda," she said. "And I go by my middle name now—Mercy."

"I love that name," she said. "It makes me think of your grandfather."

"Where's Mother and Daddy?" she asked. "Jimmy and I have some news for them."

Mercy's Face

"Oh my," Matilda said, looking from one to the other. "Your mother's upstairs, but your daddy left town."

"Where'd he go?"

"You'll have to ask you mother," she said. "Go on in the parlor—I'll get Mrs. Locke. Can I get you—may I get you something to drink?"

"No, thank you, Matilda," said Mercy. "We can help ourselves."

Mercy sat on the settee while Jimmy stood behind her with his hand on her shoulder. She reached up and grasped it and took a deep breath.

"Are you all right?" he asked.

She nodded. "As long as you're here with me."

Hazel Locke walked into the room and stiffened when she saw Mercy holding Jimmy's hand. The next look was directed at her daughter's midriff, and her head jerked up in alarm.

Mercy stood and walked over to her mother.

"Hello, Mother," she said and reached out to hug her.

Her mother clasped her arms and held her at arms-length, still looking at her mid-section.

"It's too early! You couldn't have had the baby yet," she said before it dawned on her what that meant.

"Oh, Florine, I'm so sorry," she said and hugged her and led her back to the settee. "But you have to know it's for the better. It must have been God's will."

"I don't think that's how God works, Mother," said Mercy.

"Well, no one will be the wiser," her mother continued. "You were just visiting kinfolks out of state. And there's still time to get you involved in the Cotillion."

Mercy's shoulders slumped as she looked away while her mother chattered on. "And to think that used to be the highlight of my life," she said to Jimmy.

"Mrs. Locke—" Jimmy started to say.

"This is no concern of yours," she said. "What are you doing here, anyway?"

"Mercy and I—" he began again.

"You're going by your middle name?" she turned back to her daughter, ignoring Jimmy. "My mother's name? That's wonderful, Flor—I mean, Mercy! My father would have been so proud."

Mercy looked at her mother. "What Jimmy has been trying to tell you is that we're engaged to be married."

"What?!" she said, and then shook her head. "Your father will never stand for it."

"Well, he'll just have to accept it, because it's going to happen, and very soon," said Mercy. "Where is Daddy, by the way?"

Mrs. Locke's eyes widened as she remembered. "Why, he went to fetch you," she said. "He went to Brownwood to bring you home. What are you doing here?"

"I've come back with Jimmy," she said. "We're going to live in Grace and raise horses."

"Oh, my," she said. "Horses?"

"You're not going to faint again, are you, Mother?" Mercy asked. "You're going to have to stop being so helpless and close-minded."

"What?"

"We're planning to get married a week from Saturday at the church in Grace while all of Jimmy's family are home, and I hope you and Daddy will come and put all of this behind us," said Mercy.

"Don't you know you've broken your father's heart?"

"I'm sorry, Mother—I didn't mean to hurt you and Daddy, and I'm not trying to hurt you now. I just want to marry the man I love and—"

"What about the big wedding you always talked about having? We can't do that in a week's time."

"It's not that important to me anymore," she said.

"I don't believe that—what have you done to my daughter?" she asked Jimmy. "It's always been her dream to have the biggest wedding in Waco."

Mercy untied the ribbon under her chin and pulled off her hat.

Her mother's hand went to her throat when she saw the scars.

"Now can you understand why I don't want to have a big wedding, Mother?" she said. "And Jimmy and I need to be going."

"What happened?" her mother finally found the words to speak.

"I had an accident," she said, and left it at that. She leaned over and kissed her mother on the cheek and slipped the hat back in place on her head. "I hope we'll see you next Saturday—we're planning a simple afternoon ceremony. And if Daddy won't come, get Rune and Matilda to bring you. I really want you to be there, Momma." She reached over and clasped her mother's hands.

Hazel's eyes softened. "You haven't called me *Momma* in a long time."

"It won't be the same without you," she said.

Mercy's Face

"Are you sure you know what you're doing?"

"Yes, Momma, and I've never been happier. I'm not running away this time, either," she said. "You know where I'm going, and you know the family I'm marrying into. I hope you'll make the effort to get to know Jimmy like I know him. You'll love him, too."

Hazel looked at Jimmy and then back to her daughter. "This is happening so fast," she said. "I can't take it all in. But I do know I can't miss my only child's wedding."

Mercy reached over and hugged her.

"Your father will probably have a conniption," Hazel Locke said resignedly, "but I'll be there."

Back in the kitchen, Matilda was overjoyed at the invitation and assured Mercy that she and Rune would be glad to take Mrs. Locke if they needed to.

As they walked outside, Jimmy asked Mercy if the scars were the only reason she didn't want a large wedding.

"Heavens no," she said. "But that was the only excuse I could come up with that would force my mother to let it go. A big wedding for me was her dream, too."

"I don't understand your family," said Jimmy.

"I'm sorry my mother wasn't more welcoming to you," she said, "but I'm not surprised at her reaction to our news. I'm afraid Daddy won't take it any better either."

Jimmy helped her in the saddle and stepped up behind her.

She turned to Jimmy. "I hope your father's at the hotel by now. I'm ready to go to Grace."

Jimmy smiled. "I just thought of something."

"What?"

"*Your* father has no idea what he's getting into in Brownwood," he said. "I imagine France is going to get a hold of him, but good."

Mercy raised her eyebrows and smiled at the thought. "Then maybe there's some hope for my family after all."

Chapter 40

*E*arly Saturday evening Langston Locke stepped onto the porch of the rock house. He started to knock, but stopped for a moment to listen to the sounds on the other side of the door. He backed up and stared at the house again. It looked like an ordinary house, but he could hear lots of voices inside. Maybe it was a school, or even an orphanage. But he had learned in town that Mr. Samuel ran a dry goods store. He had found the store on the town square, but it was already closed for the day. Could the Samuels do both?

And now he was here—the place Florine had come to have her baby. Maybe the Samuels would adopt it; maybe he needn't have to bring Florine home just yet. After weeks of wrestling with his pride, he had almost resigned himself to accept the baby if he still wanted his daughter in his life. Almost.

He knocked on the door. He could hear laughter.

In a moment, a young boy answered the door.

"Hello."

"Hello."

"Is your father home?"

"Yes." The boy just stood there.

"Well, may I speak to him?"

The young boy nodded and then hollered over his shoulder, "Dad, it's for you!"

Langston watched a man walk into the parlor wiping his mouth with a napkin.

"I'm sorry—I didn't hear you knock. I was wondering why Finn left the table," he said as he walked up to the well-dressed stranger and offered his hand to him. "I'm George Samuel—come on in—have you had supper?"

"Well… no," Langston said, shaking his hand. "I'd like to—"

"Well, come on in, and my wife will fix you a plate," he said as he led him into the dining room.

Langston's eyes widened when he saw the roomful of children, but Florine wasn't among them.

"Everyone! We have a guest for supper," George said. "France, would you get him a plate?"

Langston saw a petite, auburn-haired woman rise from the sea of faces and smile at him as she walked to the kitchen. He looked again around the table, wondering where his daughter was.

"Everyone, this is…" George began, and then looked at the stranger. "I'm sorry, sir—I didn't catch your name."

"I'm Langston Locke," he said. "And where's my daughter?"

The sound of a dish shattering in the kitchen was all that was heard for a moment. No one knew what to say at first, but then a little voice spoke up.

"Are you Mercy's daddy?" Caitlin asked.

"Who?" said Langston, trying to find the face that had spoken. "What was that?"

Caitlin slipped out of her chair and walked around the table to the older man. He couldn't help but go down on one knee to face the little girl when he saw her—she made him think of Florine for some reason.

France watched from the doorway, holding another plate for their guest.

"Are you Mercy's daddy?" Caitlin asked again.

"Yes, I'm Mercy's daddy," he said.

"She said she missed you," Caitlin told him.

"She did?" Langston's eyes filled.

Caitlin nodded.

"Well, where is she?"

"She went home."

"Home?" Langston reached for a chair and pulled himself up stiffly. "But I came to take her home."

"Well, sit down and have a bite first," said George. "Then we'll talk."

After supper, Ethan and the boys went outside to do their chores and the older girls started to wash the dishes. France asked Annie and Jenna to get the little ones ready for bed.

George and France stood in the parlor facing Langston.

"Where do we begin?" George asked, looking at France.

"I know where we need to start, but we have to hurry—not much daylight is left," she said, grabbing a shawl.

They led Langston out the door and walked down the road to the cemetery. The air was brisk, making them walk even faster. They came to the large, fenced area of the Samuel plot.

"Impressive," Langston said, looking at the tall monument, "but what does this empty graveyard have to do with me?"

"It's not empty, Mr. Locke," said France as she led him around to the back of the gravestone. She let him read the inscription and watched his face as he came to the last name.

He gasped when he saw it, and looked to France questioningly.

"Are these your children?" he asked.

France nodded.

"I'm sorry for your loss," he said.

She nodded again.

He looked back and read the bottom name aloud. "Langston Samuel. What a coincidence to have my name," he said.

"It's no coincidence, Mr. Locke," she said. "Mercy lost her baby several weeks ago."

Langston stared at her in shock. Then he looked back at the name. His throat felt like it was constricting.

"It was a little boy?" he whispered hoarsely.

"Yes."

"I don't understand," he said. "Did she name him out of spite for me because of that letter?"

"No," said France. "She didn't even know about the letter when she lost the baby. She gave him your name because she loves you."

A sob escaped before his hand reached his mouth to try to maintain control. But he couldn't stop the tears.

"I'd come to take her home," he said. "Me and my stupid pride. I'd come to take them both home," he said between the sobs. "And now I'm too late."

He knelt down and touched the name—his name, and wept.

After a few minutes, Langston pulled his kerchief out and wiped his

Mercy's Face

eyes and nose, and struggled to stand. George helped him to his feet.

"I need to go. I need to get back to Waco," he said.

"But the next stage doesn't come through until Tuesday," said George.

"And she's not in Waco," said France.

"What? Well, then where is she?" he demanded to know.

"She went to Grace."

"Why would she do that? There's nothing for her there!"

"Let's go back to the house and have a cup of coffee, Mr. Locke," said France. "We have a lot more to talk about."

Back at the house, France asked the children to go to their bedrooms—that they needed some privacy with Mr. Locke.

Langston sat down at the kitchen table. "Why does the baby have your name?"

"No one knew she was expecting," France said as she poured a cup of coffee for Langston. "But it broke her heart to think that the baby would be buried and forgotten. This way he'll always be remembered."

"But he's not yours," Langston said.

"There are eleven other children here in this house that I didn't give birth to, either," said France, "but we've given every one of them our name and a place to belong in this world."

"Well, how did people not know she was in a family way?" he asked. "She had to have been showing by now."

"She hid it well up until about the fifth month," said France.

Then George told him that the men that had almost robbed Mercy and Jimmy months before had shown up in town. He told Langston that Mercy recognized one of them and that he had sent her home while he went to the sheriff's office to report them. He said that Mercy's actions led to the arrest of all but one of them before they attempted to rob the bank.

"Where was the other one?" Langston asked.

George told him they had learned that the fourth man had spotted Mercy walking home and followed her.

Langston's face paled.

"His name was Hank, and he hid in our barn—probably trying to figure out a way to get to her," said France, "but she ended up walking right into his hands."

"Why did she do a fool thing like that?" Langston asked.

"Caitlin was in the barn, and Mercy went to fetch her," said France.

"What happened?" Langston asked. "Did he hurt her?"

France looked at George for him to continue—the memories of the fire still haunted her.

"He almost killed her, Mr. Locke," said George.

"What?! What happened to my daughter?" he said.

"He beat her pretty badly before the barn went up in flames," George continued. "We figured his discarded cigarette butt started the fire. Hank got out unscathed—but Mercy wouldn't leave without finding Caitlin, who had been hiding in the barn the whole time."

"Oh, dear Lord," said Langston. "But they got out in time, right?"

"We thought we'd lost them—France could hear their screams and couldn't get to them—the fire was just too hot," he said. "But back in the town square after we had arrested the others, we finally realized one of the men was missing. It was then that we learned that Hank had followed Mercy home. At that point Jimmy started running to the house."

"Jimmy?"

"Jimmy Taylor—his sister Faith works for us," George explained.

"I know them both."

"Well, he was here visiting, thank God," George continued. "He found Caitlin walking through the smoke out in the horse pen, and she pointed to where Mercy was. Jimmy crawled on his hands and knees to find her, and he got her out of there."

"And she's all right now?" Langston asked.

"It took weeks for her to heal, Mr. Locke. Her face and shoulder were seriously burned," said France.

Langston looked angry all of a sudden. "I told Taylor if anything happened to my daughter here, I would hold him personally responsible."

"Jimmy had nothing to do with her injuries," said France. "In fact, he saved her life. He cares deeply for Mercy."

"I don't need to hear that," said Langston.

"Well, you'd better hear about it because your daughter's planning to marry him," France said sternly, "and soon."

"What?!" he said. "She can't be thinking straight—did her injuries affect her mind?"

France was flabbergasted at the man's blatant refusal to face the truth. "I believe she was thinking more clearly than she ever has in her life. Unlike her father…"

Mercy's Face

"France?" said George. "You think you might ought to tone it down a bit?"

"No, George, I will not beat around the bush here," she said. "Mr. Locke, I don't know how you were raised, but I cannot believe you would even remotely consider arresting your only child just to force her to do what you wanted. You ought to be ashamed of yourself."

"I wouldn't have actually arrested her," Langston said on the defensive. "What kind of man do you think I am?"

"Well, why in the world did you send that horrible letter in the first place if you never intended to follow through with it?" she asked. "And did you know that Jimmy gave you his stallion even *after* he had learned that Mercy had lost her baby? What does that tell you about *his* character? What does that tell you about how much *he* loves her?

"Whose hands would you put Mercy in? A lying, manipulative, overly-pretentious father who worries more about his status in the community than his own daughter? Or would she be better off in the hands of a young man—not perfect by any measure, but one who's willing to sacrifice everything he has for the woman he loves? You tell me the answer to that!"

But Langston Locke could only stare wide-eyed at the petite woman standing there with her hands on her hips giving him the what for.

Chapter 41

Mercy looked toward the striking three-story red brick house in the distance as they drove the carriage through Grace. The trees along both sides of the road would've blocked much of the view at any other time of the year, but they stood quietly, stripped of their leaves with their branches seeming to point the way to the Taylor house. Mercy had always loved that house, although it wasn't nearly as massive as her parents' place in Waco. But the Taylors' house felt more like a home rather than a show place. For years she used to daydream about living in it with Justin Taylor.

She hadn't been back to Grace since the Taylors' anniversary party over two years before…with the party and the unfortunate incident with Jimmy and Allie. It was her own offhand comment that led to that heartrending situation, and the guilt was fresh on her mind. Now she was about to face Jimmy's entire family, including Justin and Allie, and she was terrified.

Mercy looked at Faith sitting in the front seat with her father, Matthew Taylor. He seemed to hold no ill-will toward her when she met him at the hotel. But the Taylors had always been gracious and polite people.

Mercy reached over and slipped her hand under Jimmy's arm, grasping it firmly. Jimmy turned and looked at her face. She was as pale as a ghost.

"You're going to be fine," he said. "They're going to love you."

"I've given them no reason to," she said. "In fact, I've given them quite a few reasons not to."

Faith reached back and squeezed Mercy's other hand. "Don't worry," she said. "Everything will be fine."

Mr. Taylor drove the carriage around to the back of the house and pulled up. Jimmy helped Mercy from the carriage and told his father he would take care of the horses.

"Why don't you get the girls settled first and then come on down to the barn," he said, helping Faith out of the carriage.

Vestal and Julia came rushing out of the house to greet them. Julia held a little blonde-haired girl in her arms. Vestal and Julia hugged everyone, and had the little girl give kisses and hugs, too. Vestal excused herself to get back to the kitchen to finish cooking supper before the rest of the herd arrived, she said. Julia told her she would be in there soon to help.

Mercy smiled at the pretty little girl in Julia's arms. She had the biggest blue eyes, and Mercy realized she had to belong to Allie and Justin.

"Where is everybody?" Jimmy asked.

"Scattered," she said. "I think Uncle John's started your father's chores; Justin and Allie are down at the river visiting with your grandmother, but they should be back in a little bit. Matt and Catherine will be here soon, and Jenny and Marcus will get here after they close the store. And Vestal and I are keeping company with Miss Grace here. It's been a year since we've seen her, and she's not a baby anymore."

Jimmy carried the trunk and other bags to the porch before he told Mercy he was going down to the barn to help his father.

"I'll be back in a little while," he said, squeezing her arm.

They watched him walk down to the barn. He untied Brave from the back of the carriage and led him to a pen. They laughed when the horse began to run and pitch, like he was so glad to be home.

"We love the name you gave him," said Julia. "It's so much better than his first name. And I love your new name, too."

"Thank you," Mercy said, pleased to know that Jimmy had shared that with his family. "My grandfather taught me that a good name is important."

"Let's go inside with Vestal," Julia said. "We're going to have a houseful tonight. Nah-kay and Castro are even going to join us."

Faith and Mercy picked up the smaller bags and followed Julia into the house. Faith told Mercy she would take them upstairs where they would be staying in her old bedroom.

Julia asked Mercy if she would mind holding Grace so she could help Vestal.

"No, not at all, if she'll come to me," said Mercy.

"She hasn't met a stranger yet," Julia said, handing her the little girl. "I'm afraid to let her run loose down here when I can't watch her every second. There are just too many things she can get into that might hurt her. All my other grandchildren are old enough to know better. And Miss Grace didn't take a nap earlier, so she's pretty sleepy. Sit over there in Vestal's rocker, if you'd like."

Mercy carried her over to the rocker in the corner and sat down with Grace. It didn't feel strange at all to hold her; in fact, it felt quite natural.

"Hi there, pretty girl," said Mercy, looking at her face.

Grace smiled at her.

"Look at all those teeth!"

Grace opened her mouth even wider, showing all her teeth. Mercy laughed and hugged her. The little girl reached up and grabbed the ribbon that tied her hat in place.

"No, no, Grace," she said, catching her hand and kissing it. "That needs to stay right there."

Grace laid her head down on Mercy's chest as she began to rock.

"She looks just like Justin," said Mercy. "How old is she, Mrs. Taylor?"

"Almost a year and a half," she said. "She'll be two years old on July twentieth. And call me Julia."

Mercy watched Julia cutting the potatoes. Her left hand was withered and useless for grasping, but she could still use it to hold the potato in place while she cut it. Mercy noticed that she didn't seem at all self-conscious about it. Julia had learned to compensate for the damaged hand, and Mercy recalled the story of how it happened. Her Apache captor had crushed it with the butt of his rifle as punishment for Julia attempting to escape with Justin not long after they had been captured.

She looked at Julia, and for the first time she caught a glimpse of the hardships she had to have endured those years she was away from her family. But no one would have guessed it now, other than the crippled hand. And she made no attempt to hide it.

Mercy reached up and pulled the ribbon, freeing the hat. She set it on the little table beside her, and glanced at Julia and Vestal to see if they were staring at her scars.

They weren't.

"Is she going to sleep?" Julia asked.

Mercy looked down to see Grace's eyes closed. She nodded at Julia and waited again for some sort of reaction. If Julia noticed her scars, she didn't show it.

Her thoughts drifted back to her last visit to the Taylor home. She wondered how she should broach the subject of her part in Allie's disappearance. Guilt had continued to eat away at her the past two years, and she wanted to make things right.

"Julia?" said Mercy.

Julia looked up, waiting for her to continue.

"I want to apologize for my thoughtless comment that caused all the trouble the last time I was here."

"Has that been bothering you all this time?" Julia asked.

Mercy nodded, close to tears.

"Honey, you didn't force Allie to go down to the river that day any more than you forced Jimmy to do what he did," Julia said. "But it's all behind us now, and no one is looking back. God has a way of turning a bad situation into something good if we let Him. And I'll always be grateful for what came out of that difficult time for us."

Mercy looked down at Grace, and tears spilled over onto her little dress. Julia put the knife down and walked over and knelt down by the rocker.

"Mercy, my family was reconciled through that ordeal, so please let it go, because I promise you, we all have."

"Even Allie and Justin?" asked Mercy.

"Even Allie and Justin," said a voice from behind them.

Mercy turned to see Allie standing in the door of the kitchen. Her dark hair was down and windblown, but she looked as pretty as Mercy remembered.

"I'm so sorry, Allie," said Mercy.

"It's all right," she said, walking over to her. "Everything turned out fine. In fact, we're all the better for it."

Julia went back to work on the potatoes, and Mercy watched as Allie pulled up a chair beside her. She seemed very comfortable around her, which surprised Mercy. She thought she would be facing an angry, bitter woman. But Allie showed nothing of the sort.

"I've been very nervous about facing all of Jimmy's family, but I was most afraid of facing you," said Mercy, wiping a tear away.

"Please know there are no hard feelings on our part," Allie said. "I realized when we met Jimmy's grandmother that God was doing something extraordinary in his life. We could've died, and Jimmy almost did at the hands of the Indeh—"

Mercy shuddered and shut her eyes, devastated by the thought that she almost lost Jimmy even before she knew him.

Allie saw her reaction and grasped her hand. "I'm sorry, Mercy—I didn't say that to make you feel worse. You had nothing to do with the Apaches attacking us. I just meant that God had his hand on us the whole time, and He didn't let us die. It wasn't easy—it was probably the hardest thing I've ever gone through, but we got it through it. And some really good things happened because of it."

"I know what you mean by that," said Mercy.

Allie looked at Mercy's scars and nodded as tears filled her eyes. "We heard you had a pretty rough go of it these past few months. I'm so sorry for your loss and the pain you've gone through. I hope you don't mind that Jimmy shared some things with us before he went back to Brownwood to fetch you and Faith."

"I'm ashamed for you to know some of those things about me," Mercy said. "I made some bad mistakes."

"We all have," said Allie. "But things are looking up, aren't they? I'm so excited that you're going to be my sister-in-law."

"You are?" Mercy asked, surprised. "He told you that, too?"

"Well, he said if you showed up here with him when he brought Faith home, that meant you said 'yes,' so I didn't know for sure until I saw you in here," Allie said. "He loves you very much, Mercy. I told him God would lead him to the right person some day. And He did."

"I feel the same about him," she said, smiling. "I've never met anyone quite like him."

They heard someone sniffing, and realized it was Vestal. Julia asked if she was all right.

"It's these blasted onions—they get to me every time."

Allie grinned at Mercy—they both could see that Vestal had her hands in the dough for her butterhorn rolls—not onions.

"She has a soft spot in her heart for Jimmy and Justin," Allie leaned over and whispered, and then said a little louder, "What do you think about this little girl you're holding?"

Mercy looked down at Grace sleeping peacefully in her arms.

"She's beautiful, Allie," she said. "Not too long ago I would've been scared to death to hold a child. But I got over that very quickly at the Samuels' house."

"Aren't France and George wonderful?" Allie said. "I'd love to see them again. I'm convinced it was no accident that we stopped by their store that day."

"I guess I wouldn't be here either if I hadn't met them," said Mercy. "They have a way of helping people get back on the right track, don't they?"

Allie nodded and smiled. Justin and Jimmy walked in the kitchen, followed by Faith coming down the stairs. She almost tackled Justin hugging him. Allie stood up to embrace her as well. Then they could hardly get a word in edge-wise with Faith telling them about her job with the Samuels and getting to teach the younger children. When she started talking about the older children, Mercy told everyone that they had better sit down because it was going to take a while.

Justin looked beyond his sister and waved a greeting to Mercy from across the room. Mercy lifted a hand and waved back as she smiled at the familiar face—the rugged good looks, the unruly blonde hair, and those amazing blue eyes—Jimmy's eyes. Then she saw Jimmy watching her and smiled even bigger with the realization that Justin seemed to pale in comparison to his younger brother.

Faith chattered on, and Allie looked over at Mercy with raised eyebrows and asked where the real Faith Taylor was.

Julia continued to help Vestal cook dinner, but she heard every word her youngest daughter share excitedly with her brothers. For years she had hoped to find something that would pull Faith out of her painfully shy self, and it was obvious that she had finally found her niche in Brownwood. But then Julia realized that Brownwood might become her home from now on, and Grace would be just a place to visit instead. That brought tears to her eyes when she thought how big and empty this house would be from now on. Her nose started to run, giving way to her emotions, and she tried to sniff quietly.

But Allie and Mercy both heard it and looked at Julia.

"Blasted onions," she said when she saw them looking at her.

Chapter 42

Jimmy stood in front of the mirror trying for the third time to tie his bowtie. He gave up and decided to get some help. He walked out of his room and started down the stairs. At the first landing he glanced out the window towards the barn and stopped. He could see Brave stomping around the pen—even pitching every so often. He thought Justin was going to saddle his horse for him this afternoon, but there he was—still in the pen—and unsaddled.

Uncle John came out of the parlor as Jimmy came down the rest of the stairs to the second floor.

"Hey, look at you!" he said. "Need some help with that tie?"

"Yeah, but I need to go saddle Brave."

"You want me to go with you?"

"If you want to."

The two men walked downstairs and out the back door and met Justin and Matthew Taylor standing there with the horses and carriages.

"I thought you said you would get Brave and saddle him for me," Jimmy said.

"Sorry," Justin said. "Change of plans."

"Well, thanks for your help, brother," Jimmy said, exasperated. "Mercy will probably shoot me if I get dirty."

"Don't tarry, though," said Matthew. "We need to leave in a few minutes."

Jimmy took off at a trot. Uncle John started to follow, but Matthew stopped him.

Jimmy started whistling to call up Brave before he even reached the barn. He saw the barn door left wide open and fussed under his breath about Justin knowing better than that. But he stopped in his tracks when a horse trotted out towards him.

It was the stallion.

"Redeemer?! What are you doing here, boy?"

The horse nuzzled him, looking for his reward. Jimmy rubbed the horse's face and his neck and saw that he was saddled. He looked beyond the horse to see Langston Locke standing in the open door. Jimmy couldn't help but glance down to see if he was armed.

Langston almost smiled, noticing the look.

"You've trained him well, Jimmy," he said. "He knows his master. I hope you don't mind that I unsaddled your other horse to put it on Redeemer."

"But I gave him to—"

"No," Langston interrupted, shaking his head. "He was never mine."

Jimmy just stood there, unsure of what to say. He turned around to see his father, brother and uncle watching them from the house.

"You didn't tell your father," said Langston.

"No, sir."

"Why didn't you? He could've stepped in and bailed you out."

"It wasn't his debt," said Jimmy. "And he's bailed me out of trouble more times than I can count. I needed to do this myself for once."

"But it wasn't your debt either," he said. "Why'd you do it, —even after you found out you didn't have to?"

"You know why I did it."

"I don't know anybody who would've done what you did."

Jimmy just looked at him.

"Well, except for your father, and probably the rest of your family when I think about it. You're definitely a Taylor," Langston said. "And I heard my daughter probably wouldn't be alive today if it wasn't for you. I'm grate-..." he started to say when his voice broke. "I'm grateful to you more than you'll ever know."

Jimmy looked at him suspiciously. Surely this wasn't the same angry man he had faced a couple of weeks before.

This time Langston did chuckle. "You don't believe me? Well, tell me if you walked away the same man after an encounter with France Samuel."

Jimmy knew exactly what he was talking about. He couldn't help but grin at the thought.

"Let me see," Langston continued, "after three days with her and that family, I'm not sure if it was the conversation where she called me a lying, manipulative, overly pretentious father who didn't deserve a daughter like Mercy that convinced me, or if it was the picture she put in my head of me as an old man all alone in this world because I was too pig-headed to see what mattered most in this life, and that's family and friends—imperfections and all."

"France Samuel is definitely a force to be reckoned with," said Jimmy. "And she loves people—not for their name or their ancestry or the amount of money they have. She and George have always accepted me from the first moment they met me, and they took Mercy in and treated her the same way."

"Well, they're better people than I am," said Langston, "but I think before I left there, my family circle grew considerably. Caitlin even started to call me PaPa, and I kind of liked that. She reminded me so much of Mercy as a little girl."

Jimmy smiled and nodded, and then his face grew serious.

"So you're here for Mercy?" he asked.

"If she'll let me," said Langston apprehensively. "Does she hate me for what I've done?"

"No, sir," he said. "Ever since her mother arrived, I've seen her looking down the road every time she walks by a window. She hasn't said anything, but I know she's been watching for you."

Langston nodded and turned away from him as he cleared his throat, and took his kerchief and dabbed his eyes. He turned back around and took a deep breath.

"Well, it's high time we get going," he said. "You don't need to be late to my daughter's wedding."

* * *

The bride's carriage was the last one to arrive at the picturesque church with the tall white steeple. Rune Bishop climbed down and assisted his wife Matilda, Hazel Locke, Faith and Mercy from the carriage.

Rune and Matilda had escorted Mrs. Locke to Grace two days before. Mr. Locke hadn't made it back from Brownwood by then, so Hazel left him a note that told him about the wedding and where she would be.

Everyone went inside the church except for Faith and Mercy. The tradition continued—Mercy wore Julia's dress, with the hem lowered to its original length. She had made her own wedding veil the day before, with her mother's help. She brushed her dress into place and looked at her friend.

"I was never this nervous being crowned in front of five hundred people," she said to Faith. "There are only twenty-five people in there, but I'm shaking like a leaf. How do I look?"

"Beautiful, as always."

"Thank you for standing with me, Faith," she said.

"You're welcome... again," said Faith as she hugged her. "That's what good friends are for, right?"

Mercy smiled and nodded, and then took a deep breath as she looked toward the doorway. Her eyes widened when she saw her father standing there waiting for her.

"Daddy?!" she lifted the veil to get a better look, and cried out as she ran up the steps and let him wrap his arms around her.

"I prayed you would come," she cried, and hugged him tight. Then she laughed through her tears. "And now I'm messing up my face before my wedding."

"Forgive me, princess?" he asked. "For being a pompous horse's behind? And I'm sorry about that monstrous letter. I hope you know I never intended to follow with it."

"I know, Daddy," she said, hugging him again.

But he needed to say more. "I was just trying to manipulate the situation. But I finally had to face the fact that you're not a little girl anymore, and I'm going to have to let you go."

"I'll always be your little girl," she said, "but a happily married one soon."

"I just want you to be happy," he said as he saw the scars on her cheek. And he knew of her deeper scars unseen. "Are you all right? I'm so sorry you had to endure all of that alone."

"I'm fine, Daddy," she said, "and I was never alone. Didn't you meet the Samuels while you were in Brownwood?"

He nodded and chuckled. "I'm quite sure my life will never be the same."

"Mine, too," she said, smiling.

"But you're still the prettiest girl in Texas," he said, and then asked quietly. "Are you sure about this?"

"I love him, Daddy," she said. "I've never been more sure of anything in my life."

Faith stepped up beside Mercy.

"You remember Jimmy's sister, don't you?"

"Yes, of course! How are you, Hope?"

Faith snickered.

"It's Faith, Daddy."

"Hope, Faith, love—I knew it was one of those."

They walked into the empty foyer, and Faith opened the doors to the sanctuary. She stood there, waiting for the music to change.

Mercy pulled the veil back down over her face, and she and her father stood behind Faith. Mercy looked at the high ceilings and the tall windows along the walls. Jimmy's sister Jenny had decorated the pews with white bows and sprigs of evergreen branches. The church looked much the same as the last time she had visited at Matthew and Julia Taylors' anniversary ceremony over two years before. The church was filled with people then, but today it held only a small gathering clustered on the first few rows. Pastor Jenkins stood in front of the pulpit, waiting to officiate.

This wasn't the big wedding she had always dreamed of.

But it was perfect.

The side door by the piano opened and Justin and Jimmy walked in and took their places at Pastor Jenkins' left.

The music changed and Faith began to walk slowly down the aisle. She turned to the left and stood at Pastor Jenkins' right. Julia began playing louder, and everyone stood and faced the bride.

Mercy's heart started racing. Her eyes quickly found Jimmy, and the way he looked at her took her breath away. Everything and everyone else seemed to melt away as she walked forward and stood in front of Jimmy.

"Who gives this woman in marriage?" Pastor Jenkins asked.

"I do," said Langston Locke as he kissed his daughter's hand before taking his place beside his wife.

Pastor Jenkins began. "Dearly beloved, we have gathered here today to witness the union of Jimmy Lawrence Taylor and Florine Mercy Locke in wedded matrimony. If anyone objects to this union, speak now or forever hold your peace."

Jimmy and Mercy looked toward their families. Silence and smiles greeted them, so they faced each other again.

"Just a moment," Jimmy said to the preacher, and then lifted the veil. "I have to see Mercy's face while we do this."

The preacher turned to Jimmy and continued, "Repeat after me…"

Mercy's Face

Mercy knew the preacher was talking, but all she heard was Jimmy's voice.

"I, Jimmy, take thee, Mercy…—to be my lawfully wedded wife… —to have and to hold from this day forward… —for better or for worse…—for richer, for poorer…—in sickness and in health…—to love and to cherish… – 'til death do us part."

The preacher turned to Mercy and said, "I, Mercy, take thee, Jimmy…"

"I, Mercy, take thee, Jimmy, to do everything Pastor Jenkins just mentioned, but I need to say more."

Jimmy smiled and looked at her questioningly.

"You and I have come from two very different lives, my love. You had a difficult time growing up; my path has been easy. But through some poor choices and tragic circumstances, God has taught me some hard lessons this past year. But at the same time He's taught me what love truly means.

"Love is patient; love is kind; love looks past the surface to the beauty inside; love can be a feeling, but even more so, I've learned that it's a choice and a commitment that goes beyond feelings; love sees the potential in each other; love means trust; love means sacrifice; and love means seeing us at our worst and still choosing to stay.

"You, Jimmy, more than anyone else, have exhibited all those things toward me, and I'm so blessed and grateful you've come into my life.

"I promise I will defend you and your name and honor, which will soon be my name and my honor. My heart is safe with you and yours with me. I am so proud to be your wife.

"You're my hero, Jimmy Taylor. You found me and rescued me in more ways than you'll ever know. But I have to warn you, though, that there will probably be some days ahead that you'll be married to a self-centered damsel—"

"And some days you'll be married to a scoundrel," Jimmy added.

Everyone laughed, and several of the wives nodded their heads in agreement.

Mercy smiled and continued. "But I promise that we'll be together always. My grandfather told me how important a good name is, and I recently learned the meaning of my middle name. My life has changed greatly since you've become a part of it, and I wanted my name to reflect that change.

"I go by the name of Mercy now, but every time I look at you, Jimmy, it is I who truly sees mercy's face."

Epilogue

The striking couple turned every head as they walked through the hotel lobby in Waco. But they seemed to be oblivious to everyone but themselves. They headed up the stairs and down the long hall to their room.

Jimmy turned the key in the lock, opened the door, and set their baggage just inside. He turned around and swept up his startled wife in his arms.

"I know this isn't our first home, but it may be a while before I get to carry you over that threshold," he said.

Mercy laughed and wrapped her arms around his neck.

"How'd you know about this?" she asked.

"Justin told me."

"He did?"

"Well, and my mother, too."

"I love your mother."

Jimmy carried her into the room and kicked the door with his foot. It hit the door frame, but didn't catch.

He walked over to the bed, laid her down, and stretched out beside her.

"You sure smell good," he said, nuzzling her neck.

"It's about time that love potion finally worked," she said, giggling.

"But I think we've been patient long enough."

Mercy began to unbutton his shirt.

Jimmy untied the ribbon under her chin and pulled off her hat. He kissed every part of her face before settling on her lips. Mercy felt that one clear to her toes.

"I wanted everything to be right between us," he said, sitting up to take off his shirt. He pulled off one sleeve, then the other and threw it towards a nearby chair.

Mercy saw the ragged scar on his shoulder and looked down to find the scar from the bullet wound on his side. She gently brushed her fingers across each of them.

"Flawed, aren't we?" she said.

"Yes," he said as he unbuttoned her dress.

She shut her eyes as he worked his way down, anticipating what was to come.

He pulled her up to slip the dress off her shoulders, baring the scars hidden beneath. She lay back on the bed, watching him look at her with those blue eyes, wondering how the color of the sky could look fiery at the same time.

"But did you realize that neither of us would be here today if not for these scars?"

"Then I wouldn't trade them for anything," she said, reaching up and pulling him back down to her.

Mercy saw something in the corner of her eye and realized someone had walked past the door, which was still ajar.

"Jimmy!" she whispered. "The door…"

She watched the movement of every muscle in his arms and back as he climbed out of bed and walked soundlessly across the room. She couldn't believe he belonged to her now… and always.

Jimmy grasped the doorknob as several women passed by, staring wide-eyed at his bare chest. He smiled and nodded politely… and then softly closed the door.

Printed in the United States
139256LV00002B/8/A

PROPERTY OF
BOERNE - CHAMPION H.S. LIBRARY
201 CHARGER LANE
BOERNE, TX 78006